THE ROAD TWICE TRAVELED

R.A. JONES

AIRSHIP 27 PRODUCTIONS

The Road Twice Traveled
© 2020 R.A. Jones

Published by Airship 27 Productions
www.airship27.com
www.airship27hangar.com

Cover and interior illustrations © 2020 Rob Davis

Editor: Ron Fortier
Associate Editor: Peggy Livingston
Marketing and Promotions Manager: Michael Vance
Production and design by Rob Davis

ISBN: 978-1-946183-82-8

Printed in the United States of America

10 9 8 7 6 5 4 3 2 1

THE ROAD
TW1CE TRAVELED

R.A. JONES

PREFACE

The story you are about to read is based on a tale told to me by an old and good friend who, understandably I think you'll find, would prefer to remain nameless.

Artistic license has been taken with the narrative as laid down by him, but not so much as to raise the possibility of having said license revoked.

It is a story that blends the whimsical with the tragical (which is indeed a word; you may look it up yourself if you like. I'll wait.).

At its heart, it is a story about *choices*. In the theoretical sense, at least, every choice that every one makes every hour of every day—potentially creates a new and different alternative time line. Billions of different choices could create billions of different worlds, different people and different events than the ones we know and think of as history.

Choices matter.

The tapestry that is a person's life is woven from a thousand, thousand threads. Think of the many changes that might occur if this tapestry could be even just minutely rewoven.

What new and different mosaic might appear upon the face of this new tapestry?

What follows is, I hope you will come to agree, a story of both the fantastic and the mundane, which are after all merely two sides of the same coin. It contains the stuff of both dreams and nightmares. It explores mysteries and actualities, and will offer few answers to either.

It speaks to life and death, and the price we pay for both.

And who knows? It might even be real.

It is most certainly *true*.

CHAPTER 1

The Saturday morning of James Francis' 65th birthday began, as did most other days for him, with the incessant and annoying "eee-eee-eee" of his alarm clock.

He hated the inhuman trilling sound of it, yet subjected himself to it repeatedly by slapping the snooze button several times. As he hit it for the final time before rising, it occurred to him that he just might consign the damned thing to the trash can.

After all, as of yesterday afternoon, he was now officially retired. Within reason, he was now free to sleep whenever and for as long as he damn well pleased.

For some reason, the thought of that brought him no more comfort than did the shrill warbling of the alarm clock.

Throwing back the covers, he swung his somewhat spindly legs off the bed. As always, the stiffness of arthritic knees caused him to wince slightly as he rose.

At the sound of a mild disturbance from outside, he limped to the window to peer through the blinds. As expected, the source of the caterwauling was one of his neighbors. It was a man several years older even than himself. His name was Crowley (or maybe it was Cooper; James couldn't really remember, nor did he much care).

Crowley fit the stereotype of the crotchety old man perfectly. No one liked him, so they mostly avoided him. At the moment, he was loudly berating a neighbor boy whose heinous offense against the codger was to have run up on Crowley's front lawn to retrieve an errant soccer ball.

"If I ever become him, Lord," James muttered, absently scratching his behind, "just shoot me. Or at least give me a bullet so I can shoot myself."

Such is the internal blindness with which most of us are blessed that James was blissfully unaware of the fact that he was already several miles down the same road Crowley was traveling.

James was in no hurry to get out and about, even on such a day as this. He had no special plans; he seldom did.

He glanced over rather than read the previous day's newspaper as he consumed what could only be loosely termed breakfast: a bowl of cold cereal washed down with a cup of instant coffee. He only bothered with the cereal to avoid stomach upset from his various prescription medications.

Afterwards, he performed the daily ritual that was about the closest he came to exercising: walking to the curb to retrieve the mail and today's paper.

There were a few other folk out and about, but none called to him in greeting, nor did he to them. Except for old man Crowley (Or Cooper. Hell, it might be Kennedy.), James knew none of them by name; neither did he want to.

He firmly believed in Frost's poetic profession that good fences made good neighbors.

He had likewise not cultivated any real friends at the accounting firm where he had toiled so mechanically for so many years. The cubicle in which he worked had been like its own, tiny world and he had seldom ventured beyond its borders. One must be possessed of curiosity before any desire to explore can exist.

At best, his co-workers could be labeled as acquaintances. Most of them wouldn't even know he had left the firm until he failed to show up on Monday.

Nearly all of the "friends" he had outside of his job had, like his money, gone to his ex-wives as part of the spoils of divorce.

As expected, there was little to be found inside the mailbox save for bills and circulars. Everybody wanted money he didn't want to give.

That was also true of the closest thing to a greeting card he found among the detritus. He knew even without opening it that it would be a reminder from his third ex-wife that her alimony check should be on its way to her.

As he frequently did, James thought on the irony behind her grounds in filing for divorce. She had sued for dissolution because he had cheated on her; on her, the woman he had been cheating *with* when wife #2 divorced him. The mistress the aforementioned third wife had discovered had sense enough to dump him in the wake of his divorce.

If asked or forced to make a choice among the three, he still preferred Barb, wife #1—and that marriage had proven to be a total disaster for both of them!

He should have known better, he supposed, than to wed when the two of them were barely in college. She'd been his high school sweetheart, though, and a nubile, sexy cheerleader to boot.

Thank God, they'd had no children; for the both of them were far too childish themselves.

So James had waited until wife #2 before making the mistake of fathering a child.

He knew there'd be no birthday card or congratulatory call from his son Michael. James had neither seen nor spoken to the self-absorbed, ungrateful bastard in ten years; not since dear old Dad had refused to "lend" the boy $20,000 to open a restaurant out on the East Coast.

Not only did Michael still hold a grudge over his father's refusal to fund his delusional dream, he also somehow managed to convince himself that James was also vicariously responsible for the ill-conceived establishment going belly-up six months after it opened!

James again thanked God; this time for the fact that—to the best of his knowledge, anyway—Chef Michael had never bred.

In what was a rare occurrence, James thought back to his own father, who had never given James much of anything save rigid rules and self-evident platitudes about working hard, saving your money, never borrowing anything and always standing on your own two feet.

James made a derisive, scoffing sound at the thought of the jewel of the ring of advice Ted Francis had passed on to him: "If you ever get a girl in trouble, I expect you to marry her."

That was the closest Ted ever came to having "the Talk" with his son. Typical of his time and his own upbringing, he was too uncomfortable with the subject matter to bother explaining to James just *how* you got a girl in trouble—or even what *kind* of trouble it was that James must never get one into.

Like most males of his generation, James had eventually figured that one out for himself. The trial and error phase had been awkward but eminently entertaining.

James never forged a particularly close relationship with his father; Ted was too hard and tough, too distant from the call of emotion for that to happen. Early in life, James decided he was not a man to be argued with. It was much easier and less fruitlessly combative to just give in to him.

It was James' father, himself a veteran, who had pushed James to join the Army right out of high school, with the thought that it would help "make a man" of him. More practically, he thought it might prove to be a career choice for James, or at the very least a source for useful veteran's benefits.

Luckily for James, the conflict in Vietnam was in its final throes at that time, and he spent the majority of his hitch serving desk duty in ordinance at a base in Georgia.

Realizing that his son was not cut out for the life of a career soldier, Ted next pushed James to use the benefits of the G.I. Bill to help pay for a college education. He even picked the college and the course of study for his offspring.

Caught in the conundrum of having a good head for figures while being simultaneously possessed of little but antipathy toward the subject of math, James nonetheless acquiesced and earned himself a degree in accounting.

This had resulted in a long, solid and steady career for James, albeit a largely empty one. Most of it had been spent with the large and semi-prestigious accounting firm from which he had now retired. He suspected that, if he should live so long, that within two years he would forget the names of everyone he had dealt with there. Within five, he might have difficulty remembering the name of the firm itself.

His father Ted was long gone, of course; cancer had taken him at an age most would consider to be far too young. James' mother Virginia, who had invested all her personal capital in her husband's existence, had outlived him by only two years. James often said that she had died simply because she wanted to. Nor did James have any siblings or other living relatives of note.

Probably just as well.

Returning from his mildly depressing trek to the mailbox, James paused at his front door and glanced back over the neighborhood. It was part of a larger housing development known as Hawthorne Hills. Located on the city's east side, it was perhaps a bit long in the tooth; but still quite nice and solidly middle class.

It wasn't nice enough to suit James Francis, though. Oh, he would be able to live comfortably and securely enough here, even in retirement. But not nearly so comfortably as he could have without the financial burden of two punitively large alimony payments.

(Thankfully, Barb—wife #1—had had the decency to eventually remarry and relieve him of that burden. The other two wives, he was convinced, would take nunly vows before doing him such a favor.)

Knowing he could have had better, should have had better, made James slightly resentful of that for which he instead had to settle.

If not for other demands on himself and his resources, he was sure he could have afforded an even better house, in an even better community.

With taller fences.

James had all of this special day to himself, but no special plans with which to fill it. At one point, during half-time of a college football game in which he had only marginal interest, he drifted out into his attached garage.

Atop a rickety workbench, scattered amidst mostly secondhand tools, sat several pieces of wood of varying lengths and widths. The plan was for those pieces eventually to come together to form a chair.

James had always felt he had a certain natural touch for tinkering with wood; in the past few years he had decided that working with it would make a good hobby in which to indulge.

Thus far, though, all he had to show for his efforts were a few partially completed projects, none of them exhibiting any particular artistry or promise to them.

He momentarily toyed with the thought of working on the chair some today, but quickly gave up on any such notion. Maybe he could just knock a few of the pieces together into a semblance of a bird feeder to hang from the lone tree in his backyard.

But then he'd have to put up with damned birds.

So instead he went back inside and watched the rest of the football game.

That evening, having finally gone to the trouble of showering and shaving, James set out in his car; ignoring its annoying knocks and pings had become almost second nature to him.

Less than a quarter mile from his driveway sat a small and slightly dilapidated strip mall. Its only occupants were a laundry, a sandwich shop and a bit of an anachronism: an honest-to-God Mom and Pop ice cream parlor.

James had been told by someone (He couldn't have told you who; he had only been half listening.) that the center had once housed a nice woodworking shop run by an old Italian gentleman. It was long gone now, having been abandoned before James moved into the neighborhood, so he could not attest to the fact that it had even existed at all.

He now looked rather longingly at the ice cream parlor. As a boy, he had loved ice cream in virtually all its forms, as was true of most kids both then and now. He seldom partook of it anymore, though. Had to watch his blood sugar.

So it was that he had never set foot inside this shop, even though it was within easy walking distance of his front porch. Not that he ever walked much farther than the distance from that porch to the mailbox at the curb.

This evening, he drove right past it again.

He had decided to splurge on himself a little this day (Better him than his ex-wives, right?) by dining at a nice, mid-ranged steak house.

As he indulged in a juicy, bacon-wrapped filet (a small one, not the more expensive large one), his blood nearly froze instantly in his veins as he heard several people singing an off-key but enthusiastic a cappella rendition of "Happy Birthday."

The chorus was not for him, of course, but rather for a young boy seated not far away with his family. As was the policy of this establishment, the beaming birthday boy was also presented with a complimentary slice of chocolate cake.

James Francis did not bother to tell his waitress that it was also his birthday, nor did he leave her much of a tip when he made his departure.

Let her get it from his ex-wives, was his less than generous attitude.

The night was still young and he had no job to concern him any longer; nor had church going been part of his Sunday schedule for quite some time. So James decided to further spoil himself by making a brief stop at a local bar on the way home: one with which he already had a passing acquaintance.

Called "Irish Mike's," it was a decent enough joint, designed and appointed in a manner meant to give it at least a semblance of the look and feel of an authentic Irish pub.

James had no idea whether or not it succeeded in such efforts. Even while in uniform he had never left the borders of the United States. Nor did he know "Irish" Mike himself or anybody else who worked at or patronized the bar. He only darkened its doors once or twice a month, always sat alone and never allowed himself to partake of more than two mixed drinks, which he nursed with the patience of an oyster.

Purely coincidentally, the route from the restaurant to the pub did take James past one of the many and virtually interchangeable Protestant churches sprinkled throughout the city. As he usually did, he allowed his eyes to dart up to the otherwise darkened church's marquee out front. Such signs often contained little messages. Most often they were fairly standard and somewhat preachy in his estimate.

"Get right or get left." "If you think it's hot *here!*"

But sometimes they were pithy, amusing, clever and even thought provoking.

The message on this particular marquee on this particular night read simply: *If you want to be loved—be lovable.*

He chuckled slightly at the thought. He figured it could be said of him that he had loved neither wisely *nor* well. But then love, like most emotions to which human beings cling, was probably over-rated anyway.

As he walked into the pub minutes later, James was mildly surprised when he saw a face that was familiar to him. It was his irascible old neighbor, Mr. Crowley (Or was it Cromwell?). Looking as sour as ever, Crowley sat alone in a booth, clutching at a tall glass of beer with both hands, as if it might otherwise fly away from him or be taken by another.

James made no effort to catch the old fart's eye or to call out a greeting to him, instead moving quickly and quietly to his own preferred spot: a stool at the far end of the mahogany bar itself. There he sat hunched over slightly, the better to avoid all other unwanted eye contact or small talk with any of the pub's other patrons. They were all strangers to him and he preferred that they remain so.

As he was close to finishing what would be his second and final rum and Coke, he jumped in surprise as a hand slapped him vigorously on the back.

James swiveled slightly on his stool and found himself looking into a smiling face he had never laid eyes on before but whose owner had now presumed to grab a seat next to James.

James couldn't help thinking that this jocular stranger certainly seemed to fit into the Irish motif of the bar far better than did most of its slightly tacky furnishings.

For, in appearance—he reminded James of nothing so much as a *leprechaun!*

CHAPTER 2

Of indeterminate age, the jovial little man sported a scraggly reddish beard, in color exactly matching that of the receding hairline on the top of his head. Equally rosy cheeks, dancing blue eyes and a broad grin showing off pearly white teeth rounded out his features.

He had a rather prosperous look about him, though this was belied by the slightly tattered, almost shabby and ill-fitting gray checked jacket hanging loosely from his shoulders,

"And how are ya doin' this fine evening, Jimmy?" the little man asked cheerfully, seemingly acting as if they were best friends. His voice carried with it a bit of an accent, though not one that sounded the least bit Irish to James' ear.

"Huh?" was all James managed before the man turned away from him and motioned to the middle-aged fellow tending bar.

"Two more rums and Cokes, if you please, Timothy!"

"Oh, no," James mumbled, starting to slide off his stool. "I shouldn't —"

"Nonsense! It's on me!" As the bartender approached with fresh drinks, the odd little man draped an arm around James' shoulders.

"T'day's the man's birthday, Timothy," the little man told the disinterested barkeep. "And he deserves a little special treatment!"

"Happy birthday, fella," the bartender said in a flat, noncommittal voice, taking his payment for the drinks and then drifting back down the bar away from the two men.

"And you just keep 'em comin', Timothy," the little man called after him. When James opened his mouth to protest, the jovial stranger hastily added, "And this man's money is no good for the rest o' this fine evening!"

"Do I know you, mister?" James managed to interject.

"No, no; not at all, Jimmy!"

"My name is James."

"Of course it is, Jimmy. I wouldn't have it any other way! Nor have ya ever laid eyes on me, before this very moment!"

"Then, why this?" James asked, lifting up his glass. His expression took on a suspicious cast. "And how did you know it was my birthday?"

"Oh, I know *lots* o' things, Jimmy," the smiling little man replied, winking and laying a finger alongside his upturned nose.

"And one o' the things I know is that a man should be allowed a little indulgence on the occasion of his 65th birthday!"

He clinked his glass against James' and toasted him. "To yer continued good health, Jimmy!"

"James."

"And may all yer lives be fruitful ones!"

The oddly endearing little man must have already been a bit too deep in his cups, James thought, as he raised his glass to his smiling lips. The last sentence he had uttered made no sense.

"Two more, Timothy!" the little man cried out, slamming his now empty glass down on the bar with a little too much force. He then extended his right hand out toward James.

"I don't believe we've been formally introduced, sir," he said with mock seriousness.

"Or informally, either." James, too, was now entering a happy state wherein the words emerged slightly slurred.

"My name, good sir, is Tipperary Rangoon Seville Oslo Cairo Nomad." The little man paused for a second to suck in fresh wind.

"The Third."

"Huh?"

"But you can just call me 'Tip'."

James blinked two or three times. "And you can call me 'Jimmy'."

"I already do," Tip replied, again winking.

"What?" A girlish, drunken giggle. "Oh, yeah. Well, you can keep doin' it." He waved a hand wildly.

"Two more, Timothy!"

The two new friends continued to converse, talking on the limited range of subjects that are of the slightest interest to the male of the species: Women. Sports. Women. Politics. Women.

"But tell me, Jimmy," Tip said at last, growing suddenly more reflective. "Havin' now lived three score and five, you must have picked up a fair bit of knowledge on life and such. Now, haven't you?"

James shrugged. "Mostly, Tip, I feel kinda like that old song I useta hear. You know the one.

"I wish I didn't know now what I didn't know then."

"Hear, hear!" Tip chimed enthusiastically, lifting his glass.

"I can't say it's been a great life," James continued, his shoulders slumping slightly.

His sodden mind sought to focus on opportunities missed or simply frittered away. Of things as they were and of how they might have been. Of decisions made for expediency's sake or for what he wrongly thought were his own best interests. Of relationships that should have been more than they were but sometimes were instead wrecked by his own actions. He tried to remember the last time he felt truly happy; grew chagrined when it proved difficult to do so. He let out a long sigh that sounded weary.

"There's no point in dwelling on the past, though," he said. "Why waste time pissing and moaning about things that can't be changed?"

"Ah…but what if they *could* be, Jimmy?" Tip asked.

"Huh?"

There was still a twinkle in Tip's blue eyes, but now they had taken on a deeper and darker aspect as well.

"Consider this hypothet—hypothet—hypothet —" Tip wiped his hand across his mouth. "Imagine this, Jimmy; just for the fun of it.

"Supposin' I could wave a magic wand in the air and send you back in time; so you could relive your life, in a manner of speaking.

"What would you do differently, the second time around?"

James stared down into his nearly empty glass, studying its contents as he gently sloshed them from side to side. Then he giggled softly.

"That's easy," he said.

"I'd bet heavy on the Jets to win Super Bowl III. I'd invest in gold when it was $35 an ounce. I'd buy Microsoft stock the first day it was offered."

"Pff!" Tip scoffed. "If all you ever wanted outta life, Jimmy, was *money*— why not just ask for a million dollars outright?"

"Could you give me a million dollars?" the slightly befuddled James asked, wide-eyed.

"I could. But I won't."

"I thought so," James said glumly, emptying his glass.

"Well, think on this instead," Tip replied, motioning to the bartender for a fresh round. "How would you explain such a sudden windfall to the *IRS*? Huh?"

"Oh. Good point, Tip."

In the next instant, though, the besotted James brightened. A smile creased his face as a fresh thought entered his mind for the playing of what he thought was simply some sort of quirky bar game.

"The idea is to send me back in time, right?"

"Right!"

"So. Would I be an old man living out the rest of his life in the 1950s and '60s—or would I literally be a little boy, starting over again?"

"Now yer getting' in the spirit, Jimmy!" Tip smiled and leaned closer, his voice taking on a slightly conspiratorial tone.

"Sendin' ya back as an old-timer would do little or nothin' ta change the course of what few years remained of yer life."

"Do I only *have* a few years left, Tip?" James blinked at this slightly sinking thought.

"Not the point, Jimmy," Tip replied dismissively. "Stay with me here. If we were to do this, you and I, I'd be sendin' you back as a lad."

"But since I'm already a boy in the 1950s, in a manner of speaking… wouldn't there be *two* of me there now?"

"Not a'tall. That's the beauty of what I'm proposin', Jimmy.

"If you agreed to let me do it, this current life o' yours would disappear right along with you; as if none of it had ever happened. You'd have a fresh, clean slate upon which you would write a whole, new story. The story of your life."

"Hmmm. But even though I'd physically be a little boy again, I'd still know and remember everything I do now, right?"

"Oh, no!" Tip spat as if the very thought was ridiculous, or at least against whatever imaginary rules dictated this funny little game.

"Such a thing would quickly drive ya mad, m'boy. Think about it for a moment. Let's say you were to return as a 10-year-old boy; livin' in the 1960s but already possessing all the knowledge that you have t'day.

"What good would it do ya?"

"A lot, I'd think," James countered. "I mean, wouldn't I be, like, the smartest boy on Earth?"

"Like yer that smart *now*," Tip replied, motioning for yet another fresh round for the two of them.

"Think, man, think. *You'd* know you were as smart and mature as any average adult was—but to the rest o' the world, you'd simply be the boy you appeared to be. Smart or no, you'd not be allowed to buy or drive a car, or vote, or get a real job, or —" Tip paused to take a sip of his drink.

"Or legally buy a drink!" He literally and visibly shivered at the very idea.

"You couldn't buy or rent a place of yer own. You'd be under the complete control of yer parents. Forget tryin' to emancipate yerself from them; children had no such recourse back then. And that's just what you'd be—a child." Now it was James who shivered slightly.

"You'd be legally required to attend school, surrounded by those who were mentally and emotionally true children. Spending hours each day studyin' subjects you've already learned and mastered.

"I don't even want to *think* about what would happen if you took an amorous likin' ta one o' yer *teachers*. You might *both* end up in jail!

"And just supposin' the grown-ups *did* recognize yer 'genius' and bumped ya straight up ta college. You'd miss all the little joys that come from bein' a child.

"And what would you have instead? You'd be a little boy thrown to the mercies of a buncha *big* boys, with their ragin' hormones and their thoughtless ways. You'd not be allowed to play sports or be invited to join any fraternities.

"And the only girls who didn't scorn ya outright would be the few who wanted ta *mother* ya." Tip sighed heavily. "What a world, what a world."

He patted James on the arm. "Ah, poor Jimmy. You wouldn't even be able to legally purchase the *gun* you'd end up wantin' ta use ta end yer own brief, miserable life.

"Another round, Timothy!"

"Geez, Tip," James groused. "Yer takin' all the fun outta this little game o' yers. What you seem to be offering sounds more like *amnesia* than a fresh start!"

"Oh, there's more to it than that, Jimmy. An amnesiac *knows* he doesn't remember things. You won't."

"So if I accepted this hypo —" James coughed. "This imaginary offer of yours—I wouldn't keep *any* of my current life? Not even the good things?"

"Aww, Jimmy," Tip tsked, shaking his head slightly. "Would you be sittin' alone in a bar on yer birthday, talkin' nonsense with the likes o' me, if there'd *been* so many good things in yer life?" James' features clouded at the words as if he had been physically slapped by them.

"You don't have to rub it in," he muttered, pushing his unfinished drink away.

"But you wouldn't lose *everything*," Tip hastily assured him.

"Oh?"

"How can I explain it simply? Think of the way that some people believe they've been reincarnated because they occasionally experience brief and murky flashes of 'memories' they attribute to earlier times and previous lives they've lived.

"Somethin' similar might happen ta you in yer new life. On occasion, you might get a vague sense of how things are to turn out. Like I say, they'd be vague—like catchin' glimpses of an egg inside a glass o' milk— but brought on by experiences of yer previous life.

"There may be times when wee little bits, just hints really, of yer knowledge and experience will play a hand in yer decision making.

"But make no mistake. You would still have to *make* those decisions. In that you would have total free will. The new future you make for yerself will be written in sand, not stone. Just as before.

"You'll again see those familiar to ya; yer ma and da. And meet new ones. And what you do can and will affect the lives of all of them as well as yerself.

"At each point in life that calls for even the most seemingly inconsequential choice, the choice you make now might be a very, very different one than that which you made at that moment in yer previous life—or it might be exactly the same one. Or one only slightly different."

"I know for damned sure one thing that would be different," James interjected forcefully.

"And what would that be, Jimmy?"

"I'd stand up more to my father. I wouldn't let the old, cold sonuvabitch run my life so much."

"So it was a bad person he was, huh? He mistreated ya?"

James sat in silence for quite some time, tapping furiously at the bar with one finger.

"I guess he coulda been worse."

"Which means he coulda been better, no?"

"We prob'ly all could be better."

"Probably. But it was himself we were talkin' about in particular. You didn't get along?"

"We got along all right."

"But not as well as you would have liked."

"No. I don't know. He was kinda like a rock, y'know? Stout and sturdy. Gave you security but no comfort. Unable to bend without breaking. Impossible to see into."

"Did you try?"

"I was a kid. I didn't know how."

"And yer darlin' mother?"

"She was just a larger kid, God love her. I have a hard time thinking of her as a separate person at all. It's like she became just another one of Dad's appendages."

"Did she love him?"

James snorted. "Oh, yeah. With all her heart. That's maybe the saddest part of it."

"And he didn't love her back, is that it?"

"Oh, I suppose he did. As much as he was able to. Like that rock, it was hard to tell. I sure never heard him tell her he loved her."

"I sometimes think we love people and are loved in return in *spite* of rather than *because* of," Tip mused before taking another sip of his drink.

"You loved the man just like yer mother did, didn't ya, Jimmy?"

"I was wrong," James replied bitterly. "Maybe *that's* the saddest part of it all."

"And did ya ever feel that he loved ya back?"

"Who knows? I've always thought that it was a lot more important to him that he be respected, even feared, than it was to be loved."

"Or to give love." James made a sucking sound with his lips against his teeth.

"He used ta call me 'Champ,' ya know? But I usually felt he was being sarcastic when he did; like he thought I was anything *but* a champion."

"Is this the first time you've ever talked about this, Jimmy?"

"I must be drunk," James said rather sullenly.

"*En vino, veritas.*"

"Whatever. Let's get back to the game." James drained his glass and cast a mildly plaintive, inquisitive glance at Tip, who promptly motioned for the bartender Timothy to bring yet another round.

"Tell me more about my new life," James prompted. Tip noticeably brightened at the prospect.

"You touched on its main aspect, Jimmy. If you go back and start out again, you'll have to fight the fight that every man does, in every existence. It's the fight to *become* a man. Yer own man: one of yer own creation.

"Absolutely nothin' will be preordained, predestined. You'll still be the ultimate master of yer own fate. As a result, you just might end up somewhere completely different than where you find yerself tonight.

"Or, you could end up slavishly following the exact same path to the exact same destination.

"I'll tell ya this much, though. Yer new life *will* be influenced by yer previous one." Tip chuckled softly. "Though you'll never really realize it.

"I'll say this much and no more, Jimmy," he continued, though James felt certain the little man still had *plenty* more to say.

"If yer the sort o' man who's able and willing to learn from mistakes and from experience, then this new life can be a better one for you, I'm thinkin'.

"If yer *not*...then yer new life'll prob'ly be little different from the one yer now drinkin' ta forget."

James' face scrunched up in thought; not an easy task given the amount of alcohol he'd imbibed.

"But if I was to turn out just the same as before," he vocalized at last, "then all this will have pretty much been a waste of your time, won't it?"

"That doesn't matter, Jimmy," Tip said with a sly grin. "After all, unlike most people—I have all the time in the world!"

James grimaced. "It —" he hiccuped. "It occurs to me there's yet a third possible course this new life could take. One you didn't bother to mention."

"And what would that be?"

"I could chase a ball out into the street when I'm ten years old and get hit and killed by a truck!"

In one of his infrequent quiet moments, Tip stared down into his half-empty glass before answering.

"Yes. That, too, is a possibility." He then straightened on his stool.

"But let's not think about that for the moment! Think on this instead, Jimmy. But don't think long: just say the first thing that pops inta yer head.

"If you had to pick just one thing, just one way in which yer life could have been different…what would it be?"

For seemingly no reason, James thought of the proverb he'd seen on the church marquee earlier that evening.

If you want to be loved—be lovable.

Fast as a fox on its heels came mental images of his parents, his son, his ex-wives and a momentary myriad of others. It was a rare and impactful moment of honest self-evaluation.

"Well," he said hesitantly, "I guess maybe I could have been nicer. Nicer to others, I mean."

"That's prob'ly true of most of us, son," Tip said softly.

Funny, James thought. Tip called him "son" even though he appeared to be at least twenty years James' junior.

"And would it be wrong," James said aloud, "to say I maybe could have been a little nicer to *myself* sometimes, too?"

"No. There's nothin' wrong a'tall with that, Jimmy," Tip replied, then nudged him lightly with an elbow.

"So long as it was *only* a little!"

Both men chuckled lightly at that.

"Y'know," James continued, "this is a fun little mental exercise; but there are some big questions that need to be answered."

"Such as what?"

"Well, first and foremost: Why would you make me such an offer?"

"Why wouldn't I?" Tip shrugged. "It's what I do, Jimmy. You might say it's my job."

"Okay. Does everyone my age receive this offer?"

"No."

"Why not?"

"I've pondered that myself. If I ever find out, I'll let ya know."

"Fair enough. How do you know who to make this offer to?"

"I just do, Jimmy."

"Hmmm," James mumbled, obviously less than satisfied with the answers he was receiving. He closed one eye, the better to scrutinize the little man with the other orb.

"Are you an angel?"

"Do I look like an angel? Or act like one?"

"How the hell would I know?" James snapped, then slapped a hand over his mouth as if fearful that the expletive might lead to him being struck by lightning.

"Are there…others…like you, Tip?"

"Yes."

"How many?"

"Enough."

James leaned closer to Tip and lowered his voice. "Is God involved in this?"

"Which god?"

James blinked in puzzlement. "There's more than *one*?"

"You people seem ta think so."

James scowled. "Yer not answering many of my questions."

"That's for you ta do, Jimmy."

"Well, here's somethin' you *can* tell me, Tip ol' boy," James said, his tipsy brain enjoying what he perceived to be nothing more than a simple exercise in what-if.

"Have you made this offer to a lotta guys?"

"Oh, quite a few, yes."

"Any women?"

"Oh, no, no, no. That's someone *else's* department."

"Hmm. And how many have accepted the offer?"

"Not so many as I'd like," Tip replied ruefully. "Most think I'm crazy, or drunk, or both and just blow me off. Some think I'm some sort of scam artist.

"Others suspect I'm a missionary, tryin' ta convince them ta be 'born again.' A couple have actually punched me in the nose.

"And once—and only once—I met a man who thanked me kindly but told me he was perfectly content with the life he'd led."

"Maybe *he* was drunk or crazy!" James jested.

"Mebbe so. Mebbe so." Tip's gaze grew more piercing.

"But some *do* accept the offer, Jimmy."

"Why?" James asked, his mind and tongue grown suddenly sharp again. "Why did they accept it?"

Tip slowly turned his glass around in circles. "Sometimes," he said at last, "it's because they're bold of heart and eager to set off on any new adventure that presents itself.

"Sometimes it's because they know they'll otherwise soon be dead anyway, with little or nothing to mark their passing. Sometimes it's because they see it as a way to forget that which they'd rather not remember.

"But mostly…it's because they're like *you*, James Francis."

"What the hell does that mean?" James snarled defensively.

Tip patted him lightly on the arm. "Don't get yer knickers in a twist, m'boy. But listen to me. Really listen to me." He took a shallow swallow of his drink.

"I'm talkin' about poor unfortunates whose lives have largely been wasted. Oh, to be sure, these people *think* they are content merely to exist. People for whom one day is very like another, in a nearly endless progression.

"You know what I mean, Jimmy. People who could have done more, could have been more…had they only tried a little harder to make the effort."

The gaze he then turned on James was more sad than judgmental.

"People whose lives—and whose deaths—will make no more of a noticeable ripple than would a single leaf falling to the surface of the ocean."

After that, neither man said a word for a full minute.

"I'm surprised only a *couple* of guys punched you," James said at last, his voice spiced with bitterness.

"No one likes to be told his life was meaningless," he muttered, the words tailing off at the end so as to be barely audible.

"Then start over," Tip said rather forcefully. "And this time…this time, Jimmy…this time try to make damned sure no one will ever say that of you again!"

James stared intently down at the remaining drops of his drink. Then, oddly, a smile creased his features and he began to chuckle.

"Damn!" he slurred. "You're *good*, Tip. You're good. For a minute there… you had me thinkin' this was all *real*!"

Tip sighed in response and slid off his stool. He did not seem to be amused.

"So, yer declining my offer, are you?"

"No-no-no-no-no!" James babbled, grabbing clumsily at Tip's arm.

"This is fun!"

"It can be," Tip agreed.

"Okay, then," James said, polishing off the dregs of his drink and slamming the empty glass down atop the bar.

"Count me in!"

"Are ya sure, now, Jimmy?" Tip's face took on a more intense, though slightly mischievous look. "Really sure?"

"THEN START OVER."

"Positiv-Positiv-Absolutely!"

Tip smiled indulgently. "Then, consider it done, m'boy."

"*Cool!*" James giggled in a way that sounded more like a snort.

Sporting a grin that looked equally silly as the one scoring James' face, and once again tapping a finger aside his nose and winking at James, Tip reached into a side pocket on his tattered jacket with his other hand and withdrew a small object.

"This will seal the deal," he said triumphantly. "Consider it my birthday present to you, James Francis!"

On the bar, directly in front of James, Tip placed a small *hourglass*. James had seen such items in a similar size before, usually being sold as three-minute egg timers.

But as he almost reverently bowed his head to more closely examine it, he saw that its wooden ends bore ornate carvings that seemed to him to speak of great age.

To his surprise, and seemingly on its own, the hourglass then began to emit a soft, pale, orange light.

"Whoa!" James bolted upright on his stool as if he had been hit with an electric jolt. "I think it's happening already! I think I'm becoming a baby again!"

"And what makes ya think that?" Tip asked skeptically.

"'Cause it feels like I'm gonna piss my pants!"

Tip put a hand to his mouth to stifle a laugh. "I think...I think that may just be a full bladder yer feelin', Jimmy. I don't know if you've noticed...but you've had a wee too much ta drink!"

"Oh." James slumped slightly.

"Oh!" He bounded off his stool and raced (as best a staggering gait would allow) down the narrow hallway leading to the bathrooms at the rear of the pub.

"Happy birthday, Jimmy," Tip called softly after him. The odd little man brought his glass up to his lips and drained it.

"And good luck to ya!"

It was several minutes later, amazed that the human body could possibly hold let alone excrete such a torrent of fluid, that James returned to his stool. He saw instantly that the little hourglass was still sitting there, though no longer glowing...but there was nary a sign of Tip. James cast his eyes all around the pub, but failed to find the funny little fellow.

"Hey, bartender (What was his name again?)," he called. Timothy walked over, bottle in hand, prepared to pour another round. James waved it off with one hand.

"The little guy I was with. What happened to him?"

The barman merely shrugged, then walked away without a word to wait on another patron. Sighing heavily and long, James slipped the hourglass into his own pocket and exited the pub by a slightly meandering path.

Perhaps it was an indication that both the hourglass and Tip were indeed magical that the inebriated ex-accountant miraculously drove himself home without inflicting any damage upon either himself, anyone else, or any property.

Not long later, he sat on the edge of his bed, staring at the unique little hourglass as it perched now on his nightstand. He had tried in vain to find the switch that would make it glow again, thinking it might make an unusual but useful nightlight.

He chuckled anew at the thought of the crazy but affable little man in the pub—and winced as the effort to laugh sent a jolt of pain through his pounding skull.

As he flipped off the room light and laid back on his pillow, he had begun to sober just enough to know that, come morning, the pain in his head would be far worse.

But the truth was that James Francis...three-time loser at love, unfulfilled bookkeeper, frustrated and lonely soul...

...Would never awaken again.

CHAPTER 3

When the two little bells atop his Roy Rogers alarm clock began to clang from the impact of the metal arm banging back and forth against them, Jimmy Francis quickly slapped the alarm off.

Not that he'd needed it's waking call: not on this particular morning, anyway. He'd already been awake for an hour, too excited to go back to sleep.

He nimbly swung his legs over the edge of his bed and was a little disappointed to see that his feet, as always, didn't touch the floor.

He grinned sheepishly; realizing it had been silly to think, to hope that he might actually have grown *taller* during the night.

Jimmy cast his gaze back upon his alarm clock and saw something else there, sitting beside it on the tall, narrow table next to his bed. Whatever it was, he felt sure it had not been there when he had slid under the covers the night before. He reached out cautiously and picked it up.

It was a small *hourglass.*

A mild pain that suddenly erupted at the base of his head made him blink and grimace slightly; then it was gone.

He was sure he'd never before seen such an object as that he now held in his hands. How, then, did he even know it was called an "hourglass?"

"What's up, Champ?"

Jimmy turned at the sound of the voice. For some inexplicable reason, he was surprised to see his father leaning in through the open doorway of his bedroom.

"You're not gonna stay in bed all morning, are you?" Ted Francis asked. "Not on your fifth birthday."

"Huh-*uh!*" Jimmy yelped. He bounded out of the bed, the small hourglass forgotten as he haphazardly set it back down on his night table.

"Who wants pancakes?" Jimmy's mother Virginia chirped as the boy rushed into the combined kitchen/dining room of their modest, two-bedroom house.

"I do!"

Jimmy climbed up onto the seat of one of the kitchen chairs set against the table, even as his father laid out three plates along with forks and knives. Jimmy frowned as he looked down at the dish Ted had placed before him.

"That's the wrong plate, Dad," he informed the elder Francis.

"Huh? What difference does it make which plate you use?"

"That's the wrong one," Jimmy repeated hesitantly.

Ted looked to his wife for help. Smiling indulgently and wiping her hands on her apron, Virginia left the stove long enough to go to the cupboard, extract a different plate and hand it to Ted.

Still puzzled, he stared at the plate. The difference, if still not the significance of it was clearly evident. Unlike the plain yellow plate he had initially placed in front of his son, this one was white, with a *picture* embossed on its inner surface.

The image was that of a forest setting. In the middle of it stood the figure of a frontiersman, clad all in buckskin. The man held a flintlock rifle, but not in the position for firing. Instead, he held the gun by its long barrel with both hands, upraised like a batter about to swat a baseball. The reason for this was evident; a painted Indian warrior, tomahawk hefted to deliver a killing blow, was charging toward the frontiersman.

Again, Ted turned questioning eyes toward Virginia, who simply gave him a resigned shrug.

"It's his Davy Crockett plate," was the only explanation she could offer.

A couple of years earlier, on its pioneering television series, the Walt Disney company had presented several episodes depicting events in the legendary life of the heroic American hero Davy Crockett, including his valiant death at the Battle of the Alamo.

The series had sparked a nationwide phenomenon. Little boys—and girls—clamored for more Crocketania. Disney happily responded with a wave of Davy Crockett merchandise: everything from T-shirts and toy guns to faux coonskin caps. Even now, such merchandise was cherished by its young owners all over America.

"Kinda silly, isn't it?" Ted Francis said. Jimmy cringed slightly at the sight of the scowl clouding his father's already taciturn features. The boy sought to diffuse it with a smile.

"Pancakes taste better on it, Dad," he tried to explain.

"Instead of being a baby about what plate you use," Ted lectured, "you should just be glad you have something to eat at all.

"There are lots of little kids all over the world who are *starving* right now, you know."

"Yessir," Jimmy replied contritely, hanging his head slightly.

"Oh, leave the boy alone," his mother said, lightly swatting Ted with a dish towel.

"*You're* not the one who'll be cleaning up the sticky mess he's gonna leave behind—*I* am!"

"Just as God intended," Ted retorted, chuckling lightly as he took his own seat. Jimmy's own spirits again picked up at the sound of his father's mirth.

In his time-tested fashion, the little boy first slathered butter (margarine, actually) atop the two pancakes his mother had stacked on his Davy Crockett collector plate. As it began to melt, a layer of chunky peanut butter, then grape jelly and finally a generous pouring of syrup joined it.

"Mmm," Jimmy moaned after shoving a forkful into his mouth. "These are 'specially good today, Mom!"

"They're the same kind of pancakes I always make, Jimmy," Virginia said with a smile. "But thanks."

Her words were informed as much by truth as by modesty, for in fact these pancakes were not discernibly different from those she liked to prepare for her two "men" every couple of weeks or so.

But though he couldn't have explained how or why, to young Jimmy today they tasted like a rare delicacy the likes of which he had not experienced in *years*.

The evening of that special day found Jimmy in his familiar and favorite position for the watching of television: lying on his belly on the carpeted floor, arms bent upwards at the elbow with his hands supporting either side of his head.

As always on that night and at that time, the family was watching *Gunsmoke*. Jimmy's mother objected to him watching this "adult" Western series, but it was Dad who dictated what was to be watched on their single, black-and-white television set.

On this particular night, though, Jimmy was too distracted to pay much attention to the doings of Marshal Matt Dillon, Chester, Doc and Miss Kitty. It had been a full day for the boy, and a good one.

Virginia Francis had hosted a small party for him, attended by half a dozen of the other kids in the neighborhood. There had been games and copious amounts of lemonade, cake and ice cream. And of course presents, which were, after all, the main reasons for bothering to celebrate birthdays.

But no gift at all had been presented to Jimmy from his own parents. To his credit, Jimmy had tried to conceal his hurt and disappointment as well as could any boy his age: which is to say, not terribly well.

Jimmy had no real sense of the relative value of money, aside from knowing it was required to pay for and buy things. He found himself now pondering the possibility that his parents were too *poor* for birthday presents. It was not a comforting thought.

As the closing credits brought the curtain down on tonight's episode of *Gunsmoke*, Ted Francis snubbed his cigarette out in an ashtray, rose from his recliner and made an exaggerated show of yawning and stretching. He had to be at the auto garage where he was one of the lead mechanics early the next day, and thus was off to bed.

As was part of his nightly ritual, Ted walked over to the chair where his wife sat under the glow of a pole lamp, sewing a patch over the torn knee of a pair of Jimmy's blue jeans.

Leaning over, Ted gave Virginia a chaste peck on the cheek and, unseen by Jimmy, gave her a knowing wink as well, causing her to smile.

By now, Jimmy wasn't even looking at the television screen anymore, lying flat on the floor with his face buried in his folded arms.

"Hey, Champ?"

Jimmy rolled over and turned his head to see his father standing in the entry to the hallway that led back to the bedrooms. Ted was holding a rather large, rectangular object wrapped in festive paper.

"You didn't *really* think me and Mom didn't get you anything for your birthday, did you?"

His face now more brightly illuminated than was the flickering TV screen, Jimmy leaped to his feet, raced across the living room and snatched the package from his father's hands.

Dropping back down to the floor on his knees with his legs splayed out to either side, the little boy tore through the concealing wrapping paper like a tornado through a trailer park. He let out a loud gasp of excitement as he fully saw what was revealed. He found himself holding in his own two hands a treasure that was almost beyond imagining.

A Fort Apache Playset!

Jimmy was beside himself. If he could have had only one gift for his birthday—this would be it.

He had become aware of its existence between the covers of a sales catalog from the Sears and Roebuck company. Within the cardboard confines of a brightly colored box was held the promise of everything an imaginative boy would need to make one of the legends of the Old West come to life (some assembly required).

Sections of plastic logs snapped together to form a square stockade, complete with a lookout post at one corner. Putting the correct tabs into the corresponding slots would create a tin barracks building to set inside the stockade. A plastic American flag flew from a plastic pole.

A couple dozen plastic soldiers and horses manned the garrison and were matched by an equal number of savage plastic Indians and their steeds. There was even a plastic teepee (presumably split-level, as to accommodate all the natives).

Like most other American boys of the time, Jimmy Francis was fascinated by tales of the West and he often engaged in pretend battles between cowboys (or soldiers) and Indians.

He was, of course, always the cowboy or soldier. Though his father had once told him that he himself might be nearly a whole one-quarter Cherokee, in Jimmy's still developing mind the Indians were always the enemy.

It didn't bother him to do so, for in truth the Indians of the cinema (who were really the only sort of Indians he knew) weren't so much *real* human beings as they were some sort of nearly mythological creatures that no longer existed: much like the dinosaurs.

Tragically, many actual Indians seemed to hold a somewhat similar view, so thoroughly had they been exterminated and assimilated into the inexorable tide of white culture.

Jimmy's was a benign bigotry, with no true animosity behind it. And in all fairness, occasionally during his many imaginary battles—it was *he* rather than the Indians who met a pretend cruel and fatal end.

And even at the tender age of five he was obtaining a growing awareness of the fact that in actual warfare the participants were not able, like equally mythical Norsemen in their Valhalla, to rise up whole and fight again another day.

What he did know, with almost religious certainty, was that he wanted a Fort Apache Playset with all his heart.

He had tenderly torn the page upon which resided the photo of the playset from the catalog and presented it to his mother along with an impassioned plea that she and his father would see fit to consider him worthy of such a prize.

Virginia did not say "no" to his request, but she did gently comment on the rather steep price required to obtain such an object of great desire.

Four dollars and ninety-five cents.

It was indeed, in the perception of a five-year-old, a veritable king's ransom. He had spoken no more about it to either parent, resigned to the fact that the family budget held no room for such extravagances.

But now, here it was! Like one who had been deigned pure in heart enough to grasp the Holy Grail, Jimmy lovingly held the prize beyond measure in his slightly chubby fingers.

Yet as those fingers flew to the taped flap at one end of the box, that mildly painful tingle throbbed in his head again as it had done that morning. He hesitated.

"What's wrong, Champ?" Ted Francis asked. "Open 'er up!"

"I can't," Jimmy said in a softly strangled voice.

"Why not? You need some help?" There was almost a look of desperation on his son's face and Jimmy looked up at Ted.

"If I open it up and play with it," the little boy said haltingly, "it won't be *mint* anymore!"

"It won't be *what*?" a baffled Ted demanded, his temper quickly starting to flare.

Even though he'd said it, little Jimmy Francis didn't truly know what the word that had just popped out of his mouth meant. But he did somehow know what it portended.

"Once I open the box and play with it," he muttered, an edge of shame that should never spike a five-year-old's tongue leaving a bitter, metallic taste in his mouth, "it'll never be worth as much again."

Both parents were left slightly stunned by this utterance, staring down at their boy slightly slack-jawed.

"Son, do you know how much that damned thing cost me?" Ted Francis finally snarled: the acid in his tone made Jimmy wince as if struck by a physical blow.

"And now you don't even wanna *play* with it? What do you plan to do—just sit there like a retard and look at the damned *box*?"

Virginia knelt down and put an arm around Jimmy's slumped shoulders. "Think about how long and how hard your daddy had to work to buy you that toy," she whispered with a note of urgency.

"I'm sorry," Jimmy said, his words catching slightly in his throat as big tears welled up in little eyes.

"Thanks, Dad," he managed to say, affecting a stiff smile as he looked up at his scowling father.

He then ripped off the tape in a single tearing motion and dipped his hand into the box.

Jimmy played with the set for a while before going off to bed. He would continue to play with it from time to time for several months.

But never with the kind of exuberance and joy that is usually the sole and transient realm of the very young.

CHAPTER 4

A block-long, open-ended alleyway ran behind all the houses lining the neighborhood where nine-year-old Jimmy Francis lived.

The mundane and utilitarian function of the alley was to provide easy access to the city's electrical utility company, for those occasions when they needed to bring in a truck and work on the power poles or lines that were spaced along the alley. It was also useful in their efforts to trim tree limbs away from those lines.

The people whose houses abutted the alleyway expended varying degrees of diligence and effort when it came to tending the stretches behind their individual houses. Some kept the grass short and neatly mowed, the fence lines clear of undergrowth. Others had allowed shrubs and bushes of various sorts to take purchase and grow along the edges.

To children, it provided a straight route from one end of the block to the other without the need to use the street and its obstacles of both parked and moving cars.

To the fertile and imaginative mind of Jimmy Francis, the alleyway also served as a portal to other worlds.

He often pretended it was some sort of isolated wilderness. On this specific, crisp fall day, toy rifle in hand, it was to him a primordial forest; and he was a frontier scout keeping an eagle eye out for hostile Injuns who might be desirous of lifting his scalp. The light brown hair that graced his head was already cut fairly short, in the fashion of the day, but young Jimmy meant to make sure it all remained firmly attached to his skull.

With no siblings of his own, and only a few acquaintances of his own age living within easy walking distance, Jimmy often found himself playing alone. Of course, such was the introspective nature of his personality that he was frequently alone even when in the company of others.

Fortunately, that was just fine with him. He had long since come to realize that he was most comfortable when he was alone with his thoughts. Even when those thoughts were the painful and vaguely disturbing ones that accompanied the mild headaches to which he had been prone since the morning of his fifth birthday.

After four years of experiencing these thankfully infrequent "spells," he no longer gave them much thought or worried about them. When he had initially complained to his parents about them, Ted Francis had accused his son of being a baby and told him just to "shake it off."

By the time he was six, Jimmy had simply stopped mentioning the headaches, either to Ted or Virginia. It was easier that way.

But he was blessed with an active mind that largely compensated for his paucity of friends. For example, with nothing more than a pair of cut-off shorts and a dull, old hunting knife he had found—sheath and all—in a trash can, he was able to take to the trees as the living embodiment of the fictional hero Tarzan of the Apes.

Having not yet read any of the actual Tarzan novels written by creator Edgar Rice Burroughs—or even being aware of their existence—the only image he had of the jungle lord was that of the grunting, Pidgin-English-speaking, near savage presented by Hollywood in a string of motion pictures that aired frequently on television. Jimmy's favorite screen Tarzan, naturally, was former Olympic swimmer Johnny Weissmuller.

Jimmy did a passable imitation of Tarzan's trademark "yodel:" the best his small lungs could manage. The nimbleness of youth made him quite adept at swinging from one tree branch to another.

So good was he that he had only fallen out of a tree *once*. And the springy, almost rubbery qualities of the young body had allowed him to bounce without a scratch.

Armed with only his knife and his courage, Jimmy of the Apes had saved many an ephemeral Maureen O'Sullivan from lions and gorillas. And from primitive, yowling natives, too: of the type that made Hollywood's portrayal of Indians seem downright enlightened by comparison.

An old yardstick, which his father had discarded after using it to stir paint, had become, in Jimmy's hands, the *sword* he used to fight his way past the Sheriff of Nottingham's guards. On many occasions, pretending to be the Outlaw of Sherwood Forest, he had hacked and stabbed his way through their ranks on his way to rescue the lovely Maid Marion.

The Adventures of Robin Hood was one of his favorite movies: Errol Flynn one of his favorite actors. And Flynn's frequent co-star, Olivia de Havilland: to young Jimmy (and even, long after, to *old* Jimmy) the actress epitomized the beauty, grace and charm of feminine perfection.

But the "weapon" in which Jimmy took the most personal pride was a pistol that at the moment was thrust into the belt of his jeans.

What made it such a source of pride for him was the fact that he had more or less made it himself. He had done so by slowly and laboriously carving its admittedly crude shape from a piece of soft wood, using a treasured pocket knife given to him by his Grandpa Taylor, his mother's father, not long before the old man passed away.

Jimmy had considered and discarded the idea of trying his hand at wood carving several times, until he happened to find this particular piece of wood among some discards a neighbor had carelessly tossed into the alley. Cradling the chunk of wood as if it were priceless ivory, and spurred on by one of his tingling headaches, he had decided to try his hand at shaping it into something else. He told no one else about the project until it was nearly finished, keeping the wood hidden beneath his bed, lest he be forced to give it up and thus admit his failure before others.

He had taken more than a few painful nicks out of his own flesh in the process of shaping the wood, literally pouring his blood and sweat into the target of his efforts. The finished product, while hardly a work of art, was unmistakably shaped like a real pistol, right down to the immobile hammer and trigger.

It had taken on an even more authentic look when, under the critical but helpful supervision of his dad, Jimmy had added a coat of dark varnish to it.

It might not have amounted to much, not when compared to professionally tooled toys, but it was all his: the product of his own hands and his own imagination.

He wouldn't have traded it away for all the tea in China.

In the process of making it, Jimmy had discovered that he truly enjoyed the feel of the blade in his hand, almost as if it were another appendage that accompanied his fleshly fingers.

He had also found himself filled with a deep and satisfying sense of accomplishment as he turned an otherwise useless and virtually formless block of wood into something else, something more.

This self-taught "skill" had already paid Jimmy several dividends. This was still what was at least perceived to be a simpler time: a time when young students in school occasionally sought to curry favor with teachers by gifting them with little "bribes" such as a fresh, ripe apple.

While riding with his parents one Sunday afternoon, Jimmy had happened to see his current teacher—a barely middle-aged woman who, despite her actual marital status, was known to her pupils as "Miss" Penny—out walking her dog.

Inspired by this, Jimmy had put his best efforts into carving a small replica of a similar dog and presenting it to Miss Penny before the start of class one day.

She made quite a fuss over it, praising its artistry and the thoughtfulness behind it in front of the entire class. A few of his less imaginative classmates seemed a bit resentful of the attention: snide comments about a "teacher's pet" were inevitable.

That didn't bother Jimmy in the least. He was quite rightly proud of himself, not the least because he knew his was a gift that would far outlast any old apple.

(Indeed, though he would never know it, a sentimental Miss Penny would lovingly display the little wooden dog atop every desk behind which she sat until the day she retired as a teacher.)

Jimmy couldn't have said for sure that the gift really earned him any special favors in school or resulted in even the slightest upward bump in his grades; but he didn't much care.

He truly liked the caring and attentive Miss Penny, and he liked that he had made her happy.

Nor did it escape his notice that, a few jealous remarks aside, most of the other kids were greatly impressed by what he had done. What *he* had done, and done alone.

The reactions of Miss Penny and the other kids to his efforts were made doubly sweet by the knowledge that they had been engendered by the product of his own mind and his own hands.

The woodcarving was also of therapeutic value to Jimmy. Even children—even those children blessed to live in a stable environment—have stresses in their young lives, coming from a variety of sources. They may be things that, to an adult, would barely rate the label of being an annoyance, but that can loom large in the mind of a developing adolescent.

Jimmy had discovered that an act as simple as just whittling a stick of wood (often done while sitting astride a branch in some good climbing tree) brought to him a great sense of relaxation, even security.

But now was not the time for such idle reverie: now he needed to be alert and watchful for any sign of the enemies who meant him harm. Clutched in his hands was his current most valued possession aside from his pistol: a toy, lever-action rifle modeled after the one used by the eponymous star of the television series *The Rifleman*.

It was in actuality a rather cheap knock-off of the authentic, licensed toys inspired by the hit show: one of many such imported from Japan. But young Jimmy Francis knew nothing of such business practices; nor would it have made much difference if he did. For when it was held in his two hands, it was magically transformed by the power of childhood imagination into a weapon that was as lethal as any known to man. To his ears, the popping sound made by the roll of caps inserted into the rifle's action sounded like the rolling thunder of an artillery barrage.

In his current self-invented scenario, Jimmy was a tough, grizzled frontiersman, drafted into acting as a scout for a troop of U.S. cavalry. It was his job to be on the lookout for any skulking "redskins" that might be lurking in ambush.

To Jimmy's mild surprise, he actually did hear a faint rattling sound on the other side of some nearby bushes.

It probably arose from something no more threatening than a sparrow or a tiny horned toad, scavenging about in the leaves; but Jimmy's agile mind instantly transformed it into a potential danger that he needed to cautiously check out.

(And if it should indeed turn out to be nothing more than a "horny toad," that wouldn't be in the least disappointing. Like many boys his age, Jimmy found these miniature "dinosaurs" to be quite fascinating. Harmless and easy to catch, he often made one his pet-for-a-day before releasing it back into the wild.)

Moving as quietly as possible, he pushed past the branches of the bushes till he found himself facing a length of chain-link fence. He took momentary notice of honeysuckle lacing in and out of the myriad gaps in the fencing.

As he drew ever closer to the fence, a new and not unfamiliar sound carried to his alert ears.

It was the sound of another child's muffled sobbing.

Keeping himself as concealed and quiet as he could manage, Jimmy pushed nearer through the foliage to investigate the source of those sobs of apparent distress. Perhaps it was someone in need of the services of an experienced and battle-hardened scout such as himself.

Drawing nigh to the fence that marked the back boundary of the nearest home, Jimmy quickly and easily identified the source of the crying.

It was coming from a little boy, partly turned away from him and huddled on the ground with his back pressed against the knobby trunk of a tall mimosa tree.

Jimmy recognized the sniffling boy, though he couldn't say he actually knew him. While his tiny, almost stunted size made him appear younger, the boy was the same age as Jimmy: a student at the same school.

He was, by most standards,, an odd little fellow. Jimmy knew that much about him, though he had never personally witnessed any purported weird behavior. *Others* said so, and Jimmy chose to believe them. There were, after all, far more of "them" than there were, of this little geek.

The boy's name was a perfectly normal sounding one: Dickie Watson. Because of the reddish hair, freckles and protruding ears attached to a head mildly disproportionate to his little body, though, most of the other guys had taken to calling him *"Howdy Doody"* after the popular TV puppet. They called him this right to his face, on those rare occasions when they deigned to speak to him at all.

Not that he had much choice in the matter, given that he was one and small and they were many and big. But little Dickie took the teasing well, usually responding to it with no more than a smile and a shrug of his slender shoulders. His good-natured personality and the fact that only shame would accrue to the act of whipping such as he spared Dickie from most physical bullying; certainly from the worst.

He tended to keep to himself, more as the result of the teases and taunts than because of any innate desire to be alone. More often than not, if anyone took note of him at all they would see his face buried in the pages of some book.

Jimmy started to back away from the fence. Whatever had upset Howdy was of no concern to him: certainly none of his business. There was nothing to be gained by sticking his nose into another's affairs. But there could be something to lose, in terms of his own standing in the third-grade community, if he was seen in the company of such a social pariah.

He'd barely begun to shuffle backwards when a familiar but no less annoying little stab of pain erupted at the back of his neck. Gritting his teeth, he reached around to rub the sore spot.

Dickie Watson had his legs bent upward, his arms wrapped around them. His head was bent forward between his knees as if in an effort to muffle the sound of his crying.

"Hey!"

Dickie's head snapped up, his expression clearly showing how startled he was suddenly to hear an unexpected voice calling down to him from above.

Jimmy Francis was inwardly rather proud of himself. He had managed to climb the fence and make the short jump from it into the mimosa tree without Dickie having heard him. Proof in his own little mind that he would have made a great Indian scout in real life.

"I'm Jimmy Francis," he called down.

"I know," Dickie replied, wiping his nose on the back of his shirtsleeve. "Wotta you want?"

"Can I come down?"

"I guess," Dickie shrugged, rising to his feet as Jimmy climbed down a few branches before letting go and dropping lightly the rest of the way to the ground.

"What's wrong with you?" he then asked, with the honest bluntness of most children before time and conventions beat it out of them.

"Nothin'," Dickie said defensively, turning his face away in embarrassment.

"Then why are you crying?"

"I'm not crying! I'm not a baby!"

"I didn't say you were," Jimmy responded gruffly. "But I saw you crying." Dickie made no reply to that.

"Did someone hit you?"

"No."

"So why are you crying?" Jimmy pressed.

"'Cause we're all gonna *die*, okay?" Dickie wailed, spinning to again face the bigger boy. "Ya happy now?"

Jimmy frowned, staring in puzzlement at the distraught boy. He may be more than just a geek, Jimmy thought.

He might be *nuts*!

"What makes ya think we're gonna die?" he asked, keeping his voice slow and calm so as not to cause further upset.

"You wouldn't understand."

"I might. I don't read as many books as you do, but I ain't no dummy, either."

Dickie said nothing, but Jimmy felt sure he wanted to.

"C'mon. What is it?"

"It's something I heard my mom and dad talking about," Dickie finally declared.

"Do you know what's happening in *Cuba*?"

"Uh…no," Jimmy rather reluctantly confessed. "What's Cuba?"

"It's an island where Commies live. You know what Commies are, don'tcha?"

"Of course I do," Jimmy snorted.

Everybody in America knew what Commies were. Mostly, they were Russians, who seemingly were monsters with no goal in life other than the dropping of atom bombs on the United States.

Like all schoolchildren in America, Jimmy had repeatedly gone through the preparedness drills at school that were euphemistically called "Duck and Cover." When the alarm bell sounded, each pupil dropped to his knees beneath his desk and covered his bowed head with his hands.

The children indulged the grownups by unflaggingly going through this exercise—even though they knew full well that neither a desk nor their clasped hands would provide the least bit of protection if they happened to be unfortunate enough to be at or near Ground Zero.

"Well," Dickie now expounded, "Cuba must be crawling with Commies. And they're about to shoot missiles at us!"

This was an understandably simplified explanation of what would come to be known to history as the Cuban Missile Crisis; but little Dickie's narrative was sufficient for the moment.

"I heard my dad tell Mom that there wasn't really any place that would be safe from 'em." Dickie sniffed to hold back fresh tears.

"So we're all gonna die!" he logically concluded, his voice choking.

Jimmy squinted; not because of the prospect of nuclear annihilation but because of the dull throbbing that had again arisen in the back of his skull.

"No, we're not," he said softly but firmly.

"Huh?"

"We're not gonna die," Jimmy repeated.

"How do *you* know?"

"I just do, okay? President Kennedy won't let it happen"

"How will he stop it?"

"I don't know. But he will."

"You sound awful sure."

"I am. We stopped the Nazis; we can stop the Commies, too."

Amazingly, even though he was just a little boy himself, the certainty in Jimmy's eyes and tone of voice proved to be assuring to Dickie. He rubbed a little more snot from his nose onto the back of his sleeve and managed a wan smile.

"Why don't we eat some honey?" Jimmy now suggested. "That'll make you feel better." The logic of this assertion was dubious at best, but to Jimmy the ingestion of anything sweet was bound to make life look a little rosier.

"Where we gonna get honey?" Dickie asked.

"From your honeysuckle vines," Jimmy said, pointing toward the foliage-covered back fence.

"What do you mean?"

"You never got honey from honeysuckle?"

"No."

"Boy, you've been readin' the wrong books," Jimmy said rather condescendingly. "Let me show ya."

He did just that: deftly demonstrating how to extract a precious drop or two of the sweet nectar from the vines' blossoms.

"Pretty good, huh, Howdy?" he said, then immediately realized he had blurted out the derogatory nickname. "I mean, Dickie."

"It's okay," the small boy said, smiling. "Don't tell the other kids, but I like 'Howdy' better than I do 'Dickie'."

"Really?"

"Yeah. I think it sounds kinda like a cowboy name. You know, like the way they call Hopalong Cassidy 'Hoppy'."

"Yeah," Jimmy said. "It does." The turn in the conversation reminded him of what his original mission had been before the interruption of Commies, A-bombs and honeysuckle.

"You wanna play cowboys and Indians with me?" he asked, hoisting his rifle.

"Sure," Howdy replied eagerly. "Just let me go get my gun!"

Within a few days, the Cuban Missile Crisis did indeed end short of bombs flying and the world quickly settled back down to its Cold War normalcy.

Duck and Cover.

About that time, in the cafeteria of Bryant Elementary School, Jimmy Francis was partaking of what in the 1960s would be considered a nutritious lunch, along with a few of his buddies. One subject of their mealtime discussions was the number of days remaining before their next release from the confines of academia for Thanksgiving break.

Jimmy glanced up to see little Howdy Watson standing and holding his own lunch tray nearby, looking expectantly at him.

By way of response, Jimmy quickly dropped his eyes back down to the table, pretending he had not seen Howdy.

Almost instantly, a wave of shame washed over him, accompanied by yet another of those tingling if transitory aches in his head.

"Hey, Howdy!" he called out. Howdy, eyes also downcast, had already begun to turn away; but now looked back at Jimmy.

"C'mon over!" Jimmy invited, pointedly ignoring the scathing glares he was receiving from the other boys at the table.

"Hi, guys!" Howdy chirped as he plopped down next to Jimmy: obviously delighted by the invitation and eager to accept it.

He was a smart little boy, though, and fully aware that he was not really welcomed at the table by most of the others. Buoyed by Jimmy's gesture of acceptance, though, he decided to respond differently to the others' hostility this time.

"I don't know why you guys look at me so funny," he said, holding up a single French fried potato and waving it slightly for emphasis.

"I'm really just like you, you know. I look like you. I talk like you." He glanced at the French fry. "I even eat like you."

At that point, imitating a simple yet time-honored magic trick he'd picked up in one of his many books, Howdy appeared to shove the French fry up one of his nostrils (while actually palming it)—then began moving his jaws as if he was chewing it up before swallowing. To further nail the illusion, he deliberately produced a prodigious burp (the ability to do so on demand being much admired by boys of a certain age).

Unable to help themselves, the other little boys at the table began to laugh loudly. One laughed so hard that a squirt of milk shot from one nostril.

"Look!" Jimmy said, getting into the spirit of the moment and pointing to the boy. "Joe must eat with his nose, too!"

This engendered even more laughter, causing yet another of the boys at the table to expel a rather loud fart.

"Ew!" another boy yelped. "Chris must eat with his *butt!*"

In the face of such sophisticated humor, the laughter around the cafeteria table grew even more raucous: so much so that one teacher on monitor duty cast a suspicious eye upon the boys.

Little Howdy Watson would never become terribly popular around the school; he'd certainly never be considered one of the "cool" kids. But after that day in the cafeteria, the worst of the bullying came to an end. Even the name "Howdy" became just a title rather than a mark of derision.

He had made one true friend, in the person of Jimmy Francis. A relationship that might well have never existed at all became a bond that would carry both of them through life.

CHAPTER 5

It was a pleasant Saturday, not long after Jimmy Francis turned ten.

The morning cartoon shows he still greatly enjoyed had ended and he had taken that as his cue to retreat to his small bedroom. He was lying on his belly atop his as yet unmade bed, reading a copy of the latest issue of his favorite comic book: *Amazing Spider-Man*.

His pal Howdy had failed in most of his efforts to transform Jimmy into the kind of avid reader he was; but it had required little effort to convert him at least into a follower of these garish, four-color epistles.

Hearing a noise outside, Jimmy swiveled his gaze to peer through the partially opened blinds of his window. Out in the driveway, he saw his father carrying various types of fishing tackle out to the family station wagon.

Brief fishing trips to a small, nearby lake were among Ted Francis' favorite pleasurable activities. He had long since given up on asking his son to come along with him as an exercise in futility. Being that angling was an amply solitary activity, he'd felt no great compulsion to press the issue.

At least the boy had a moderate interest in playing baseball. That was something, Ted thought.

...READING A COPY ...OF HIS FAVORITE COMIC BOOK...

Inside the house, Jimmy returned his attention to his comic book. His head dropped between his shoulders and he groaned almost inaudibly as one of his mystery headaches suddenly made its presence felt.

Because of the tingling sensation associated with these bouts, Jimmy had come to think of them dismissively as being his very own "spider sense."

Ted Francis was taking a final mental inventory. He had packed his large and well-provisioned tackle box as well as three fishing poles of various types. A small ice chest held three cans of beer and a bottle of Pepsi. As usual, wife Virginia had also insisted on sending him off with enough sandwiches to feed Cox's Army.

He closed the tailgate of the station wagon and couldn't conceal his surprise when he turned around to see young Jimmy standing there. In addition to his usual weekend ensemble of blue jeans and T-shirt, the boy was also wearing a favored New York Yankees baseball cap.

(Geography aside, half the boys in America wanted to be Mickey Mantle: hence, they were Yankees fans.)

"What's up, Champ?" Ted asked, eager to be on his way.

"Nothin'," Jimmy replied, lowering his gaze to scratch the back of his head. "I was just wondering if I could come with ya today."

"Yeah?" Ted made no effort to hide the suspicious expression on his face. "How come?"

"No reason. I just thought it might be fun."

"You sure?"

"Yeah." Jimmy scuffed the toe of one tennis shoe across the concrete of the driveway. "You know...I got nothin' else ta do."

"Okay. Well, let's get goin', then."

The forty-five minute drive to tiny municipal Lake Iola passed mostly in silence punctuated only occasionally by meaningless small talk. Ted remained suspicious of his son's motives. Those suspicions grew when, upon reaching a likely spot along the lake's shore, Jimmy declined to accept the use of one of Ted's fishing poles.

"Well, son," the man asked, "if you don't wanna fish—why'd you wanna go *fishing*?"

Jimmy responded with a slightly exaggerated shrug.

"It's kinda like you always say, Dad. It doesn't really matter if you catch anything or not, so long as you get to relax and enjoy the fresh air. That's what I'm doin'."

"Uh-huh," Ted said. He was more likely to believe in UFOs than in this explanation, but chose not to let that deter him from what he was there to do.

A short time later, he noticed that Jimmy had gotten up and drifted away a short distance down the shoreline. Pulling off his shoes and sox and rolling up the legs of his blue jeans, the boy waded out into a shallow pool of water, from which rose several stalks of stiff reeds. With the help of his ubiquitous pocket knife, Jimmy sawed off about six inches from the top of one such stalk.

Returning to the spot near where his father sat in a lawn chair while watching the corks from two separate fishing poles bob on the surface of the lake, Jimmy plopped back down on the ground, sitting cross-legged.

After holding up the stout but hollow reed and peering as if through a telescope, Jimmy then began to use his knife to start drilling small holes along the length of one side of the reed. He then cut off one end of the reed at a slight angle.

"What on earth are you doin', son?" Ted asked, his curiosity getting the better of him and diverting his attention away from his poles.

By way of response, Jimmy put the slanted end of the reed in his mouth and blew. A distinct whistling sound came out the other end, varying in pitch and tone as he then played his fingers over the holes he had drilled in it.

"It's a flute, Dad," he said cheerfully, blowing a few more slightly sour notes.

"Hnnh," his father grunted. "Have you ever made one of those before?"
"Nope."

"So, you don't really know what you're doing?"

"I guess not," Jimmy replied. Looking slightly downcast, he bent his head and blew a few more notes from the pipe.

"Not bad," Ted said, much to Jimmy's surprise.

"If you want, when we get back to the house we can slather a little lacquer on it: make it look a little jazzier."

"Cool. Maybe I'll make some more while we're here. You know, a couple extra to give to my friends."

"That's fine, Champ. But why not try *selling* them instead?"

"You think I could?" Jimmy asked, the idea never having entered his juvenile mind of its own volition.

"You could try. I don't think you'd get much: maybe a nickel. But nickels can add up. And they'd be all yours.

"Let me tell ya somethin', son. A man always feels better about himself and about life in general when he's got a little walking around money in his pocket."

Jimmy liked the idea, gazing down at the simple whistle in his hand in a whole new light.

"Now that I know it works," he told his father, "I thought I might try something else, too."

"Like what?"

"It's somethin' I saw in one of Howdy's books."

"That kid's kinda squirrelly, ain't he?" Ted interjected.

"A little. But he's okay. Anyway, you take four or five of these reeds, cut 'em to different length, and sorta glue 'em all together."

"Really?"

"Yeah. I think they call it a *Pan Flute*."

"Hmm. Well, it sure wouldn't hurt to try. There's plenty of reeds over there, yours for the picking. You can cut ya a whole bunch of 'em if you want and we'll bring 'em home with us. If you can get one of them—what'd ya call it?"

"Pan Flute."

"If you can get one of 'em put together and it really works, who knows? You might be able to get a *quarter* for it."

"Wow." In a day when a penny still had purchasing power of its own, the thought of having twenty-five of them at once was enough to infect a child with copper fever.

Jimmy quickly took up another reed and began to work on it, before casually looking up at his father, who had picked up one of his poles to give the cork a little bob or two he hoped would entice a fish.

"Did you ever think of naming me Ted, Junior, Dad?"

Ted glanced over his shoulder at Jimmy, then returned his attention to the pole in his hands.

"What makes you ask that, son?"

"Oh, nothin'. I got a couple of juniors in my class, that's all."

"Yeah, I thought about it. It's what I wanted to do. But your mother wouldn't let me."

"How come?"

"Oh, she said something about letting you grow up to be your own person, instead of just a little version of me."

Jimmy chuckled. "I don't think I'd like it if people called me 'Little Ted'."

"I don't guess I would, either, Champ."

"So why'd you call me James?"

"It's a good, strong name. Solid. 'Sides, I always liked the actor James Stewart."

"Ah." Jimmy now also knew how he came by his *middle* name.

The boy went silent then for a few minutes, working industriously on his next reed flute. Finishing it, testing the sound that came from it and finding it to be satisfactory, he set both flute and pocket knife to one side.

"Dad?"

"Yeah?"

"Can I ask you about somethin'?"

Ted Francis emitted a low, disgruntled groan. He placed his fishing pole on the ground, lodged between two rocks to hold it upright at an angle. He fished a pack of Marlboros out of his shirt pocket and used a Zippo lighter to ignite the end of one of the cigarettes. He took a deep drag, holding it in his lungs for several seconds before exhaling.

"I knew there had to be a reason for you suddenly wanting to tag along today," he said, his voice sounding resigned.

"What do you mean?"

"You're wanting to have the *sex talk*, aren't you?"

"Huh? Eww! God, no!" The very thought of discussing such an intriguing but darkly forbidden subject with his father was repellent to the boy.

"Good. Good." Ted visibly relaxed, then looked at his son with some sternness.

"Besides, there's really only one thing you need to know about that."

"Just one?"

"Just one."

"What is it?" Jimmy asked, a curiosity he had not felt at all a minute earlier now beginning to well up inside him.

"It's just this: If you ever get a girl in trouble...by God, you're gonna do the right thing and marry her!" He tossed the smoldering butt of his cigarette out into the lake.

"You got that?"

"I got it," Jimmy gulped.

"Good." Ted again took one of his fishing poles in his hands.

"Now what was it you *did* want to ask me?"

For a moment, Jimmy forgot what he had wanted to ask before their unexpected digression into the mire of matrimony. He took another moment trying to formulate adequately what he wanted to ask and how he wanted to ask it, then decided to just let it flow.

"Was it really bad for you in the war?"

Ted Francis' face took on a darker, more solemn cast than it had carried before.

"I don't like to talk about that, son."

"I know you don't, Dad. But I wish you would. Even just a little."

"How come?"

"Because you're my dad. And because I might have to go to war some day, too."

"I hope not, boy."

"Me, too." Jimmy knew he was in too deep to stop now.

"You were there at D-Day, weren't you? On one of the beaches?"

"How do you know about D-Day?"

"I got a book from the library."

(That was partly true; but partly, Jimmy just *knew*. The way he seemed to instinctively know about other things from time to time. Things normally beyond the ken of a boy his age. He just knew.)

"But I wanna know more than just book stuff. I wanna know about you."

Still holding his pole in one hand, Ted used the other to shake a fresh cigarette from his pack and light up.

"Yeah," he said at length. "I was at Omaha Beach."

"Were you a'scared?"

Ted fixed him with a hard stare before answering. "Would you have been?"

Jimmy moved his own eyes away to gaze out over the lake. "Yeah."

"Then you'd have been smart. Yeah, I was scared. We all were. I 'spect the Germans were, too.

"It was hell on earth, son. Bullets flying everywhere. Bombs going off. Men screaming their lungs out."

"God," Jimmy sighed. "How do you get over somethin' like that?"

"You don't, Champ. You just live with it as best you can." Ted deeply exhaled smoke.

"Let's not talk about it anymore, okay?"

"Okay."

Nor would they—that day. But a gap had been bridged, and upon it Jimmy would build. From time to time, in bits and pieces, he would come to know more about his father's life experiences. Not just in the War, but in the Great Depression that preceded it.

Jimmy learned how his father had felt compelled to leave school after the eighth grade in order to help support his family. How Ted and his younger brother Wayne—who would be killed in the Pacific Theater—had made money by diving for lost golf balls at the municipal course, cleaning them up and reselling them. These stories and more Jimmy gleaned from his father. Along with stories, Ted imparted what knowledge he had accrued.

With knowledge came understanding, and from understanding grew knowledge.

From both comes wisdom.

Ted Francis began to look at the boy differently in the course of their conversations: almost like he was a little friend in addition to being his son. Someone he grew increasingly at ease with when talking about a wide range of subjects.

"Dad," Jimmy said on that day at the lake that started it all, "can I tell you somethin' and you not get mad?"

"That depends. Have you done something wrong?"

"No."

"Then I probably won't get mad."

Jimmy took a deep breath, but let the words flow out along with the air. "I think you should tell Mom you love her more often."

"Oh, you do, do you?" Ted replied, suppressing a grin.

"Yeah."

"Why?" The hint of a smile now faded. "Did Mom say something to you?"

"No."

Ted frowned slightly. After flipping away the remnants of his Marlboro he took the time to light up a fresh cigarette before he spoke again.

"Your mother knows I love her, Jimmy. Why else would I work so hard to pay the bills and to keep a roof over our heads and food on the table?"

"I know she knows, Dad," Jimmy said, tapping the side of his head lightly. "In here." He then tapped his breast.

"I just think she maybe needs to know it more in here, that's all."

"Ya do, huh? And just what is it that makes you think that?"

"I dunno," Jimmy replied, not wanting to tell his dad about the tingling little headache he was feeling right now. Ted thought, not for the first time, of what an odd little boy it was that he had fathered.

"But I think it's true," Jimmy continued, his youthful brow furrowing slightly.

"You don't have to do it all the time," he explained to his father. "Just every once in awhile. Just let her know you 'preciate her.

"I dunno, tell her you like her cooking or the way she cleans the house. Maybe give her some candy even when it ain't Valentine's Day. That kinda stuff." The child looked expectantly up at the man, but could read nothing in his stoic face.

"Does any of that make sense?"

Ted's expression did change now: to one of mild puzzlement.

"How long have you been thinking about this, son?"

"Not too long. Why?"

"It just seems kinda, I don't know...*deep* for a 10-year-old. You're *sure* Mom didn't put you up to this?"

"God, no. She'd prob'ly be embarrassed if she heard what I just said."

"I reckon she would. I know *I* am." Ted flipped away the less than half smoked cigarette and turned his attention back to the fishing pole in his other hand.

"You know," he said finally, "it probably wouldn't hurt for *you* to do that sorta stuff for Mom more often, too."

The slight grin he threw toward his son showed the boy his father wasn't angry or scolding. Slightly abashed, Jimmy ducked his head and scratched the back of it.

"*Whoa!*" his dad yelped as the tip of the rod in his hand suddenly bowed deeply downward.

"Looks like I got a big'un!"

"Let me help!" Jimmy shouted, leaping to his feet and moving toward his father.

In his haste he failed to notice that the large stones lining the shoreline were wet and covered with patches of slimy moss. As the heel of his right foot came down on one such patch, it slipped out from under him. The boy did a half gainer and plunged into the lake's cold waters.

Having had time enough only to gulp in a shallow breath before breaking the surface, Jimmy momentarily panicked as he plunged deeper. A harsh bubbling sound assailed his ears and he had difficulty keeping his eyes open.

Instinct prevailed when thinking failed. The boy extended his arms and began to pump them up and down. At the same time he flipped his bare feet back and forth until he felt himself beginning to rise.

The instant he broke the surface of the lake and desperately sucked in a wheezing rush of air, he felt strong hands latching onto his shoulders. With a single jerk, Ted Francis pulled his son from the grasp of the water.

Jimmy lay where he fell, spitting and coughing up water he'd swallowed and wiping at his stinging eyes. His breathing was rapid and shallow, while his heart well-nigh threatened to burst from his tiny chest.

As both pulse and respiration slowly returned to normal, Jimmy became aware that his father, having tumbled to a sitting position after plucking the boy from the water—was *laughing*.

"What's so funny?" Jimmy snapped angrily. Ted's laughter subsided, ending in a hacking cough.

"Nothing, son. Nothing," he gasped. "It just struck me, though—that you're the biggest catch I've ever fished outta this damned lake!"

Much as he didn't want to, Jimmy found himself laughing along with his father.

"Well," he managed to sputter, "just so long as you don't throw me back in!" Ted laughed so hard at that he had to hold both hands over his aching belly.

Back home a couple hours later, as the pair trekked up the walkway leading to their house, Ted placed a hand on Jimmy's shoulder.

"I appreciate that you made the effort to go fishing with me today, Champ," the father said. "But, uh...you don't ever have to do that again, okay?"

"Thanks, Dad," Jimmy replied, grinning up at his father. Ted then made an exaggerated pucker with his lips.

"And do *you* need me to say I love you every once in a while, too?"

"Eww!" Jimmy's features screwed up and he pulled away slightly, causing Ted to smile. "No, I'm good, Dad." (For all his sudden and youthful enlightenment, Jimmy was still of the mind that guys simply didn't say such things to other guys. If you wanted a fella to know you liked him— you lightly punched him on the arm.)

As they entered the front room of the house, Ted gave his son a light "noogie" atop his head.

"Go change outta those soggy clothes and get ready for supper." He lowered his voice slightly.

"And let's not tell Mom I nearly let you drown, okay?"

"Gotcha."

Jimmy lingered in the living room though: long enough to see Ted enter the kitchen where Virginia was at the counter, cutting up lettuce for a salad.

"We're home from the hunt," Ted announced. As he drew near to his wife, he patted her lightly on the butt and kissed her on the cheek. Virginia jumped slightly, but then leaned her head against Ted's shoulder—

never missing a stroke as she sliced away at the lettuce. Jimmy smiled as he watched.

But then, still not heading immediately to his bedroom, he tiptoed across the living room to where sat the one and only telephone in the household. Slowly and quietly, he dialed a familiar number.

"Hello?" said an equally familiar voice, picking up after the third ring. Perfect.

"Hey, Howdy. It's me."

"Hey, Jimmy. What's up?"

"Listen. You're a pretty smart fella."

"That's what I keep telling you."

"Shut up!" Jimmy hissed. "I got a question for ya."

"Okay. What is it?"

Jimmy looked over his shoulder to make sure he was still alone in the room and out of earshot of his parents. He next cupped one hand around the telephone receiver before whispering into it.

"How do you get a girl in trouble?"

CHAPTER 6

Jimmy was patiently arranging his troops on the battlefield.

Which was to say, he was lining his toy soldiers up in rows on his bedroom floor. His was a most diverse army: including cowboys and Indians amongst the more suitable World War II plastic figures.

Only Jimmy was aware that this was a doomed brigade. Once he got them all lined up in their rows, they would then be subjected to heavy artillery fire: meaning Jimmy would begin to mow them down by shooting at them with rubber bands.

Though he could not have told anyone, including himself, why, Jimmy had always been fascinated by Lost Causes and Last Stands: Custer at the Little Bighorn, the Texians at the Alamo, the 300 Spartans at Thermopylae. Occasionally, when playing alone outdoors, he would pretend to be an entire squad of soldiers: "dying" again and again until the attacking Indians had wiped out his entire command.

Before he could commence the opening barrage of this particular massacre, however, his father poked his head in and knocked on the open doorway.

"Hey, Champ. You wanna go out in the backyard and play a little catch before supper?"

"Sure!" Jimmy chirped, jumping to his feet and grabbing up his baseball mitt.

He enjoyed tossing the ball back and forth with his dad. Not for the physical activity it afforded, but because it always came with conversation.

Ever since they had made their fishing trip together a few months prior, Jimmy had noticed a subtle but definite change in his father. It was a change for the better, too, in the eyes of the boy.

Ted had seemed to soften slightly, become more relaxed. He was still tough as an old boot, yet was less stiff and unyielding in his demands and in his behavior around Jimmy and his wife Virginia.

Best of all, Ted had slowly begun to talk more often and more openly with Jimmy. Mostly about his war experiences at first, but later just about things in general. He was open and responsive to Jimmy's many questions (so long as they didn't concern S-E-X).

It was a change Jimmy liked and appreciated.

Something was a little off on this particular day, though. Jimmy sensed it in various ways. His dad usually didn't smoke while they played catch, but today he'd lit up a Marlboro before the first pitch was thrown. Nor did he say a word for several minutes. When he did at last speak, it was clear he was a bit ill at ease.

"I got somethin' I gotta tell ya, Jimmy," he finally said.

"What's that, Dad?"

"Well…something's happened. And in a way, you had something to do with it."

Jimmy's throat tightened. "Did I do something wrong?"

"No. No. Nothin' wrong." Ted was clearly struggling for words. "You remember that talk you and me had out at the lake? About how I should treat your mother?"

"Uh-huh."

"I took your advice."

Jimmy had already noticed as much, as well as what he perceived to be a warmer atmosphere around the Francis household.

"It was good advice," Ted admitted. "It, uh, well, it made Mom a lot happier." He paused, slapping the baseball into his mitt a time or two, smiling slightly. "A lot happier. Anyway—" he went into a slow wind-up, preparatory to throwing the ball.

"You're gonna have a baby brother or sister, Jimmy."

Luckily, the pitch Ted threw was slightly off the mark, for Jimmy was too stunned to raise his arm and attempt to catch it. It narrowly missed his head before sailing past and rolling clear to the back fence.

"Whoa…" he exhaled. Then he too smiled.

"Do I get to pick which it is?"

Ted chuckled. "Nope. Nor me, either. That's up to God and Mother Nature."

Jimmy trotted back to retrieve the errant baseball. By the time he returned to his previous spot, a new and mischievous thought had sprung into his wiry brain. He made sure to keep the ball in his possession when next he spoke.

"This reminds me of a question I've been meaning to ask you, Dad."

"What's that?" Ted lifted his gloved hand to indicate he was ready for Jimmy to make the next throw. Instead, the boy just stood with a slightly silly grin on his face.

"Did you get Mom in trouble before you married her?"

For a pregnant moment, there was silence and Jimmy felt a sinking sense of impending doom.

"Damn you!" his father shouted, throwing his baseball glove at the boy. It struck him and he fell to the ground, doubled over.

Not from pain, but because he was beginning to laugh uncontrollably. The giggling sounds that can only be matched by those of another child or by the babbling of a rushing brook rippled out around him.

Ted Francis trotted over and threw himself down atop his son, not in an unduly rough way. The two of them began to roll around on the ground, with Ted applying the requisite "noogies" to the top of Jimmy's head.

Both were still laughing when they stopped rolling around and assumed seated positions on the ground. Ted was gasping so deeply that he began to cough harshly, finally spitting out a small wad of phlegm.

"You oughtta stop smoking, Dad," Jimmy said, now growing serious. "Those things are bad for ya."

"Yeah, you're right, Champ. I've been meaning to quit."

But with one of his long-ingrained flashes of mild pain, the little boy had the sinking feeling that his father would never fulfill that pledge.

CHAPTER 7

"Jimmy! Can you come into the kitchen?"

Engrossed as he was in putting the finishing touches on a handmade picture frame he hoped to gift to his mother for Christmas, Jimmy thought he knew what the summons presaged and wasted no time in hiding his handiwork and taking off double time toward the kitchen. Virginia Francis took great pride in her talent for preparing home-cooked candies for the holidays, and today's task was the cooking of the season's first batch of rich, dark fudge. With her in the kitchen was the youngest addition to the Francis family, two-year-old Chuck.

Jimmy had taken to calling his baby brother "Scooter" due to the fact that, even before he was truly crawling, the infant had devised a method of mobility by simply "scooting" his tiny bottom across the floor. The nickname would stick to him permanently.

Scooter was seated in a high chair decorated with appliques depicting various Warner Brothers cartoon characters: Bugs Bunny, Daffy Duck, Porky Pig and others. He was happily engaged in using both hands to disperse a bowl of banana pudding just about everywhere except into his mouth.

Jimmy leaned over and kissed the toddler atop his head as he passed the chair. There had been some concern on the part of the Francis parents that, especially given the rather wide age difference, Jimmy might resent the baby, or at best be indifferent to him.

Instead, for reasons he himself would have been hard pressed to articulate, Jimmy had almost instantly accepted Scooter into his life. The baby seemed to be as much a gift to him as it was to their parents.

Moments before Jimmy's arrival, Virginia had removed the bubbling fudge mixture from atop the stove and was using a wooden spatula to spread it out into a pair of shallow pans to cool. She then held out the pan and spatula, both caked with the remnants of the fudge, toward Jimmy.

"Anybody wanna lick the bowl?" she asked disingenuously.

"You know it!" Jimmy chirped, hopping atop the nearest empty countertop and accepting the rapidly cooling pan from his mother. Licking the still warm remains of the homemade fudge was one of the many forms of heaven on earth that too often go unnoticed and unrecognized once the appreciation and wisdom of youth fade.

As he sat on the countertop devouring the delicious dregs of fudge, Jimmy took pleasure in watching his mother as she continued to bustle about the kitchen. She was gathering the necessary implements and ingredients for her next sweet confection, divinity.

"Can I ask you somethin', Mom?" Jimmy said, smacking his lips around the spatula. The question was possibly sparked by one of the boy's little "tingles." He barely noticed them after so long, but they usually led him down interesting paths he might otherwise have passed over.

"Of course, sweetie."

"Why did you marry Dad?"

"What an odd question," she chuckled. "I married him because I loved him, naturally."

"Well, yeah," he persisted. "But, *why*? I mean, what sort of things does a fella need to do before a girl falls in love with him?"

"And why do you want to know that?"

"I dunno," he shrugged. "Just about every man I know, except maybe weird ol' Uncle Carl, is married (True enough, given the social taboo regarding *divorce* that was still prevalent at the time), so I figure, some day I'll prob'ly get married, too."

"I hope so," Virginia said airily.

"So I figure it might come in handy if I know what kinda guy girls like. And you're a girl."

"I am indeed. Thank you for noticing."

"So I thought maybe you could tell me what girls like."

"You don't already have a particular girl in mind, do you?" his mother teased playfully.

"Maaa! O' course not!" In truth, Jimmy *had* found himself looking at girls with a slightly different eye of late. He still didn't like them as well as he did comic books or baseball, but he was beginning to see that they had a certain appeal in their own way.

"Well, let's see," Virginia said, seeing that Jimmy was earnest in his questioning.

"I think a sense of humor is very important," she began. "And he should be smart. Not necessarily book smart: just life smart.

"Girls like a man who's generous. And someone she can at least sometimes share her thoughts with.

"A man should be thoughtful and considerate," she continued, though Jimmy saw her hesitate briefly and flow flush in the cheeks, "when it… when it comes to the *physical* part of their relationship."

"You mean *sex!*" Jimmy gleefully chimed in.

"Do you want me to let Scooter lick the divinity bowl?" she threatened mildly.

"Naw. He'd just get most of it in his hair, anyway. Go on, Mom."

"All right. Let me see. When a woman speaks to a man, she wants to really be *heard*. And taken seriously."

"Does Dad do all that stuff?" Jimmy asked, clearly skeptical.

"Oh, maybe not *all* of it," his mother conceded. "Not all the time, anyway. But he tries; I really do think he tries the best he can. And that counts for a lot, too."

She lowered her eyes to look at the mixture she was vigorously beating in a bowl, then lifted her head to gaze out the kitchen window before continuing.

"But I have to tell you, baby, that in the end love sometimes doesn't make a whole lot of sense.

"It seems to me that people love each other just as much in *spite* of their *flaws* as they do *because* of their *virtues*.

"That may not make sense to a little boy," she said wistfully. "But it's true."

(In actuality, it made perfect sense to the boy. In fact, he felt as if he had already heard almost the exact same words before, from someone else. Whom, he couldn't quite remember.)

"So how do two people know for sure that they're gonna stay in love *forever*?"

"Oh, they don't. Nobody does. That's one of the things that makes falling in love so scary." She smiled softly at her eldest son, ran her hand through his hair and down his cheek.

"If you live long enough," she told him, "you're probably going to break someone's heart; and someone's going to break yours."

"That sounds awful," he observed, scrunching up his nose.

"It is, sweetheart. But that's just the way it is. That's life. Just try to live it the very best way you know how. That's all you can do."

"What's up?" Ted Francis interrupted the moment, strolling through the kitchen doorway.

"Oh, me and Jimmy have just been talking about love and marriage," Virginia explained.

"You haven't gone and gotten some little girl in trouble, have you, Champ?" Ted asked his son with mock seriousness.

"Dad! Ted!" Jimmy and Virginia shouted in unison.

Ted walked over to Jimmy, who made a half-hearted attempt to pull the pan of fudge remnants away as Ted reached out and scooped out a dollop with one finger.

"Son," the man said after licking off his finger, "I can tell you all you need to know about marriage in a single sentence. It's the same one my daddy told me." He surreptitiously winked at Jimmy before continuing.

"Just remember that when you marry a girl, you agree to take her for better or for worse." He gave an exaggerated shrug.

"And it don't ever get no better!"

Virginia Francis fairly launched herself across the small kitchen and began to whack her cowering husband with a dishtowel. The laughter coming from both Ted and Jimmy made her whack all the harder.

Though the ruckus and commotion was all in good fun, little Scooter—observing it all from his perch atop the high chair—did not recognize it for what it was. His lips quivered, he began to whimper and then gave in to a full-blown crying fit.

Jimmy hopped down from the countertop; Dad had stopped the brutal assault upon his person by wrapping his arms around Virginia, pinning her arms to her sides. Now she began to howl—though hers were mixed with giggles as Ted began to kiss her repeatedly on the side of her neck.

Ignoring them (adults could be such children), Jimmy gathered some fudge drippings onto one fingertip and popped the digit into little Scooter's mouth. The toddler's crying ceased immediately as he began to savagely suck on the sugary finger.

That's how life should always be, Jimmy thought as he watched his baby brother suckle contentedly.

Simple enough that all its problems could be solved with a cheekful of chocolate.

CHAPTER 8

"C'mon, ever'body," Ted Francis barked. "Let's get a move on."

It was a nice, sunny summer Sunday, and Ted and his wife Virginia, with a reluctant five-year-old Scooter in tow, were heading out the door. Virginia's mother had been ailing, and they planned to bring fresh soup and spend the afternoon with her.

As he opened the front door, Ted was mildly irritated to see Howdy

Watson headed his way up the walkway. Though he was now fifteen, Ted could swear the little oddball had not grown an inch or an ounce since the day Jimmy first brought him home like some stray puppy he'd found wandering the streets.

"Don't you have a home of your own?" Ted growled.

"Sure," Howdy replied, ignoring the man's tone. "I sleep there." The boy was dragging a red-and-white ice chest behind him; he couldn't have carried it, even empty, for it was nearly as big as was he.

"I thought you and Jimmy were staying around the house today," Ted said, sounding somewhat suspicious.

"We are, sir," Howdy replied, ever polite to his elders: a trait Ted thought his oldest son would do well to emulate.

"Then why the ice chest?"

"'Cause I'm in charge of the essentials: soda pop, lunchmeat, bread. Jimmy's supposed to provide chips and snacks."

Ted heaved an exasperated sigh, though, in fact, he didn't object to Howdy's presence. He actually kinda liked the little goof.

"You're not planning on spending the whole summer here, are you, boy?"

"Heck, no. I figure this'll just about get us through the day." He tapped the side of his head with one fingertip.

"And this way, we'll never have to leave the TV, except to go to the bathroom!"

"You two damned lunkheads just make sure to *do* that," Ted said gruffly. "There'll be hell to pay if I come home and find one of you has gone and peed on the *carpet*!"

Howdy just laughed and pushed in past the adult; after all these years, he was well accustomed to Mr. Francis and his irascible ways. For some reason, he seemed to find Ted's crankiness to be an endless source of amusement.

"Hurry up, Howdy," Jimmy said rather impatiently from the short hallway that extended from the living room to the front door.

"I've got the set tuned to CBS," he continued. "I don't think anybody does the space stuff better than Walter Cronkite."

"Me, either."

"What's so important that you plan to stay glued to the television for the rest of the day?" Virginia asked innocently.

She frowned slightly as Jimmy and Howdy both looked at her as if she'd been living in a cave her entire life.

"Just the biggest event in human history, Mom," Jimmy said somewhat condescendingly. "Today's the day we walk on the Moon for the first time!"

"Oh. That's nice." She bent to take Scooter's hand. "We'd better get going, Ted."

To her surprise and annoyance, Scooter pulled free of her grip. "I don't wanna go."

"Of course you do. You love your grandma."

"I wanna stay with Jimmy."

"Let's go, Virginia," Ted roughly prompted.

"Come on, Scooter."

"I wanna stay with Jimmy!"

Sighing heavily, Virginia cast a plaintive look at Jimmy, who in turn looked at Howdy, who for his part simply shrugged.

"Will you be good?" Jimmy asked his little brother.

"Uh-huh."

"Uh-huh." Now Jimmy sighed before looking back at his mother. "I guess he can stay if it's all right with you."

"All right. Just don't get so lost in space that you forget to keep an eye on him."

"They'll be fine, Mother," Ted said, taking her by the elbow and practically dragging her out the front door.

"Can we go to the Moon some day?" Scooter asked his older sibling, holding his hand as they walked into the living room.

"Maybe some day, bubba," Jimmy replied. "I sure would like to."

"We can all go together," Howdy joined the chorus. "We'll be the *Three Space Musketeers*."

"*Mouse*keteers," little Scooter "corrected" Howdy.

"That, too!"

Jimmy Francis had always been interested in life as it existed in the past, especially in his movie and TV viewing: Westerns, swashbucklers, medieval tales. You name it—*The Searchers, Captain Blood, Ivanhoe*—he was enthralled by it.

But he also pondered the future and the stars and what each held in store for mankind. *Forbidden Planet, The Day the Earth Stood Still, It Came From Outer Space*: all these cast a spell over him as well. Howdy's engulfing interest in America's true life budding space program had proven contagious, becoming yet another shared interest between him and Jimmy.

As could have been expected and anticipated, Scooter fairly quickly lost interest in the hours of commentary, interviews, charts, graphics and commercial breaks that preceded the actual Moonwalk. But, true to his word, he remained well behaved throughout the day, occupying himself by playing with his toy cars and trucks: content to just be in the company of the two older boys.

And eating. The sandwich fixings Howdy had packed in being the closest they had to actual nutritious food, the three boys picked up the slack with junk food: chips, candy and the like. The ambrosia of the gods for children. It would be upon Virginia Francis, on returning later that day, to cope with the sugar rush that had Scooter practically bouncing off the walls by that point. Yet he somehow calmed himself at the crucial moment, planting himself on the floor between Jimmy and Howdy when the ultimate endeavor occurred. All three boys sat in silence, slack-jawed, their eyes glued to the screen of the television set as grainy images of astronaut Neil Armstrong hopping down to the lunar soil were beamed around the world.

Forever after, and because of the choppy quality of the audio message being beamed hundreds of thousands of miles from the Moon, Jimmy and Howdy would have a friendly disagreement over whether Armstrong's first, historic statement was "that's one small step for man," or "that's one small step for a man," as he intended.

But each boy was in full agreement that they had been blessed to witness firsthand what had to be one of the most important and epic moments in all of human history.

Time, complacency and even indifference have perhaps dimmed the significance of that achievement in the minds of many people, surrounded as they are by so many wonders of technology and stellar exploration.

But to those who lived in the years before it and who now saw man bounding around upon an alien orb, it was both a dynamic and climactic moment: almost as if they were witnessing the final step of a journey that began when Adam and Eve took the first steps outside the bounds of Eden.

Sleep was a long time coming to Jimmy Francis that night of the first Moon walk. He lay awake in bed, holding in his hands the piece of wood he had begun carving on a week earlier. When finished and painted, it too would be a rocket ship.

He didn't even try closing his eyes at first, needing them to stare out his window and up into the night sky at the face of the Moon. On this night, for the first time ever, there were men resting on its surface and looking back at him.

If such a thing as this were possible, he thought…then maybe so were many other things.

...WHEN THE ULTIMATE ENDEAVOR OCCURRED.

CHAPTER 9

The high school seniors were congregated at the city's assembly center, all bedecked in tuxedoes and formal dresses for their prom. Graduation ceremonies would follow soon on its heels.

But a few miles away, at Will Rogers High School itself, a more casual dance was in progress: this one being for the benefit of that year's class of juniors.

Seventeen-year-old Jimmy Francis had his eager eyes set on one girl in particular: a comely, auburn-haired cheerleader named Barb Newburg.

(He no longer possessed the knowledge that, in his previous odyssey through life, Barb was the girl with whom he shared his first, disastrous marriage.)

He did know that, because of her looks and her status high above on the teenage social ladder, most boys were intimidated by her and so afraid of the shame and stigma of public rejection that they kept their distance from her on such occasions as this.

Unlike these others, and given that Barb was at the moment without a steady beau, Jimmy was willing to gamble that this would make her eager to accept any reasonable offer to dance that she might receive. Her own awareness of her desirability and fear that this and her status might be damaged if she appeared unwanted just might be all that was required for someone like Jimmy to be an acceptable, if fleeting, partner.

Granted, "jocks" were her usual dish of choice, it appeared. Jimmy wasn't exactly that; but his position as second-string second baseman on the school's baseball team, he figured, should prove sufficient to impress the girl.

Watching her standing amidst her small coterie of best girlfriends, hands behind her back and swaying back and forth to the sounds of recorded music by the Beatles, Barb looked ripe for the picking. Screwing his courage to the sticking post, Jimmy started toward her.

And promptly, inadvertently, bumped shoulders with another girl as she walked past him.

"Excuse me," she said in a soft and shy voice. She barely glanced at Jimmy, for she was more intent on not spilling any of the contents of the two, small crystal glasses of punch she was carrying.

"No problem," Jimmy assured her with a shrug.

Normally, that would have been the end of it; Jimmy would have almost instantly forgotten such an incident of almost literally two ships that pass in the night, and resumed his personal voyage toward Barb Newburg.

But now one of his little jolts to the head decided to land at the base of his skull. Rubbing the back of his neck (a gesture even those who knew him best thought was merely a nervous habit, for he spoke to no one of these flashes of pain to which he was prone), he turned back to look again at the girl with the punch glasses.

He knew her, though just barely; her name was Kathy Brown. Tall, with long, dark hair she wore parted in the middle, she was not a bad looking girl, though an overly prominent nose kept her from being what most would consider pretty. She was more than a bit on the skinny side, too.

The corners of Jimmy's lips curled barely upward. The thought of the girl's slight figure reminded him of an exchange of dialogue from an old Spencer Tracy and Katherine Hepburn movie he had recently watched on television with his mother (who adored Hepburn).

"There ain't much meat on them bones," one male character had observed of Hepburn.

"No," Tracy said sagely, "but what's there is *choice!*"

Jimmy had never spoken more than a few perfunctory words to Kathy Brown, but she seemed to him to be a friendly person. She always had a smile she was ready to share with everyone. More than once, he'd heard others refer to her as "sweet:" a characterization that could be the kiss of death when applied to any boy hoping to score serious points with the ladies, but a term of praise when applied to the female of the species.

Alas, Kathy was also absent from school fairly frequently, amidst rumors that she suffered from a variety of ailments and illnesses. The less kind among Jimmy's male classmates "joked" that she would be dead before she was laid.

Jimmy frowned. Maybe the tingling in his head was telling him that this cruel joke was all too true.

The girl must have had a pretty good brain in her head, though, he reckoned. Despite her frequent illnesses and absences, he'd often seen her name among those who had made the principal's Honor Roll. While he made better than average grades himself—excellent grades in wood shop and math—Jimmy's own name had never appeared on the Roll.

"Hey, buddy."

Jimmy smiled and shook his head as he turned to see Howdy Watson approaching him. Ever the one to make a statement—albeit usually the wrong one—Howdy was the only boy to show up at the dance in a suit: one so garish and brightly colored in mismatched hues as to be more appropriate in a circus than at a high school dance.

To Jimmy, this was just Howdy: a good guy who made a good friend. To most everybody else, he was an oddity, a source of amusement. Howdy pretended to be content with that, always ready to join in with the laughter.

Jimmy knew better.

He knew Howdy would give away all he owned just to be "normal."

He was too young yet to have learned that normalcy is highly overrated.

And he, too, was a regular occupant of the principal's Honor Roll. Such was the fiber of his own character that Jimmy never held this against Howdy.

"Nice party," Howdy said, sipping at a glass of punch. "Who were you staring at?"

"Nobody. I just bumped into Kathy Brown, that's all."

"Hmm. I hear she's sweet."

"So they say." Jimmy punched Howdy lightly on the upper arm.

"Hey, why don't the two of us grab a couple o' girls and go cut a rug out on the dance floor?"

"Help yourself," Howdy replied. "I doubt there's a girl here who'd dance with me."

"Dressed like that—do you blame 'em?"

Howdy chuckled. "Philistine. I'm just ahead of my time, that's all."

"Yeah. About a hundred years ahead."

"And yet I still let you hang out with me, young James. You go on and dance; I hear some cheese balls over on the snack table calling to me."

Ready now to resume his original campaign strategy vis-à-vis Barb Newburg, Jimmy straightened his clothes, exhaled into a cupped hand to make sure his breath wouldn't offend, and turned in her direction.

Only to find that he had waited too long and seemingly missed his window of opportunity.

Thad Richards, star running back on the varsity football team, six feet of muscle and ego—had beaten Jimmy to the punch. Jimmy saw Thad and Barb exchange a few words, laugh a little and then head out to the dance floor together.

Disgruntled, Jimmy's first inclination was to just leave the dance altogether. Maybe grab Howdy and go take in a late movie or stop in at their favorite pool hall.

The throbbing in his skull increased in intensity.

CHAPTER 10

"**H**i."

Kathy Brown and her girlfriend had been engaged in conversation when Jimmy Francis approached and they both looked at him with slight puzzlement.

"Hi, Jimmy," the second girl said.

"Hello, James," Kathy greeted him.

He chuckled. "God. Only my *grandma* calls me 'James.'" I like 'Jimmy' better."

"All right."

With that, the conversation pretty well died.

"Nice dance," Jimmy said at last. Both girls nodded.

"I'm gonna go get some more punch," Kathy stated, assuming Jimmy was wanting to get her girlfriend alone and wishing to excuse herself from the scene as quickly and gracefully as possible.

"Don't go," Jimmy said quickly, taking her a bit by surprise.

"I came over to see if you'd like to dance." When the young lady clearly hesitated to answer, Jimmy felt sure he'd made a mistake and would soon be making the dreaded walk of shameful rejection back across the floor.

"I know you don't know me very well," he stammered in an attempt to save face for both of them. "So if you'd rather not—"

"She'd love to!" Kathy's friend pronounced a little too loudly and a little too eagerly, giving Kathy a slight shove toward Jimmy.

Smiling, he put a hand on the small of her back and led her toward the dance floor. He didn't notice when Kathy looked back over one shoulder and shot her girlfriend a dirty look. In response, the other girl smiled broadly and flashed the thumb's up sign.

The only actual dance style Jimmy had ever learned was *The Twist*, which was largely out of style by this time. Fortunately, what mainly took its place was equally simple: so long as you could shuffle from side to side and wave your arms slightly in anything remotely resembling being in rhythm to the music, you could usually get by without knowing any of the actual popular dances of the day.

What Jimmy lacked in expertise and confidence he mostly made up for with an enthusiasm that was contagious and brought a smile to the face of his partner. Both laughed lightly as the current song ended.

"You wanna grab another glass of punch now?" Jimmy asked. Strangely, in the course of just a three-minute dance, he had found himself feeling nicely comfortable in the presence of this young woman who did indeed strike him as being very sweet.

"Sure," she replied honestly. And it seemed completely natural to both to hold hands as they walked together toward the punch bowl.

For several minutes, as they sat and sipped the fruity brew, Jimmy entertained Kathy by carrying on a running and humorous commentary on the contortions of some of the other couples out on the dance floor. He found that Kathy's musical laughter had retained some of the tinkling magic that even his little brother Scooter had now lost as he left childhood behind him.

(However others may choose to define it, Jimmy would contend that true childhood was gone forever once a boy or girl stepped through the classroom door on the first day of kindergarten. From that moment on, a person begins to be burdened by *responsibility*—the serpent in the garden that forever strips a being of the innocence of the kind of unbridled joy required to elicit truly beautiful laughter.)

At a moment when Jimmy paused to take a sip of punch, Kathy studied his profile.

"Why did you ask me to dance?" she said softly.

"Beg your pardon?" he replied, though he had heard the question perfectly well.

"We barely know each other," she stated. "So what made you ask me to dance?"

"Are you sorry I did?" he came back, growing concerned with the direction she was headed.

"No. I just want to know why, that's all."

He thought on that for a moment or two (If more such pauses were taken during conversations, fewer of them would end in acrimony.) and then gave her a wry smile.

"Have you ever seen the movie *The Magnificent 7*?" he inquired.

"Noo," she replied, naturally puzzled.

"There's a story in it about a man who one day just stripped off all his clothes, jumped into a patch of cactus and began to roll around. People asked him that question, too: Why'd you do that?" He paused again, took another sip of punch.

"So, why *did* he do it?" Kathy pressed.

Jimmy grinned. "The man said: 'Cause it seemed like a good idea at the time'."

He held his breath as Kathy scowled at him for at least three "Mississippi's," then relaxed as he saw the corners of her pretty mouth begin to move upward of their own volition. A slightly unladylike snort issued forth and she began to giggle so hard she was bent over at the waist.

Then her head snapped up as the strains of a popular romantic ballad began to flow from the PA system.

"Oh. I *love* this song!"

"Then let's get back out there and dance," Jimmy said, rising to his feet.

"Are you sure?" she asked, knowing that this song would call for them to slow dance. Jimmy held a hand out to her.

"It seems like a good idea."

Other than the need to avoid stepping on your partner's toes, the slow dance required even less skill to perform than did the fast dance. The boy put his arms around the girl's waist, she put her arms around his neck and they swayed lightly back and forth while turning in a slow circle.

Most importantly, it provided them with a socially permitted and acceptable way of achieving moderately close contact.

With his head nestled against hers, Jimmy could inhale the fresh smell of Kathy's hair, the slightly florid aroma of her conservatively applied perfume. He liked the feel of her, and when he pulled her slightly tighter against him, she offered no resistance.

"I'm glad I jumped into this cactus patch," he whispered to her.

"So am I," she sighed.

Neither noticed when they continued to dance for several moments after the song stopped.

A short time before the dance officially ended, Kathy reluctantly told Jimmy she was going to have to leave in order to meet the Saturday night curfew imposed upon her by her father. Jimmy offered to drive her home and she gladly accepted.

It was not exactly a chariot that awaited them without, but rather a pale blue, 1955 Plymouth. It was the only one Jimmy's father Ted had ever purchased brand new rather than used; and so long as one didn't mind treating it to a fresh quart of oil every week it still performed serviceably.

Following her easy directions, Jimmy got Kathy home in plenty of time to meet her curfew. They again held hands as he walked her to the front door.

"I had a really good time tonight," Jimmy said, standing awkwardly on the porch, wondering for no more than the most fleeting of moments if it would have, could have, been any better had he spent it with Barb

Newburg instead.

"So did I, Jimmy." The girl held her hands together in front of her, swaying lightly from side to side.

He cleared his throat, momentarily fearing to look at her. "Maybe we could get together again some time," he managed to get out at last. "You know…grab a burger and a movie or something."

"I'd like that," she replied almost instantly, though to Jimmy it seemed to take her interminably long to respond. The invisible hand squeezing his heart now released its grip.

"Me, too," was all he could think to say.

"Me, too," she repeated, and both laughed nervously at the silliness of it all.

"Okay," he said, taking a step away and then stopping. "I'll, uh, I'll get your phone number at school Monday and we'll talk."

"Okay. Good night, Jimmy."

"G'night." He made no effort to kiss her farewell. Besides being too scared to make such a move, he felt sure that this was a prize worth taking the time to know better first.

The straightest route back to his own home took Jimmy through a neighborhood with which he had little familiarity (and no knowledge that it was the part of town where his previous self had so grudgingly lived before that fateful night at Irish Mike's).

Along the way, he encountered a small strip mall that appeared to have only two tenants. One was a small ice cream parlor (a place to take Kathy, perhaps?). The other had a hand-painted sign over its entryway.

Santini's Woodworks—Hand Crafted.

On impulse—meaning at the urging of one of his pesky tingles—Jimmy turned into the center's well-tended parking lot. Both businesses were closed, as he knew they would be, but this would not prevent him from peering into the display window at Santini's.

Next to an ornately carved chair sat a chest chiseled with baroque patterns. Atop the chest was what appeared to be a jewelry box. Though made of wood, it seemed to glisten like purest silver. The artistry of the work nearly took Jimmy's breath away.

Jimmy had barely entered his home and locked the front door behind him fifteen minutes later when the telephone in his living room began to ring. Not wanting to wake his parents, he dashed as best he could through the semi-darkness to snatch up the receiver before its third ring.

"Hello?" he said in a muffled voice.

"Did I see you leave the dance with Kathy Brown?" Howdy Watson asked without feeling the need for any preliminary greeting.

"Yeah."

"Sooo...?"

"So what?" Jimmy snapped irritably.

"So...did you get to first base?"

CHAPTER 11

Monday afternoon saw Antonio Santini intently working on the piece of wood that would eventually become one of the legs for a custom ordered high chair.

He paid scant attention when he heard the sound of the bell over his shop's front door tinkle. He didn't bother to look up, knowing that one of his clerks would handle the needs of whoever had entered.

"Mr. Santini?"

Slightly annoyed at the interruption, Santini glanced up to see the youngest of his two clerks standing in the curtained doorway leading back into the work area.

"What is it, Dale?"

"It's some kid. He says he wants to speak with you."

"What does he want?"

"All he'll say is that he wants to talk to you."

"Did he at least tell you his name?"

"Oh, yeah. Jimmy. Jimmy Francis."

"Jimmy Francis." Santini tapped the top of his workbench with one slightly gnarled finger. "I don't think I know him."

"I don't think he knows you, either," the clerk replied. "He just asked to see the man who made the things in the front window."

"Is he a salesman?"

"I don't think so."

Santini's head drooped. "All right. Send him back."

The teenaged boy who pushed through the curtain moments later struck the woodworker as being a good-looking boy, well groomed. He also looked slightly nervous and was clutching a cloth bag with both hands.

Jimmy hadn't known what to expect. What he saw was a little old man ("Old" being a relative term when viewed through the eyes of youth.

Santini was only in his mid-40s.) with mounds of curly, graying hair atop his head. His eyebrows were nearly as bushy as the moustache parked atop his lips. His dark eyes, peering at Jimmy over a pair of spectacles that appeared about to slide off his aquiline nose, bore a look of kindness.

"Hello. How can I help you?" Santini asked, his English plain and easily understandable though his accent still rang with the sunny sounds of his Italian homeland.

"I stopped by here the other night on my way home," Jimmy explained. "I don't think I've ever seen anything so beautiful as what you have in your front window."

"Oh?" Santini sat up just a bit straighter, pride glistening behind his spectacles. "You have a good eye. So...you came back to look some more?"

"Yeah. Did you make all those things out there yourself?"

"With these two hands," Santini boasted, holding them up for Jimmy to see. "And the grace of God."

Jimmy nodded. His mouth opened slightly, then closed, as if the words were dammed up behind his teeth.

"You wanted something else?" Santini prompted.

"Can I show you something?" the boy asked, holding up the sack he was carrying. "It'll only take a minute."

Santini glanced over at the work awaiting his attention, and then back at the boy, studying his face as if he was selecting the right cut of wood to craft. "Sure," he said with a shrug.

From within the sack, Jimmy extracted several samples of his own handiwork: a pan flute, carvings of dogs and cats, a few small boxes. He lined them up on a countertop, then stepped back.

"I carved these myself," he declared.

Pushing his spectacles farther up his nose, Santini slowly and closely examined each piece, turning them over in his weathered hands. He cleared his throat softly before looking back at Jimmy.

"Welll," he said at last. "They're not terribly good."

"Oh." Jimmy felt himself flushing from the roots of his hair to his toes. He began to hurriedly scoop the products of his hands back into the sack.

"Wait, wait, wait," Santini said gruffly, lightly slapping at Jimmy's hands. "They're not terribly *bad*, either."

"You don't have to be nice," Jimmy said defensively.

"Why would I be? I don't even *know* you!"

The truthful absurdity of that statement caused Jimmy to laugh nervously. Santini's features softened as well.

"You wanted me to be honest with you, didn't you?" the older man said.

"Apparently not," Jimmy admitted sheepishly.

"Let me finish," the woodsmith continued. "What I mean is that these knick-knacks are rather crude in their execution. That's to be expected. You taught yourself to carve, correct?"

"Yes, sir."

"And it shows: it shows. But the work also shows *promise*. It's up to you whether you ever fulfill that promise."

"Would you teach me, Mr. Santini?"

"Why?"

"What do you mean, why?"

"Why do you want to learn to carve wood? Machines do it faster, easier."

Jimmy's features wrinkled in concentration for several moments before he attempted an answer.

"Machines don't have hands or hearts. They don't have souls. The things you make, I can tell; they may be functional but they're more than that. Each one is a piece of you. A work of art.

"That's what I want to do. I want to make art. I want to give away a thousand pieces of myself."

Santini could do naught at first but stare at the boy in amazement. "How old are you, son?"

"Seventeen."

"You talk like you're seventy."

"Maybe I am—inside."

"Maybe you are. And I should call *you* 'sir,' eh?" Santini smiled but shook his head slightly.

"But I'm no teacher, except maybe by example. Are you still in high school?"

"Yes, sir. For another year."

"Okay. All right. Here's what I suggest you do. Take any art classes you can find. And we have a good technical school right here in town. When you graduate high school, enroll there for a year or two."

"Oh," Jimmy replied, unable to hide the dejection he felt. "Well, thank you." Santini frowned again as the boy turned to leave.

"Wait, wait, wait," he said, waving Jimmy back.

"Now I have the question for you. Do you know how to work one of those...the noisy money machines?"

"You mean a cash register?"

"That's it, yes."

"Yeah, I can do that. I ran a register at Burger Barn last summer."

"I'm sure it was a wonderful experience."

"Eh. It was okay."

"Enough with burgers. Here's my thought. I could use a little help, maybe. Selling the nails, the screws, the hinges—all the ugly things that help keep the place open. Someone to sweep the floors. Who can run the clackety money machine."

"I could do all that," Jimmy said eagerly.

"Of course you can. Anybody can. But I want no lazy boys."

"I'll do my best."

"All right. I believe you. It would only be part-time. I'll pay you two dollars an hour. If that's no good, you can leave now."

"Sounds good to me," Jimmy said, not adding that this wage was nearly double the amount he'd been paid at Burger Barn.

"Good. Good. And maybe, when we're slow or you're not working, you can come back here and watch me. Maybe learn a little."

"I'd like that, Mr. Santini."

"H'okay. You go now. Wait!"

Santini picked up a small wood sculpture that Jimmy, in his haste had failed to return to his sack. Before handing it back to the boy, the old wood carver turned it over in his hands, examining it more closely.

"What is this?" he asked, holding it out to Jimmy. "A cow?"

"It's supposed to be a horse," the boy replied glumly.

"Hmm." Santini scanned it again, then looked at Jimmy over the rim of his spectacles with a critical eye.

"Are you sure you wouldn't rather be a *plumber*?"

CHAPTER 12

"Dad? Can I talk to you for a minute?"

Ted Francis put down his evening newspaper, frowning as he looked up at his oldest son.

"I thought I told you to get a haircut."

"I did," Jimmy mumbled, brushing one hand through hair that still came down just slightly over the tops of his ears and the back of his shirt collar.

"Well, if you paid for it, you got cheated."

Jimmy didn't want to talk about hair: that could lead to an argument about hippies and politics and these were the furthest things from his mind at the moment.

High School graduation was only a couple of weeks away and Jimmy wanted to discuss what would come next for him.

There had been a time, when he was a younger boy, when he wouldn't have even considered attempting to start such a dialogue with his father. Dad was the undisputed head of the household and everyone in it did as he said.

But Ted had mellowed—not totally, but some—in the intervening years. Starting with their talk about the older Francis' war experiences, father and son had found it easier to engage in real and varied conversations. As he grew and matured, Jimmy had also grown more confident in his own opinions, his own judgments. Now, he'd decided, was the time to put that to the test.

(Such was the intimidating figure his father cut, though, that Jimmy was not sure if the tingle at the back of his skull was one of his intuitive and prompting flashes—or simply a nervous headache brought on by dread!)

"Here's the thing, Dad," Jimmy started, knowing that with his father it was best to dive right in with both feet.

"I know you want me to join the military as soon as I graduate...but that's not what *I* want."

"Is it the war in 'Nam that's got you worried, boy?" Ted said, tapping the newspaper now resting in his lap. "'Cause it sounds like it's winding down pretty fast. President Nixon'll have us completely outta there in no time."

"And what a waste of blood and money it's been," Jimmy observed soberly.

"I think you're right," Ted replied, much to Jimmy's surprise. "But I don't recall ever hearing you say that *before*...when it was *other* boys who were over there fighting and dying."

Anger flared inside Jimmy's belly, but he suppressed it lest it lead them too far astray from what he wished to discuss with his father.

"You're right, Dad. I didn't. I should have, but I didn't. But I'm no coward. If I get drafted, I'll serve as best I can.

"But I won't volunteer."

"It doesn't have to be the Army," Ted persisted. "You could always join the Air Force or the Navy. You might learn a trade there; you'd earn some veteran's benefits for sure."

"I know that's what you did, Dad, and that it was a good and helpful thing for you. I'm just saying it's not right for *me*."

"Uh-huh. And do you know what *is* right for you?"

"I think so. I hope so." Jimmy pulled an envelope out of the back pocket of his jeans and waved it slightly.

"I've been accepted for fall classes at the technical school here in town. I'm going to study carpentry and woodworking." He made no mention of the art class he had managed to enter in his final year at Rogers, or the weekly sculpting class he found available at one of the town's recreation centers and had already been attending.

"When I'm finished with school, Mr. Santini has promised to take me on full time at his shop."

"There's no real money in that, Jimmy: working for some poor old man in a little, rundown shop," Ted said with a grimace.

"How's this instead? You've always been good at math, have a way with figures; your momma tells me you've been helping her keep our checkbook balanced for years.

"With the right schoolin', you could become an accountant, work your way up to making a damn good living."

"Maybe so. But the truth is, I hate math, Dad. And I'd hate like hell to have to do it day after day after day for all my life."

"That's why it's called *work*, son. It's not supposed to be *fun*."

"But it's not supposed to suck the livin' *soul* outta ya either, is it?"

Ted responded with what almost sounded like the muted growl of some caged jungle cat. He set his newspaper down on the floor, then extended his hands toward his son: one palm up, the other down.

"Take a good look at these, Jimmy." Even the merest glance would have plainly shown them to be rough and callused. The ends of the fingers were blunt, nearly squared.

"No matter how hard I scrub, no matter what kind of soap, what kind of solvent I use, I can never get them completely clean. There's always a little grease, a little grime in the pores.

"I want something better for you."

Unconsciously, he rubbed those beefy hands together: a grease monkey Lady Macbeth, forever unable to remove a damned spot.

"I've told you some of what my life was like during the Depression," he said to Jimmy. "I had to drop out of school after getting no further than the 8th Grade."

"You're still one of the smartest men I've ever known," Jimmy assured him, eliciting a slightly weary smile from his father.

"I quit school to help out my family," Ted went on. "But jobs were few and far between even for full-grown men with educations.

"So I did whatever I could. I'd dive into the water hazards out at the municipal golf course and fish out balls that had been lost there. I'd clean 'em up good and resell 'em at the clubhouse.

"The good thing back then was that things were cheap. You could buy a loaf of bread for a nickel—if you could scrape together a nickel.

"Sometimes you couldn't. More than once I stood in line at a free soup kitchen with my momma."

"I don't know how you guys survived," Jimmy almost whispered.

"You do what you have to do, son. That's life. But y'know, just bein' a boy and all…sometimes I preferred *hunger* to the *shame* I felt standing in those soup lines. Makes it hard for me, even to this day, to ask anybody for even small favors." He gazed intently at his son.

"You can see why it would mean so much to me to have a boy of mine go to college, can't you?"

"Sure. I understand." Jimmy playfully slapped his father on the knee, feeling the urge, the need, to lighten the mood.

"But, hey; I'm not your only hope. Scooter seems to be pretty smart. Maybe he'll go to college!"

"I hope so. 'Cause, like you—he ain't ever gonna be a pro ball player. The way he hangs on to his momma's skirt, I just hope he learns enough to become a decent *cook*!"

Ted leaned back in his easy chair. As the light from the nearby lamp struck his face at a different angle, Jimmy thought that his father looked older and more tired than he remembered.

"I guess every father wants his sons to have a better life than he had: to be a better man. That's what I want."

"I know you do. And I appreciate it. But any man who does honest work for honest wages can take pride in the job he does."

"Where'd you ever hear *that*?" Ted asked gruffly.

"*You* told me, Dad."

"So *that* you listened to." Ted looked at the boy in a way Jimmy wasn't used to seeing.

"We've talked a fair amount about a lot of things over the last few years, Jimmy. You've given me reason to respect your point of view—some of the time."

Jimmy grinned (not knowing that in the life he'd first led, there had been no such conversations, only long periods of mutual silence that were a different sort of communication).

Ted lit up a cigarette and exhaled the first puff in what was more of a sigh.

"You know I can't help you much with tuition and such. Between the bills and that damned bean sprout of a brother of yours needing a new pair of tennis shoes every three months…there's not much to spare. I'm sorry."

"It's all right, Dad. I understand. I intend to keep working at Mr. Santini's while I go to school." He hesitated slightly before going on.

"And, uh, you think it would be all right if I keep living here? Just till I can afford to go out on my own?"

"I think that'd be all right, son," his father replied with nary a pause. "Just so long as you remember that this is *my* house. Mine and your mother's. It ain't no hotel and it ain't no restaurant.

"But as long as you're willing to live by the house rules…well, you're welcome to stay here the rest of your life."

"That sounds fair to me, Dad. Thanks."

Near the doorway leading into the kitchen, just out of sight, Virginia Francis had been listening to every word. Knowing this possibly acrimonious dialogue was imminent, she had feared for the worst.

Now, she smiled as she dabbed at the corners of her eyes with a dishtowel.

"And, son, the next time you see that damned barber of yours," Ted said sharply, once more disappearing behind his retrieved newspaper.

"Tell him to actually *cut* a few hairs!"

CHAPTER 13

"**H**ave you come to any sort of decision, Howdy?"

Jimmy Francis and his pal Howdy Watson were in attendance at one of the many small parties being held the night of their high school graduation. Kathy Brown, Jimmy's date as always, had excused herself to go to the powder room, leaving the two young men to their discussion.

Jimmy had already enrolled in courses at technical school, beginning in the fall; his chosen path was clear and as yet unwavering. But Howdy had seemed to bounce back and forth as to his own future planes: one day he'd facetiously declared he was going to become an astronaut, the next he might seriously consider some sort of teaching career.

"I think I have," he said in response to Jimmy's query.

"Money's kinda tight in the Watson household," he said. "Same as in yours. So I think I'm gonna enroll in the community college downtown."

"Sounds like a plan," Jimmy said, not knowing if Howdy was serious or not. "Any idea what you'd major in?"

"I think so. I had a nice, long talk with the guidance counselor at Rogers a couple weeks ago."

"We really *have* a guidance counselor?" Jimmy only half jested. It was a running joke at the high school that there was actually nothing more than an empty office with that tag screwed to its door, so seldom did there seem to actually be anyone there and available for counseling.

"Believe it or not, yeah," Howdy said with a grin. "He really helped me become aware of all my possible options.

"So I think I'm gonna study computer programming."

"Really?" Jimmy said quizzically. "No offense, buddy, but that sounds kinda *dumb*. I mean, no more computers than there are—what are the odds of finding any work in that field?"

Howdy shrugged. "Maybe not too many—now. But I have a feeling it's gonna grow."

"Phew. I hope you're right."

"And if all else fails," Howdy said with a slightly askew grin, "your old job at Burger Barn is probably still available!"

An hour later, Jimmy's old Plymouth was parked along the shoulder of a narrow country lane just outside the city limits. Jimmy and Kathy Brown were lying together atop the front hood, gazing up into a night sky whose full beauty stood revealed even this short distance away from the obscuring lights of the more urban areas.

Jimmy's interest in the heavens had not diminished since he sat enthralled before his television set watching Neil Armstrong bounce on the surface of the Moon.

To some, gazing up at the endless firmament may have given them a sense of personal insignificance. It had an opposite effect on Jimmy, filling him with a grand sense of being part of the eternal.

"What are you thinking?" Kathy asked him. Since the night they had shared their first dance, the young couple had continued to be just that: a couple.

"I was thinking that the stars look close enough to touch tonight," Jimmy replied, gazing dreamily upward. "And that if I could, I'd reach up, grab one and give it to you."

With a sigh, Kathy rolled onto her side and snuggled closer to the boy. He put an arm around her and drew her even closer.

"What about you?"

He grew slightly nervous when she did not reply immediately. She'd seemed a little off this past week, more withdrawn, and this concerned him.

"I've decided to go to nursing school, Jimmy."

"I'm not surprised," he said, though he kept to himself his idea that this decision had been most likely influenced by the many doctors and nurses with whom Kathy had become acquainted during the course of the treatments for the persistent ailments that had plagued her short life.

"I've, uh…I've been granted a partial scholarship."

"Hey, that's great!"

"Is it, Jimmy?"

"Well, sure. Isn't it?"

"I'm not sure. It's to Macon College."

Jimmy stiffened slightly. "Isn't that in Red Bluff?"

"Uh-huh."

"Whoa." Red Bluff was a bit more than a hundred miles to the west.

"Looks like we'll have to make the most of this summer, then," he said, trying to sound upbeat.

"Is that all we have left, Jimmy?" she asked so softly he could barely make out the words.

"What do you mean?"

"Are we gonna call it quits come fall? Or just slowly drift apart during the school year?"

Jimmy was instantly and deeply perturbed by the thought and by the tremor in Kathy's voice that told him she was fighting to hold back tears.

"Why do things have to change at all?" he demanded. "We'll have the telephone and the mail. Weekends and holidays, too; Red Bluff's not that far away."

"Everybody in our situation says things like that, Jimmy," she replied. "And they mean them when they say them, too. But next thing you know, they've gone off in different directions. I've seen it happen."

"Well, it's not gonna happen to us," he insisted. "We won't let it!"

"Are you sure?"

"Of course I'm not! But I am pretty sure that if we go forward *expecting* to break up—we probably will. Do you *want* us to break up?"

"No!" she said emphatically.

"Well, neither do I." As had become his wont, he paused, concentrating on how best to make his words come out right.

"I'm not talking about getting married or anything like that. Not yet. We're both too young, too poor and needing and wanting more education. That sound about right to you?"

"Uh-huh," she replied softly.

"But I do want to be with you, Kathy. And if the time ever comes when I feel different—I'll be honest with you about it."

"All right."

"Oh!" He slid off the car hood. "There's somethin' I almost forgot." He moved to retrieve a small box from inside the auto's glove compartment. Climbing back atop the hood, he handed it to Kathy.

"Oooh," she murmured as she removed an object from within.

"I made it myself," he boasted.

In the palm of her hand, the girl now held a rose: one sculpted from a piece of cherry wood. Nestled within its petals was a heart, and inside the heart were engraved the initials "JF" and "KB."

"I love it, Jimmy," Kathy said, gently cradling the wooden rose in both hands. "And I love you."

"How could you not?" he quipped.

She rolled onto her side and began to slap at him lightly. He laughed as he fended off the taps, then wrapped his arms around her.

"Y'know," she said in an airy tone that was belied by a look of little hurt in her eyes, "it's customary to say, 'I love you, too'."

"Would you mind if I didn't, just yet?" he replied, growing suddenly serious.

"Why not? What's wrong?"

"There's not a thing wrong with you," he quickly assured her. He again struggled slightly to find the right words.

"I'm just not real sure, real certain in my own mind about what love really is, what the word really means." He chuckled self-consciously.

"Hell, my dad uses the same word to describe how he feels about Mom—and about pizza!

"I mean…well, look at Howdy's parents."

Just over a year ago, Mrs. Watson had awakened one day to find that her husband had packed a bag and made off in the middle of the night. Until that horrible moment, everyone—especially Howdy's mother—thought that the couple were perfectly content and secure in their marriage.

Now she struggled just to pay the rent, aided by the little Howdy was able to bring in.

"So I never want to say those words to anyone," Jimmy concluded, "until

I'm absolutely sure *I* understand them—and sure I mean 'em. I mean all the way into my soul.

"So…give me some time, okay?"

"Okay," Kathy acquiesced reluctantly. "But not *too* much time. You wait *too* long –" she scowled slightly. "You wait too long—and *Howdy's* liable to start looking good to me!"

Having so declared, she stared at Jimmy silently, intently—and then they both burst into peals of laughter.

After, she lay close beside him, resting her head on his lightly rising and falling chest.

"I *do* know that I *want* you, Kath," he said, gently stroking her long hair. "And I *think* that I *need* you."

She raised her head and smiled wanly. "Then I guess that'll have to be enough…for now."

"For now," Jimmy repeated.

Kathy lowered her head and the two of them kissed: lightly at first, then with more urgency. Almost of its own volition, Jimmy's hand slid up to cup the small but firm roundness of her breast and she moaned softly into his mouth.

He felt his own excitement growing quickly, achingly; but he and Kathy, by tacit agreement, had always stopped short of much else than this.

This time, though, as he began to slide his fingers away from her breast the girl grabbed his wrist and pulled his hand back to where it had been resting.

"I don't want you to stop, Jimmy," she whispered.

"Are you sure?" The fact that he cared enough to ask spoke volumes to the eager girl.

"You don't want Howdy to lose his cherry before you do, do you?" she asked, her eyes twinkling like they were two of the myriad stars dancing above the two teens.

Again, they both broke into laughter. When it subsided, Kathy kissed Jimmy lightly on the tip of his nose.

"I'm sure," she told him earnestly. "More sure than I've ever been of anything."

And so it was that, with the hood of an old Plymouth for their bed and the sparkling vault of the night sky for their canopy, the two of them made slow and tentative but passionately genuine love.

CHAPTER 14

"Jimmy?" Howdy Watson said, his voice trembling. "Wake up, man!"

Six months earlier, the two staunch friends had decided to take the plunge and move out of their respective homes and take a small place together. It was only a small, garage apartment, but to the two youths it was a landmark in their path to full adulthood.

Jimmy's parents had tried to talk him out of making the move (Yes, even his father Ted, in his usual gruff and roundabout fashion) but had finally acquiesced to his wishes. They assured him that he was welcome to return if the monthly expenses proved to be too much for him.

At age twenty-one, though, Jimmy Francis was now working full-time for Mr. Santini, having completed his trade school courses (while continuing to educate himself by taking sculpting classes at the town's Remington Museum).

Nor was he simply another one of the clerks at the wood shop. Such had been the rapid improvement in his skills that Mr. Santini had not only promoted him to assistant manager but had also begun to let Jimmy assist him with some of his commissions. Recently, a child's rocking chair that Jimmy had undertaken to build alone managed to pass muster, under the critical eye of Santini, who finally, grudgingly (so he protested) conceded that Jimmy just *might* have what it takes to be a real wood carver.

Jimmy's mother had teared up just a bit, as mothers will do, on the day he moved out: repeating the offer to gladly take him back in at any time. Jimmy didn't deign to tell her that he thought poor Howdy's mom would be far less inclined to make him a similar offer; thus he felt compelled to make a go of things for his buddy's sake.

He was thinking less kindly of that buddy on this early Sunday morning as Howdy shook him like a dog would a loose sock it had sunk its teeth into.

"What is it?" Jimmy grumbled. "What do you want?"

"It's your mom, Jimmy."

"Huh?" All cobwebs were instantly swept from his mind.

"She just called. Your dad's collapsed in the hallway at home and he can't get up. She needs you!"

"Has she called for an ambulance?" Jimmy asked, leaping from his bed and hurriedly pulling on a pair of jeans.

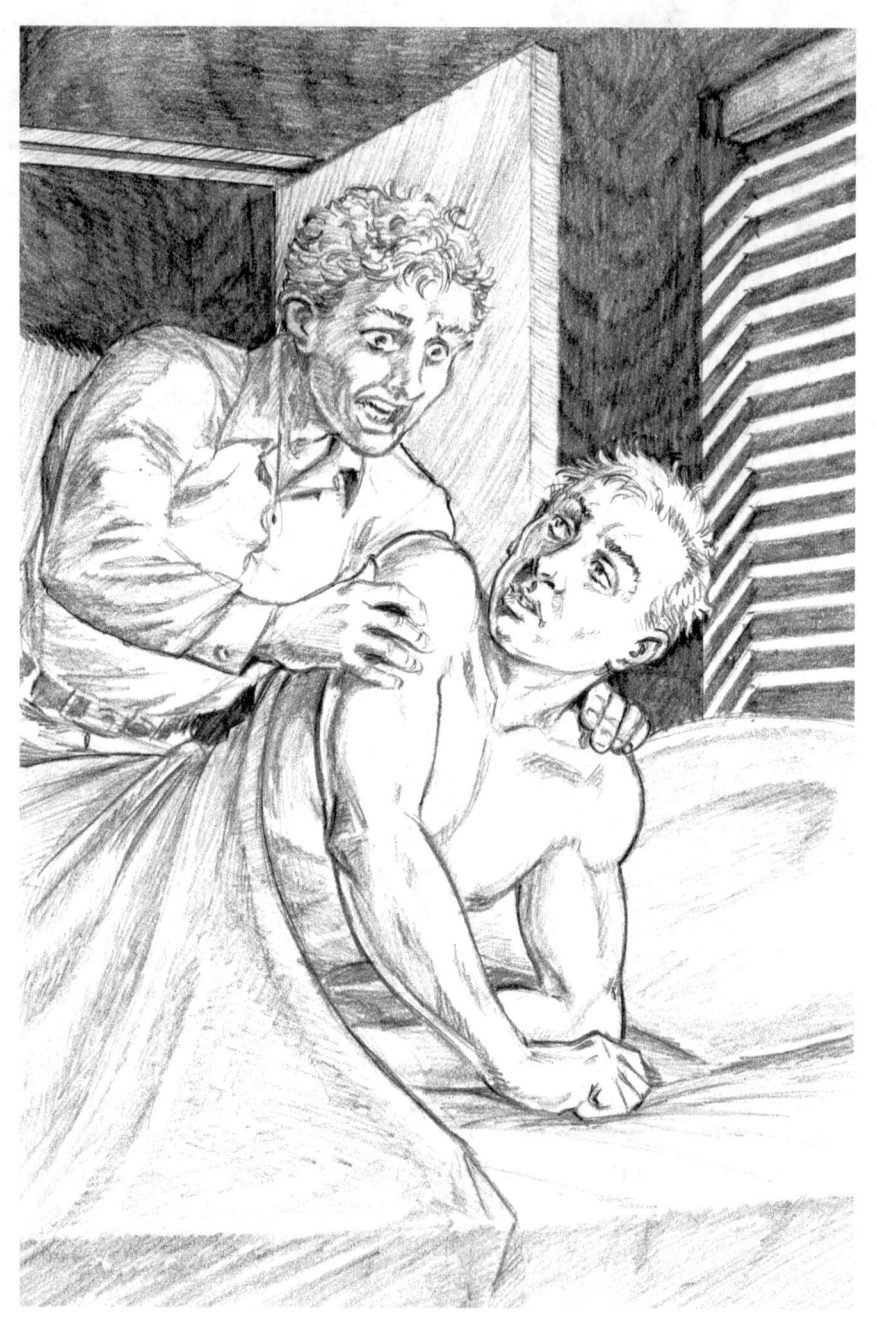

"JIMMY! WAKE UP, MAN!"

"Not yet. She said she wants to see if she can help him first."

"Stubborn old woman!" Jimmy swore, reaching for the car keys kept lying in a shallow dish beside his bed. Howdy grabbed him by the wrist.

"I think I should drive, Jimmy."

The second the two of them stepped through the doorway of the Francis home, eleven-year-old Scooter practically tackled Jimmy, wrapping both arms tightly around his older brother.

"Hey, pal," Howdy said, gently pulling Scooter away from Jimmy. "Why don't you and me go wait in the living room."

Sniffling loudly in an attempt to keep the moisture welling up in his eyes from becoming full-blown tears, Scooter looked up at Jimmy, who smiled and nodded his head.

"Mom?" he then called out.

"Back here, sweetheart," Virginia called from the back of the house.

Jimmy stopped when he was but halfway down the hallway. The sight of his father—so strong, so insistently self-reliant—lying sprawled on the floor while a kneeling Virginia hovered over him, was almost more than Jimmy could bear. His own knees threatened to give way and he placed a hand against the wall for support.

"What happened, Mom?" he asked when at last he too took a knee beside the fallen Ted.

"I'm not sure," she said haltingly, her voice quivering as she reached out and gripped her son's arm with surprising strength.

"When your father got up this morning, he complained that he wasn't feeling well. He went into the bathroom for a little while." Her lips began to tremble.

"I thought maybe he'd picked up some sort of stomach virus. That happens, you know?"

"Yeah, I know."

"But when he stepped out into the hallway, he just..." She made a vague sweeping motion with her free hand. "He just collapsed!"

"Dad?" Jimmy said in a voice deliberately overloud. "Dad? Are you all right? Can you hear me?"

Ted Francis' head lolled from one side to the other, letting Jimmy know he was at least semi-conscious. His lips moved, but whatever words he sought to mumble were unintelligible.

"My God, Mom," Jimmy said, rising to his feet. "Why haven't you called the paramedics for him?"

His mother looked up at him, wringing her hands together. "You know how he is, Jimmy. He hates hospitals with a passion. I kept hoping he'd come out of it."

"Well, he hasn't, has he?" Jimmy said in a tone he hadn't meant to sound so harsh and judgmental.

"He needs more help than we can give him, Mom," he continued more gently. "I'm calling an ambulance."

Virginia reached down to stroke Ted's cheek, then turned pleading eyes up toward Jimmy.

"All right," she said. Her face took on a more resolute expression.

"But I won't let strangers see him lying helpless on the floor. That would kill him. Help me get him up and into bed." She looked up to see Jimmy blankly staring down at his father, seemingly hesitant to make a move.

"Jimmy!" she barked. "Help me!"

As if waking from a stupor, he again knelt so as to raise Ted to a sitting position.

"C'mon, Dad," he urged. "We've got to get you up."

With minimal assistance from the frantic Virginia, Jimmy pulled his father to his feet and managed to half carry, half walk him the few feet to his bed. Taking the time to cover her husband in a blanket, Virginia then went for the phone.

She was beside Ted later as the paramedics lifted him into the back of an ambulance. They helped Virginia get in as well before taking off, lights flashing, for Saint Paul's Hospital. Close behind the ambulance, Howdy drove Jimmy and Scooter.

The three of them were left to pace and fret in a waiting room area at the hospital for what seemed to be more than the hours it actually was. All leapt to attention when a haggard looking Virginia Francis finally came out to talk to them.

"They're still running tests on Ted," she informed them. "But they have him stabilized. They should be moving him to a room in Intensive Care before long and then we'll all be able to see him."

"He'll be all right," Jimmy sought to comfort her, squeezing her arm lightly. He was puzzled by the odd look she gave him in return.

"Boys," she said, glancing over at Howdy and Scooter. "I need to talk to Jimmy alone for a minute.

"Let's go see if we can find us a vending machine," Howdy said to the youngest boy. At the same time, Virginia led Jimmy outside to a patio most often used by those visitors who felt the need to smoke.

"What the hell's the matter with you?" she snapped as soon as she was sure they were alone and out of anyone's earshot.

"What do you mean?" Jimmy asked. He had never heard such venom in his mother's voice, nor known her to use even the mildest of profanities.

"Back at the house," she said in a rush. "It was pretty obvious you didn't want to help me get your father off the floor."

"No," he whispered.

"What—did you think you were too *good* to help him when he needed you the most?"

"Too good?" her eldest repeated, his voice choking as he began to fight back tears.

"Oh, God," he moaned. "I'm not good *enough*!"

Now it was her turn to feel puzzled. "What do you mean?" This time, Jimmy didn't pause to search for the right words; he simply spoke from the heart.

"He's the one who always carried *me*, Momma," he gasped. "It just wasn't right, that's all. I didn't have the right to carry him." He fiercely wiped away a tear.

"I felt…so ashamed."

"What? No."

"You don't understand, Momma. Not for myself. For *him*. He was always so strong, so tough. He has so much pride. He would have been so ashamed, knowing he was being lifted and held up by me. So ashamed. I just know it." He shook his head strongly.

"I'm sorry if I let him and you down."

"Oh, Jimmy," Virginia said, reaching out and rubbing his arm. "You're so wrong. You're the first person Ted *would* turn to for help, when he really needed it. He looks up to you so much."

"He looks up to *me*?" Jimmy said incredulously, rubbing one hand over his eyes to wipe them dry.

"Yes," his mother insisted. "Oh, you know how you men are. He'd never say that to you: not in so many words, anyway.

"But he was proud as could be when you made your own decision about your future: even more when you stuck to it, worked hard and became self-sufficient." She gazed back the way she had come.

"What'll we do if we lose him, Jimmy?"

"We won't lose him, Momma," Jimmy said with a confidence he didn't feel in the least.

"He'll be all right. We all will."

CHAPTER 15

Jimmy caught himself just as his body began to pitch forward. He had literally fallen asleep while standing on his feet: such was the sheer exhaustion overwhelming him after nearly forty-eight hours.

The previous evening, Howdy Watson had finally convinced young Scooter Francis to come home with him and get some food and rest, but Jimmy and their mother Virginia had stayed at the hospital all night and into the next day, keeping vigil over the somnambulant Ted Francis.

Just a few hours before, a doctor had pulled Virginia aside and talked to her about the results of the various tests that had been conducted on Ted since his admittance to the hospital. Of all he said, the stunned woman would remember but one word clearly.

Cancer.

If Ted Francis had not so religiously avoided doctors throughout his adult life, they might have discovered the legacy of his heavy smoking while it was still only in his lungs.

But by now it had metastasized, spread throughout his body until finally reaching his brain.

There was nothing they could do now save make his final hours as comfortable as possible.

Jimmy tried rubbing the exhaustion from his eyes as a nurse came bustling into Ted's room on her regular rounds. After checking the various tubes and monitors attached to him, she leaned over the patient.

"Mr. Francis?" she said, speaking loudly in hope of slicing through the stupor that had possessed him since he had fallen to the floor at home.

"Do you know where you are, Mr. Francis?" His head lolled slightly and his eyes seemed to squint, but no words issued from his mouth.

"Do you know who this is, Mr. Francis?" she pressed, pulling a reticent Virginia close to the bed. Ted managed to make some strangled sounds but his attempt at a response was unintelligible.

"Do you know who this is, Mr. Francis?" the nurse loudly repeated, dragging an even more hesitant Jimmy to the side of the sickbed.

Ted seemed to make an effort at focusing his glazed eyes and a slightly drunken looking grin gamely tried to turn up the corners of his mouth.

"Friend," he murmured, in a low but clear voice. Then his eyes closed and his head sank back more deeply into his pillow.

For as long as he himself would live, Jimmy would fervently choose to believe that for that moment his dad had known exactly what he was saying. It would be the last coherent utterance Ted Francis ever spoke.

Six hours after he said that one word…he was gone.

CHAPTER 16

Antonio Santini was becoming a little peeved.

Jimmy Francis' lunch hour officially ended fifteen minutes ago. He should be back behind the front counter, relieving Santini, to resume his personal work. Instead, the boy was still holed up in a separate little room also located at the rear of the store.

Not long after his father had died the previous year, Jimmy had asked Mr. Santini if he could make his own personal use of the small room, which until then had been merely a seldom-employed storage area.

That arrangement had been fine with Santini, though his curiosity became naturally aroused as Jimmy started spending more and more of his free time in there. That curiosity became suspicion when he discovered that Jimmy had taken it upon himself to install a *lock* on the door leading into that room.

Leaving the front area to the other clerk on duty, Santini stormed back to the rear of the store and began banging on the door of Jimmy's private sanctum.

"Damn!" he heard a voice exclaim from inside.

The old man then heard the lock clicking from the other side. The door opened and he saw Jimmy standing there, sucking on the end of his bleeding left thumb.

"Sorry, Mr. Santini," Jimmy mumbled around the wounded digit. "I guess I lost track of time."

"What's going on in there?" Santini demanded, trying to barge into the room.

"Nothing's going on," Jimmy assured him while also deftly sliding over to block the older man's passage.

"No? Then, what's that?" Santini pointed over Jimmy's shoulder. Atop a small worktable that was the room's only furnishing, Santini could see a variety of the shop tools always kept on hand. They surrounded some unseen object that was covered by a dark chamois cloth.

"It's nothing," Jimmy insisted.

"Let me be the judge of that, eh?" Santini said, finally pushing past Jimmy.

"It's really nothing," Jimmy protested. Ignoring him, Santini snatched away the concealing square of cloth and let out a slight gasp.

What Jimmy had been attempting to keep concealed from the old craftsman now stood revealed to be a nearly finished wooden *sculpture*, standing almost eighteen inches high.

The figure was of a Native American male, holding in his left hand a feathered lance. A blanket draped over his shoulders covered much of his body. Where the blanket hung down over his right arm, which was held across his breast, the figure's head was bowed. Nearby lay a sheaf of papers bearing various conceptual drawings of the statue.

"You did this?" Santini asked, continuing to look at the sculpture rather than at Jimmy.

"Yes, sir," Jimmy said. "But not on company time, Mr. Santini." (The old man had long ago given Jimmy permission to call him just "Tony," but that always seemed too disrespectful to the younger man.) "I've worked on it weekends, lunch hours, after closing. I'm almost finished.

"I call it *The Last Warrior.*"

Santini didn't reply for a full three minutes as he examined the statue with a critical eye, running his fingers across its curves.

"It's good, Jimmy," he pronounced at last. "*Very* good." He at last turned back toward his anxious protégé.

"What do you intend to do with it?"

"I don't know. Maybe give it to someone as a gift."

"*Or,*" Santini said cagily, "we could display it in the front store window. Maybe sell it, eh?"

"You'd let me do that?"

"What 'let'? I was thinking maybe we could make some sort of business arrangement."

Well aware that the old man had been known to squeeze a nickel so tightly that the image of Jefferson wept, Jimmy eyed him somewhat suspiciously.

"Meaning what, exactly? If we sell it, you keep part of the money?"

"Exactly!" Santini grinned and put a fatherly hand on his shoulder.

"Like what: ten percent?" Jimmy asked tentatively.

"Actually, I was thinking more like twenty-five percent. After all, I give you a place to work. You use my tools, my electricity."

Jimmy frowned.

"Fifteen percent."

Santini's hand left his shoulder.

"I took you in: taught you all I know."

Pause.

"Twenty percent."

"Fifteen percent," Jimmy repeated.

"Yer bustin' my balls here, Jimmy," Santini sputtered, waving his arms. "Like a son I treat you…"

"You wouldn't charge your son a commission at all."

"You don't know my son."

"Fifteen percent," Jimmy said, standing his ground. "Or I work in my home, sell my statues at the Flea Market, and keep all the profits for myself."

Realizing that he was beaten, Santini gave a weary shrug. "Fine. Just for you—and my father would disown me for this—fifteen percent."

The two men shook on it. It was the only contract either would ever need.

"You mentioned your son, Mr. Santini," Jimmy said as he gently covered up his statue. "I don't think I've ever heard you talk much about him."

"Dominic. He's a good boy." Santini sighed softly. "But he never had any interest in the family business or in living here. 'The middle of the middle of nowhere,' he always called it.

"So he took off to New York City first chance he got. Now he's a big shot: a fancy schmancy lawyer."

Jimmy smiled. Despite Santini's dismissive way of talking, Jimmy knew the old man was proud of his son and his accomplishments. Dominic and his father took turns flying out to visit each other twice a year.

"But enough of this," Santini groused, clapping his hands. "I'm not paying you to be my headshrinker. Your lunch hour ended twenty minutes ago.

"So go—go do some *real* work!"

CHAPTER 17

Kathy Brown, dressed immaculately in her crisp whites, walked briskly down a corridor of Hillcrest Hospital.

She'd been working there as a nurse for a year now, since shortly after graduating from college. But it had taken only her first week there to convince her that this was truly what she was meant to make her life's work.

She smiled brightly the moment she caught sight of Jimmy Francis waiting for her in the facility's front lobby; he held a gaudy colored paper sack in each hand. The smile vanished as she drew closer and could see he had an odd expression on his face.

"What's wrong, Jimmy?" she asked, grown suddenly concerned. She knew he didn't really like coming here, or to any other hospital. Not since his father died.

"Nothing," he replied quickly, his own smile now assuring her. "I was just watching you as you came toward me. I don't know why, but I just don't think I ever fully realized before just how *tiny* you are."

"That comes from being as sickly as Tiny Tim most of my life," she only half jested.

"But I *have* always known just how *pretty* you are," he declared, leaving her too true joke behind.

"Now I *know* something's wrong!" she said, slapping him on the upper arm.

"Hey! Don't go beatin' on a man who's brought you burgers, fries and soda from your favorite place!" He displayed the twin paper bags as if he were a supplicant making an offering at an altar.

"It's such a pretty day, I thought we could just eat here, out in the garden area."

"That sounds nice, Jimmy," Kathy said, circling his left arm with her right arm and leading him onward.

It was indeed a beautiful day for eating out of doors. But Jimmy was far quieter than normal as they partook of their simple fare, and Kathy decided to press the issue.

"Something's on your mind, Jimmy." It wasn't a question. "You might as well tell me what it is."

He scratched the back of his head (at the spot where his mysterious tingles always originated) and smiled at her rather sheepishly.

"We've been together for quite a while now," he began. "I think it's been good—don't you?"

"Uh-huh," she said, seemingly only half listening to him as she scooped a bag of warm French fries out of the larger sack that held them.

Initially irked by her response, or lack of same, Jimmy's features suddenly took on a look of revelation.

"You've known ever since that first time we made love that I was in love with you, haven't you?" His tone was almost accusatory.

"Oh, I knew it well before that happened," she replied matter-of-factly, popping a fry into her mouth before adding, "or else it *wouldn't* have happened."

"Then why haven't you ever said anything?" What Jimmy had imagined would be at least a somewhat tender and romantic moment (at least as romantic as one can be while downing junk food in a hospital garden) had taken a sharp turn onto a road that led he knew not where.

"I had already told you what I had to say; told you how I felt," she explained, using a voice one might employ when speaking to a small and slightly slow child.

"It was up to you to come to terms with how *you* felt."

Feeling like his wheels were returning to firmer ground, Jimmy smiled. "Well, now I guess we *both* know!" Then the smile gave way, just a bit.

"But it's been a while since you said it to me. Your feelings haven't changed, have they?"

"A little, maybe."

"Oh?" He was now clearly concerned.

"Yeah." She was peering into the sack from which she had extracted her food. "Did you think to bring any ketchup for these fries?"

"How have your feelings changed?" he pressed, while simultaneously handing her a small, plastic ketchup container.

"Now that I know you better than I did that night," she replied, dipping a fry into the ketchup, "I think I love you a little bit more than I did then."

"Whew!" He exhaled nearly enough air to inflate a balloon.

"I know it took me a god-awful long time to say the words," he admitted, reaching out and taking one of her hands.

"But now that I have, I intend to repeat them as often as I can." (His smile was for this moment, but also for that moment so long ago when, alongside a placid lake, he had offered his father the same advice.)

"And I'm gonna do my best to not just *say* that I love you—but to *show* that I love you."

"You already do," she assured him, reaching across the small table where they sat and popping one of her fries into his mouth. He lowered his head slightly as he chewed.

"If you want to be loved—be loveable," he murmured under his breath.

"What's that?"

"Oh...just somethin' I must have heard once." He straightened and moved his hand to a shirt pocket.

"Which reminds me, for no particular reason: I made something for you." He opened his hand and Kathy saw he was holding a small, wooden *ring*, part of its band being carved in the shape of two interlocking hearts.

"Did you make it yourself, Jimmy?" Kathy asked breathlessly.

"I sure did."

"It's beautiful!"

To her stunned amazement, Jimmy then slid awkwardly out of his chair, dropping down on one knee as he took hold of Kathy's left hand and slid the ring onto her finger. As he had taken painstaking time and care to insure, it fit her perfectly.

"Now that we've finally got all that 'I love you' stuff settled," he said, striving mightily not to let his voice quiver, "don't you think it's about time we got married?"

"Why?" was her unexpected response, softened slightly by the clearly mischievous look on her face. "Have I gone and got you in trouble?"

They both began to laugh almost hysterically, to the point where Jimmy noticed that Kathy's laughter had changed to loud sobbing. Overcome with emotion, unable to speak, she simply began nodding her head furiously before throwing herself into his arms.

"Oh," he told her when the laughing, crying and kissing had subsided sufficiently for both young lovers to catch their breaths, "and just so you know; I intend to replace that with a *real* ring as soon as I can. One you help me pick out.

"I just thought this one would be appropriate for the occasion."

"I love it," she said fervently, holding her hand out to examine it at arm's length.

"And no matter how many other rings I might ever get—this one is never leaving my hand!"

CHAPTER 18

Jimmy Francis had not set foot inside Calvary Cemetery since the day his father Ted had been buried there.

But he was there now; it had been in the midst of one of his long-accepted headaches that the impulse had come upon him to do so.

Even having now done so, he couldn't bring himself to go directly to the site of Ted's grave. The area of the cemetery in which it lay was called the *Sorrowful Mother* section. Jimmy's parents had selected two plots there, side-by-side, because it sat atop a small knoll that was shaded by the spreading branches of a towering elm tree. They always said they chose this spot because it would offer them such a lovely "view" of the rest of the cemetery and of the wooded hills running just to the north of it.

In the middle of this section of graves was a small, man-made sort of round grotto. There, two curving concrete benches sat in front of a plaster reproduction of Michelangelo's magnificent statue, *The Pieta*.

Jimmy had always loved the original, considering it to be one of the most brilliant and beautiful works of art ever to be rendered by the hand of man. The image of a mother cradling the lifeless body of her grown son who was so horribly murdered was one of the most powerful ever imagined.

Jimmy took the time now to study the reproduction closely. As an artist and budding sculptor himself, he recognized and admired features usually lost on most observers. Almost lovingly, he ran his fingers over the face of the Virgin Mary. He was awed anew at the skill with which Michelangelo had managed to give the grieving mother an expression that was at once sad and accepting, knowing as she did that her son Jesus had made this ultimate sacrifice, paid this ultimate price, for the salvation of the world.

Tears were misting Jimmy's eyes as he turned away and made the short walk to where his father lay. He had briefly considered bringing flowers with him to lay on the site, but quickly dismissed the notion. Dad wasn't a flowery sort and would probably criticize him for wasting his money.

Jimmy stood there rather awkwardly at first. He was unsure of what to do with his hands. He tried holding them together in front of him, but that felt too much like he was praying. Thrusting them into his pants' pockets felt worse. He kept his eyes up.

"So..." he finally said out loud, instantly feeling foolish for speaking to a dead man. "I'm getting married, Dad," he continued anyway.

Only now did he look squarely down at his father's grave marker, almost as if expecting a reply to rise up from it.

The marker, set flush to the ground, was a simple but nice one: bronze and supplied to the family for free by the Veterans Administration. Jimmy could see a few, small, dry clods of dirt sprinkled across it; probably thrown onto it while custodians mowed the grass around it.

Though inadvertent and innocent, Jimmy felt it to be somewhat disrespectful. He lowered himself to one knee and used the back of his hand to sweep the dirt away.

He then almost tenderly brushed his fingertips across the raised letters of his father's name. Surprisingly, doing so brought him a feeling of comfort—and of being comfortable. He went all the way to the ground, until he was seated cross-legged in front of the grave marker.

"You'd like Kathy, Dad; I know you would," he said. He grinned crookedly. "And she'd put up with you, for my sake. That's the kinda girl she is. Her and Mom get along great."

Beginning to feel almost like he was literally conversing with his father, Jimmy chuckled. "Hey, I came across an old Spanish proverb awhile back that I think you'd get a kick out of. It goes something like this:

"Whether a man ever marries or not...he'll live to regret it.

"Don't tell Mom I repeated that to ya. Besides, I think that old Spaniard was wrong."

Jimmy spent nearly half an hour talking to Ted. He told him about how Mom and Scooter were getting along. He told him about how much he enjoyed his work with Mr. Santini.

He talked about Kathy and his concerns about her health. He even gave Ted an update on how the Yankees were doing that season.

On impulse, as he finally rose to leave, Jimmy kissed the tips of two fingers and lightly pressed them to his father's headstone. Ted wouldn't like or approve of such a display of affection between two men; but Jimmy figured he'd just have to live with it.

So to speak.

Within a week of this visit, Jimmy began his most ambitious sculpting effort to date: a 3'-by-3' reproduction in wood of Michelangelo's *Pieta*.

Mr. Santini—who, in a momentary lapse of effusiveness, declared the finished statue to be itself a minor masterpiece—would sell it to the pastor of the Catholic church he attended, for display in its rectory.

(Jimmy, though he would likely have characterized himself as being a "believer" in a general sense, had never attended any church religiously. Like his father, he often said that the only occasions that would prompt him to darken the door of any particular church were "marryin's and buryin's.")

Over the course of time, Jimmy would gain a fair reputation among art lovers of a certain type. Even so, he would never seem to achieve quite the level of skill or reputation to make a decent living from his works of art alone.

And that was all right by him. He loved his art and the sense of achievement and peace it brought him, and he never wanted it to become a "job." He also liked the practical nature of the other woodworking that he and Mr. Santini did. He wouldn't have traded his time spent with the old man for either love or money.

His job brought him sufficient amounts of the latter—and Kathy gave him ample supplies of the former.

CHAPTER 19

Chuck Francis was only half-heartedly watching the small portable television in his bedroom when the soft knock came at its open doorway.

"Can I talk to ya for a minute, Scooter?" his older brother Jimmy asked, poking his head through the portal.

"Sure, bubba," Scooter said, his face lighting up with a smile.

Jimmy entered and took a seat on the edge of his brother's bed, near the chair in which Scooter sat.

"As you know, the wedding's coming up pretty soon," Jimmy reminded him. "I never knew how much work went into puttin' one o' these shindigs together. Thank God Kathy and our mothers are doing most of the work.

"But that still leaves one job strictly on my shoulders, and I haven't managed to get it done."

"What's that?"

"I haven't picked my best man."

Scooter looked at him with mild puzzlement. "What do you mean? Isn't Howdy gonna be your best man?" The thirteen-year-old had certainly and understandably assumed as much, considering that Jimmy and Howdy had been the best of friends for over half their lives.

"Oh, sure," Jimmy acknowledged, staring out the window. "I've already asked him to be *one* of my best men."

"*One* of 'em?" Scooter queried. "You mean you can have *more* than one?"

"You can have as many as you want." Jimmy now turned his eyes toward his brother. "And I was hoping *you'd* be the one standing next to me with the wedding rings, buddy."

"Really?" Scooter gushed, obviously thrilled at the prospect of standing up for the big brother he fairly worshipped.

"That'd be *great!*"

"I think so," Jimmy said. He had bowed his head, and when he raised it back up Scooter could see a slightly worried expression on Jimmy's face.

"There's just one possible problem, Scooter."

"Wotta you mean?"

What the younger boy didn't know is that a few days earlier Jimmy had received a concerned phone call from their mother. Virginia had told him that she was worried about the direction Scooter's life seemed to be in danger of taking.

For no reason she could discover, he had begun to slack off in his schoolwork, and was now receiving grades reflective of that. Occasionally, he would skip school altogether, in order to hang out with some older boys of whom Mom did not approve.

"It's like this," Jimmy now explained. "Me and Kathy want to get married in July. But because of restrictions on when she can take off from her duties at the hospital, we've had to schedule the wedding for a weekday afternoon."

Scooter scowled slightly. "Okay. Why should that be a problem?"

"Well, it isn't—for *me*." Jimmy had thrown out the bait: now he had to hope he had a deft enough hand to set the hook.

"Here's the thing, Scooter. When I mentioned it to Mom the other day, she told me you were having a little trouble in school."

"What kinda trouble?" Scooter said tersely.

"She didn't really say," Jimmy fibbed. "All she said was that it looked like your grades might be such that you'll have to take summer school classes to make up the lost credits.

"If that happens…well, I wouldn't want you to miss any classes on account of me. So, you might not be able to be at the wedding at all!"

"I'll be there," Scooter said in a soft voice, following a long pause.

"What about your grades?"

"There's still plenty of time left in the semester. I'll just bring my grades up so I don't haveta worry about summer school."

"Are you sure? 'Cause I sure do want you to be the one standing next to me that day." Jimmy reached out to pat Scooter's knee.

"It would mean the world to me, bubba."

"I promise, Jimmy," Scooter said earnestly. "No matter what it takes, I'll do it and I'll be there."

"That's good enough for me," Jimmy stated firmly, rising to leave. "I know you'd never deliberately let me down. I appreciate it."

"OKAY. WHY SHOULD THAT BE A PROBLEM?"

Jimmy congratulated himself silently (but hopefully not prematurely) as he left the young teen's room. He was sure that if he had just butted in to Scooter's affairs, lectured him like a parent about the need to straighten up and fly right, the boy would have stubbornly resisted on pure principle. This way, it would seem more like it to him that this was all his own idea.

And when the day came, it was Scooter who stood beside Jimmy and handed him the wedding rings. Scooter, who beamed with pride and joy when his big brother kissed the bride.

By any reasonable standards, the wedding was a lovely affair that went off smooth as glass. By saving and planning carefully, the newlyweds would even be able to honeymoon on a five-day cruise of the Caribbean.

During the reception that immediately followed the ceremony, Jimmy managed to find a few minutes alone with his other best man, Howdy Watson.

Howdy was doubly happy on that day. First, because he loved Jimmy and Kathy like family and took joy in their bliss. Second because, after holding down a number of unrelated and unfulfilling jobs for variable but short lengths of time, he had finally landed a post working with computers. The rest of the world was finally starting to catch up to him.

A locally owned oil and gas company had decided to add a computer system to their corporate headquarter building in town and Howdy had successfully applied for one of the new positions this opened up.

"I have to admit," he now confessed to Jimmy, "I feel a little jealous today."

"Why's that?"

"Oh, I guess I just envy what you've found with Kathy. I'm beginning to think that'll never happen to me."

"Don't think that way, buddy," Jimmy replied, placing a fraternal hand on Howdy's shoulder. "You just haven't met the right girl yet, that's all."

"I *meet* plenty of girls," Howdy said glumly. "That's easy. The hard part is finding the one who'll give the time of day to a scrawny, homely twenty-three-year-old Trekkie who still collects comic books."

"Stop it," Jimmy quipped. "You're turning me on."

"Yeah, yeah," Howdy said in pretend annoyance, shaking his shoulder to dislodge Jimmy's hand.

"But from now on—that's *Kathy's* job!"

CHAPTER 20

For no particular reason, Jimmy Francis awakened with a start in the middle of the night.

As he lay on his back looking up at the ceiling, he found that he was breathing harder than normal. He rolled over onto his left side only to discover that the other half of the bed was unoccupied.

Rolling around to his right side, he smiled lightly as he saw light coming from under the closed door of the adjoining bathroom.

Now nearly five months into her first pregnancy, his wife Kathy often complained that her bladder had shrunk to the size of a grape, so often was she compelled to empty it.

The young couple had not taken any particular birth control precautions since their honeymoon; both were in agreement that they wanted to have children. Even so, it had taken three years for Kathy to conceive.

Jimmy now lay awake but with his eyes closed: thinking upon fatherhood and all the responsibilities but also all the joys he knew or hoped would accompany it. When he heard the bathroom door swing inward, he opened his eyes and rolled to his side.

He could see Kathy only in silhouette, framed by the open door. She appeared to be sagging against its frame.

"Jimmy," she called out weakly. "Help me. Something's wrong."

"What is it?" he asked anxiously, throwing the covers off.

"I'm *bleeding*!"

CHAPTER 21

Howdy Watson had broken several traffic laws as he raced to reach the hospital.

When Jimmy had called him, he had been unable to give his best friend many details about Kathy's dilemma. Howdy didn't need any.

His car had barely stopped rolling before Howdy shoved the gear into park, turned off the ignition and bolted toward the automatic doors leading into Hillcrest's emergency room. A nurse seated behind a reception desk called out to him but her voice failed to register on his roiling brain and he rushed right past her.

Quietly but quickly, Howdy began prowling the maze of corridors, realizing too late that at the very least he should have stopped at the front desk long enough to ask for directions.

Just as he was about to give up and retrace his confused steps, he caught a glimpse of a familiar face. The door at the end of the hallway down which he was currently rambling was closed, but had a thin vertical glass pane that allowed for a limited view of what lay beyond.

Even from a distance he could recognize Jimmy Francis, who appeared to be in taut conversation with a white-coated doctor.

Howdy couldn't hear what was being said, of course, but as he drew closer he saw Jimmy's face suddenly assume a stricken look. His legs seemed to threaten to buckle beneath him and he clutched at the doctor's arm in an effort to keep from collapsing to the floor.

Howdy quickened his pace, only to be pulled up short by a stern-faced nurse interjecting herself between him and the door.

"That area's restricted," she warned. "Only doctors, staff, patients and their family members are allowed back there."

"But I'm *like* family!" Howdy blurted, immediately and inwardly castigating himself for not simply lying and claiming to be Jimmy's brother.

"I'm afraid 'like' isn't good enough, sir," the nurse replied.

"My friend needs me, dammit!" Howdy protested.

"Is there a problem here?" Unnoticed by Howdy, an armed security guard had now put in an appearance. Oddly, and despite the fact that his right hand was hovering uncomfortably close to his holstered pistol, the guard's features actually looked slightly less stern than did those of the nurse.

"I don't think so," the nurse told the zealous guard. "I was just about to show this gentleman where the nearest waiting room is."

Howdy continued to look anxiously back over one shoulder as the nurse took him by one arm, turned him around and marched him away.

The young man could never have told you how long he sat in that waiting room, each minute crawling by like a glacier migrating to the sea. He considered calling Jimmy's mother, but thought it best to wait till he knew exactly what was happening. So instead he sat alone.

He was bent forward, arms on his legs, head down facing the floor when at last he sensed the presence of someone standing over him. He raised his eyes to see Jimmy looking down at him with the blank numbness of a shell-shocked soldier.

"It was a boy, Howdy," Jimmy managed to mutter. "I was gonna have a son."

"Oh, Lord," Howdy choked, feeling his throat constrict and his eyes well over. He reached out to grasp Jimmy's hand, pulling him unresistingly down to a chair beside him.

"She had a miscarriage," Jimmy said in a monotone. "They don't know why."

"And Kathy? Is she –?"

"The doctors told me they have her stabilized. They ran a few tests just to be sure before taking her to her room. She's there now." His lips continued to move soundlessly for a moment before he turned a plaintive gaze toward his sympathetic friend.

"Why would something like this happen, Howdy? Why?"

"I don't know, Jimmy," Howdy said, reaching out to place a gentle hand on his buddy's arm.

"I don't know if anybody knows," he continued, struggling mightily to find the right thing to say. "I guess we just have to hope God has a reason that we don't understand."

"*God*?" Jimmy snapped, startling Howdy by roughly jerking his arm away. There were tears in his eyes, but behind the tears it was anger that flashed brightly.

"There *is* no *God*, dammit!"

Howdy flinched, as if he had been physically slapped by the words. "C'mon, Jimmy. Don't say that. I understand; you're upset."

"You don't understand anything!" Jimmy snarled. "What kind of a god would allow something like this to happen? What kind of a 'plan' requires an innocent, unborn baby to *die*?

"No. There's no God, Howdy." His shoulders slumped. "There's only life...and death."

He then began to sob softly as he buried his face in his hands, and Howdy reached out and rubbed a comforting hand over his back.

"How's Kathy handling this?" Howdy asked at last.

"I don't know," Jimmy replied in a tone of defeat. He felt Howdy's hand stop moving.

"What do you mean you don't know?"

"I just...I just haven't been able to bring myself to go in and see her, talk to her yet." He felt Howdy remove his hand entirely.

"You...damned...*coward*!"

Jimmy's head snapped up to look at Howdy. What he saw to his amazement was a look of sheer outrage and revulsion such as he had never seen exhibited by his easygoing friend. The stinging virulence of his hissed utterance twisted Jimmy's insides.

"You're sitting here feeling sorry for yourself," Howdy accused, "wasting time cursing a god you claim doesn't even exist—while Kathy's lying alone there in the bowels of hell somewhere.

"Left alone...while she tries to come to terms with the worst thing that's ever happened to her. With a loss that's even greater for her than it is for you." With one hand he made a waving motion in the general direction from which Jimmy had come.

"Now you get off your ass," he commanded in a voice that would brook no debate, "and go be with your wife."

Looking dazed, Jimmy rose stiffly to his feet, took a few steps and then turned to look plaintively at his best friend.

"What'll I do, Howdy?" he pleaded. "What'll I say to her?"

"You do whatever she needs you to do," Howdy instructed, his tone finally softening. "You tell her you love her no matter what—and you mean it.

"The rest'll take care of itself, in time."

Jimmy nodded hesitantly. "Thanks, man. I don't know what I'd do without you."

"Well, just thank that non-existent God of yours that you'll never have to find out. Now, get goin'

"I'll be out here when you need me."

CHAPTER 22

The door leading into Kathy Francis' hospital room might well have weighed a ton, so difficult was it for her husband to push it open and enter.

He stopped just a step into the room, looking at his wife. He had never seen her look so tired. She lay in bed, her head turned to one side, looking through the window at a sunrise whose beauty meant nothing to her, hoping perhaps that its glow would have healing properties.

The movement as Jimmy began to tentatively walk across the room caught her eye and she turned her head to watch as he slowly approached. He stopped beside the bed and for an uncomfortably long period of time neither spoke a word.

"I'm sorry!" they both blurted out at once.

As if he'd been poleaxed, Jimmy fell to his knees and dropped his head onto her bed.

"I'm sorry, sweetheart," he repeated. "I'm sorry I wasn't here sooner."

"Shh." Kathy lightly stroked his hair. "It's all right. You're here now." Her voice broke slightly.

"Besides...I'm the one who should be apologizing."

"What do you mean?" Jimmy asked, raising his head.

"It's my fault," she gasped as tears began to fall. "It's all my fault that we lost the baby!"

"No...don't ever think that," he begged. "Never. Never, never."

"I must have done something wrong," she persisted.

"You didn't. I'm sure of it. These things just happen sometimes. There's nothing you could have done to prevent it."

"How can you be so sure?"

"Because I know you, babe. I know you would never do anything wrong or bad that could have hurt him." His hands clenched.

"Maybe it was *my* fault. Something in my genes or something."

"No." Kathy weakly slid over on the mattress, tugging Jimmy's arm and silently urging him up onto the bed beside her. As gently as he could, he took her into his arms and she rested her head on his chest.

"Let's not blame each other, Jimmy," she whispered.

"All right."

Neither could have said with certainty how long they lay there like that, each drawing silent comfort and strength from the other. There was no need to share thoughts that were virtually identical.

At some point a soft tap came at the door and Kathy's attending physician respectfully entered the room. Dr. Adams was middle-aged but somehow seemed older in the faint light coming from above Kathy's bed.

His was not, Jimmy thought but did not say, the face of a bearer of good news.

"How are you doing?" he asked Kathy as he approached, a weary but benign smile on his lips.

"All right, I suppose," she replied cautiously. "When do you think I can go home?"

"I'd like to keep you here for a day of observation," the doctor replied, and Kathy's grip on Jimmy's hand tightened. "Maybe two. You can use the rest."

Jimmy lightly kissed her atop her head, his own demeanor darkening as he detected a slight change in the physician's expression.

"We've, uh, we've gotten the results back on some of the tests we ran earlier," Adams said.

"I know this isn't a good time, Kathy, Jimmy." He inhaled deeply.

"But I really feel that both of you need to know what the tests show."

Out in the waiting room, Howdy Watson had finally given in to his own physical and emotional exhaustion and was curled up in a ball on a small sofa, sleeping.

With a start he awakened, his sleep disturbed by the very silence that should have abetted it. Blinking the slumber from his eyes, he gazed up to see a shaken, ashen-faced Jimmy standing over him.

"What is it, buddy?" he inquired, rising from the sofa and wincing slightly; one foot had gone to sleep and was now painfully tingling with the returning flow of blood to it.

Jimmy's face twisted and tears began to seep from beneath closed lids. Howdy circled him in his arms.

"We're never gonna get another chance, Howdy!" Jimmy sobbed.

"What do you mean?" his comrade asked, pulling him down so they were seated side-by-side on the sofa.

"We just got more bad news from her doctor," Jimmy explained numbly.

"One of the tests they ran." He grimaced. "She's...she's got some sort of congestive heart problem."

"Oh, God," Howdy gasped.

"It's funny," Jimmy murmured, "but in a way the miscarriage may have actually saved her life. Dr. Adams said the stress of going full term, the strain of delivery...likely would have killed her."

"Is there anything they can do?"

"They can't heal it, no."

"So, she's...she's gonna...?" Howdy couldn't bring himself to say the final word.

"No. Not right away, anyway." Jimmy straightened himself. "With rest, proper diet, mild exercise and medication...the doctor says she can live a reasonable number of years." He bit down on his lower lip.

"But, no...she probably won't be growing old with me, Howdy." His frame sagged again.

"And there'll be no more pregnancies."

Howdy put his hand on the back of Jimmy's neck and rubbed it. (Right on the spot where I get those damned tingles of mine, Jimmy thought. Why hadn't one of them warned me about this?)

"Do you need to get back in with Kathy?" Howdy asked.

"No. Not right away. They gave her something to make her sleep. They told me she should be out for a few hours at least."

"Then why don't we get outta here for a while, get you some fresh air," Howdy suggested.

"I don't know if I should," Jimmy replied, looking back the way he had just come.

"Just for a little while. Clear your head a little."

"Okay."

" I just got one question," Howdy said.

"What's that, buddy?"

"Does this place validate parking?"

"Dude, this really isn't a good time for jokes," Jimmy chided. But then, despite himself, he chuckled lightly: felt guilty for doing so.

"I know, Jimmy," Howdy assured him. "But sometimes, that's when you need the jokes the most!"

CHAPTER 23

Half an hour later, Howdy Watson was seated on one of the concrete benches at Calvary Cemetery, staring intently at the full-sized reproduction of *The Pieta*. He would periodically shift to one side or the other, changing his perspective while maintaining eye contact with the statue.

Close by but out of earshot, Jimmy Francis once again sat cross-legged on the ground before his father's grave: once again talking to his spirit.

These ethereal conversations had become sort of a habit for Jimmy, if only because the visits with his father always left him feeling at least slightly better. He spilled out his troubles to Dad, but also happily shared the joys.

There was no joy today.

"I feel kinda lost, Dad," he said, having already delivered the worst of the news.

"I just don't know what to do. And that makes me angry somehow. I mean, a man—a husband, a father—he's supposed to know the right thing to do all the time, isn't he?"

After staring at the headstone for a long, silent moment, Jimmy smiled slightly.

"But *you* weren't right all the time, were you? No offense," he hastily added.

"I know in my *head* that I didn't do anything wrong. Neither did Kathy." He grasped for words.

"But somewhere inside—maybe not so much in my heart as in my belly—I feel like I screwed up." A slightly more placid look came over his face as an unbidden memory flashed to the surface of his brain, along with his familiar tingling pulse at the back of his skull.

"I remember what you told me one time as a kid. You told me there were only two things a fella needed to do when he'd made a mess of things.

"Clean up the mess…and try your best never to do it again."

He tilted his head slightly upward to stare at the rustling leaves of the nearby elm. He understood completely why his parents had fallen in love with this spot.

"That's what I'm gonna do, Dad. I'm gonna do everything I can to get Kathy and me through this and make us whole. And I'm gonna do everything I can to show her I love her, no matter what."

As had by now taken on the aspect of ritual, Jimmy kissed his fingertips and pressed them lightly against Ted's headstone.

He then rose to his feet and walked over to where Howdy still studied the statue of Mother and Child.

"Hope I didn't keep you waiting too long," Jimmy said as he took a seat next to Howdy.

"Not at all," Howdy replied, not averting his eyes from the sculpture before him. "Y'know, I actually came to a realization while I was sitting here and looking at the statue."

"Yeah? What's that?"

Howdy turned toward him, arching his eyebrows and wearing a silly grin. "The Virgin Mary was kind of a *hottie!*"

The suddenness, the total inappropriateness of the comment blindsided Jimmy.

Despite himself, he began to laugh: loud and hearty. At one point, though, the laugh ceased to be one of mirth and became one of near hysteria. It in turn developed into deep, wracking sobs as he threw his arms around the best friend he'd ever had.

Clutching Jimmy to him tightly, Howdy finally allowed himself to also succumb to grief, bursting into tears himself.

Afterwards, they made two more stops before returning to the hospital, though both dreaded the prospect.

They went to see Jimmy's mother.

And then to see Kathy's.

CHAPTER 24

College sophomore Chuck "Scooter" Francis sat alone in his dorm room. It was a warm day, bordering on being downright hot, but as was usual, the dorm's air conditioning units were doing an inadequate job of maintaining a comfortable temperature. In hope of stirring up a little breeze Scooter had raised a window and propped open the door to aid in circulation.

He was supposed to be studying for an exam, and indeed had been, but had decided he'd earned a brief reprieve from the books. He pushed his wheeled, swivel-backed chair from under his desk and, using his feet, propelled himself over to where his small, portable television set sat atop a dresser.

It seemed that the younger of the Francis boys had inherited his brother Jimmy's desire to build things—though his own ambitions were of a grander scale and did not require him to actually construct with his own hands.

It was an architect he aspired to be, his vision to design buildings that would soar so high as to rival the legendary Tower of Babel.

He had just settled back in his chair to watch an episode of the popular comedy series *Three's Company* when a voice called to him from the open doorway.

"Working hard as ever, I see."

Scooter's face lit up as he swiveled to see his brother Jimmy standing in the corridor just beyond the doorway.

"Don't just stand there, bubba," he said, leaping out of his chair. "C'mon in!"

The siblings shook hands warmly and Scooter motioned for his brother to avail himself of the room's only other chair.

"In a minute," Jimmy replied, placing both hands on his hips and arching his back with a slight groan. "I've been sitting too long today."

"What brings you a hundred miles from home in the middle of the week?" Scooter inquired.

"Business, mostly. I just got finished delivering a hand-tooled hope chest to one of Mr. Santini's customers.

"Long as I was in the neighborhood, I thought I'd drop in on my little brother and see if he was free to grab some pizza—my treat."

"I'm always up for free food; you know that." Though as tall or maybe a smidgen taller than Jimmy, Scooter was a good twenty pounds lighter. Which made his ability to put away copious quantities of food without ever gaining an ounce of weight all the more annoying.

As Scooter went to his small closet to select a fresh shirt, Jimmy quietly closed the dorm room door behind him, even as his expression took on a slightly more serious mien. He stepped closer to the chair he'd been offered even as Scooter plopped down on the edge of his bed and began to slip on a pair of tennis shoes.

"So," Jimmy began, trying his best to sound nonchalant and unrehearsed. "Mom's been a little worried about you, Scooter."

Scooter dropped his second shoe on the carpeted floor and heaved a deep sigh. "I had a feeling this was more than just a social call. What is it, Jimmy?"

"Oh, you know how Mom is. She's just feeling a little neglected by her baby, that's all."

"Aw, geez," Scooter moaned.

"Well, now," Jimmy pressed on, "you gotta admit that you've pretty much stopped writing or phoning her lately. And you didn't even come home for spring break."

Scooter put on his final shoe and began to tie it. "You know how it is, Jimmy."

"Not really, no. Tell me." Jimmy now moved to the chair; turning it and straddling it backwards with his arms folded and resting atop its back.

"I don't know," Scooter said defensively, clearly flustered and jittery. "Just…things."

"Is it a girl?" Jimmy asked in a tone more hopeful than accusatory.

Scooter chuckled, though the sound of it was almost mournful. "There's no girl."

"Oh, God. Please tell me it's not *drugs*."

Scooter smiled wanly as he shook his head. "No. Oh, I'm not quite the straight arrow." He chuckled again, somewhat inappropriately, Jimmy thought. "Not as straight as you've always been, bubba.

"But I seldom indulge in more than a couple o' beers on a Saturday night and a little weed when it's offered.

"Hell," he chuffed, "I can't *afford* to have a drug problem!"

"Is *that* the problem, kiddo?" Jimmy continued to probe. "Money? I could probably—"

"No, no." Scooter waved the offer away with one hand. "I'm getting by all right." Though he wasn't supposed to know, Scooter was already aware of the fact that, since the death of their father, Jimmy had always slipped a few bucks here and there to their mother for her and Scooter. He wasn't about to solicit or accept even more.

"Are you sure it's not a girl?"

"Positive. To be honest, Jimmy," he grimaced slightly, "I don't really like women very much."

"Lots of men don't like women, Scooter. Hell, from what I'm told, a fair number of *women* don't like women!"

"You just don't understand, Jimmy. Can't we just let it drop?"

"We *could*—but you know that just means the next visit like this you get will be from Mom herself."

"God!" Scooter exclaimed. "That's the *last* thing I need!"

"Don't tell me you're mad at Mom. Is that why you've been avoiding her?"

"No. I love Momma just as much as you do."

"Then come on, bubba," Jimmy cajoled. "Tell me what it is and we'll go from there."

Scooter combed his fingers through his hair and let out a sigh of exasperation.

"All right," he said at length. "But you gotta promise me you won't repeat a word of this to Mom. I mean it, Jimmy. You gotta swear."

Jimmy wasn't at all sure he wanted to make any such promise blindly. But seeing the adamant, almost panicked expression on his little brother's face led him to nod curtly.

"Like I said," Scooter began, "my problem isn't with women." His eyes took on a pained cast.

"It's with men."

Jimmy frowned, his brow furrowing with anger. "Is some guy picking on you?"

"No," Scooter replied, his voice rising. This wasn't working at all the way he would have liked.

"It's just that…what I'm trying to say is…I mean that I…that I'm…" At a loss for any further words, he simple looked at Jimmy expectantly, waving his hands like he was a contestant in a game of charades.

"Oh. Oh, geez!" Jimmy's eyes widened with sudden realization.

"Scooter...are you tryin' to tell me you're a *queer*?"

Scooter slapped one hand over his face to hide the blush that was spreading across it like a wildfire.

"See? See?" he stuttered. "*That's* why I didn't want to talk to you or Mom about it!"

"Oh, my God. You *are* queer." Jimmy looked unabashedly dumbfounded.

Scooter scowled defensively. "I don't like that word, Jimmy."

"Okay. What's the *right* word?"

"Gay."

"Gay?"

"Gay."

"Gay."

"Gay. And yes, I like men. You happy?"

To his surprise, Jimmy responded by grinning broadly and reaching out to tousle Scooter's hair.

"Do any of 'em like you back?"

Scooter slapped his hand away, blushing even more deeply as he flattened his hair back into place.

"What the hell's that supposed to mean?" he asked rather snappishly.

"Well, let's be honest here, squirt," Jimmy said smugly. "In this family, I pretty much inherited all the good looks."

Rather than issuing a stinging verbal rebuttal, Scooter fixed his brother with a look of puzzlement.

"You seem to have gotten over your initial shock awful quick, Jimmy."

His brother shrugged. "To be honest again...a part of me may have already suspected as much."

"Oh? This should be good. What sort of things tipped you off?"

"C'mon! I'm not saying you have a limp wrist, a lisp and swish when you walk. But you've always been a bit uncomfortable around girls. Never really dated. Either keeping to yourself or hanging with other guys. Not a sissy, but a million miles from macho."

"God, bubba," Scooter scoffed. "You've just described *Howdy*! He's not gay, is he?"

Jimmy cocked his head to one side. "Why—you interested?"

"Ew! No way!"

"Yeah. Just as well. He's as straight as I am—just awfully awkward, socially. Poor guy still hasn't found a girl who realizes how much he has to offer."

"No offense," Scooter said. "I mean, I like Howdy a lot...but do you really think there *is* such a girl?"

Jimmy chuckled softly. "Y'know, I've never believed in that romantic notion that there's only *one* perfect person for each of us. But sometimes there aren't a lot.

"But I do think there is at *least* one—it just takes some of us longer to find that one than it does others."

"Do you think that's true for guys like me?" Scooter asked.

Knowing the question was sincere, Jimmy pondered it a moment before responding. "I imagine so. Haven't you had any luck in finding someone yet?"

"I haven't really tried very hard," Scooter admitted. "I'm still kinda—kinda working things out in my own mind."

"I gotcha. Just be careful, Scooter. There are a lot of hurtful people in this world: gay, straight or in between. And I can tell you right now that I won't be happy if one of 'em tries messin' with my baby brother." He pointed a warning finger at his sibling.

"Above all, don't forget the advice Dad gave us."

"Yeah?" Scooter said warily. "Which jewel of wisdom was that?"

"Try not to never let all your brains go to the head of your pecker."

Both young men enjoyed a laugh at that, but Scooter quickly grew serious again.

"Oh, God. If Dad was still alive...he'd hate me, wouldn't he?"

"Probably," Jimmy replied honestly. "At least for a while; he'd raise nine kinds of hell about it. And he'd be wrong for doin' that.

"I loved the old man, bubba. You know that. I still do. He was a good and decent man, and I'd like to think I learned a lot from him: that the best of what I am came from him.

"Like most of us, though, he was a product of his time and his upbringing. You've got to recognize and understand that. But that doesn't mean you have to accept and agree with everything he said being gospel.

"That's something everybody has to do at some point: judge the values and opinions of their parents. Decide which ones they want to adopt for themselves and which ones they want to throw away. That's what it means to grow up; to become a man or woman in your own right."

Scooter looked at him plaintively. "I don't know what I'd do if *you* hated me because of this, Jimmy."

"Never happen," his brother assured him, then closed one eye and fixed him with a baleful glare from the other.

"Just don't ever tell me you're a Red Sox fan, too."

"Yankees forever!" Scooter exclaimed. He smiled warmly at Jimmy.

"Thanks for being such a good sport about this."

"Hey—if something makes you happy and it doesn't hurt anybody else, I got no problem with it."

"I shoulda known you'd feel that way."

"Yeah, Scooter. After all these years—you shoulda."

"I'd have saved myself a few sleepless nights if I'd talked to you sooner."

"Everything in its own time, I guess."

"I guess." Scooter grimaced slightly. "Speaking of which; don't tell Mom about this, okay? That's why I've been avoiding her lately. I was afraid she'd be able to tell something was wrong with me. And you know how she can be: like a dog worrying a bone. She'd have kept at me till she pushed me into saying what I didn't want to say.

"I'll tell her myself, I promise—when the time's right. When I think we're both ready."

"Okay," Jimmy concurred, though this was quickly followed by a look of annoyance. "But for God's sake, pick up a phone once in a while and give her a call, will ya?

"The poor woman keeps bouncing back and forth between worrying that you've joined some kind of cult—and fretting that you just don't love her!"

"You're exaggerating for effect, I hope?"

"Not by much." The smile he now gave his younger brother was one more of warmth than of mirth.

"There's something you have to understand, Scooter. You're Mom's lifeline."

"C'mon."

"I mean it. If not for her need to finish raising you up, I really think Mom mighta just given up and died herself after Dad passed away. That's how much her own life was tied to his.

"That's how much it's tied to *you*."

Scooter was left at a loss for words, so he said nothing.

"I don't know about you, bubba," Jimmy broke the silence, rising up from his chair, "but I'm still hungry for pizza."

"Sounds good to me," Scooter replied cheerfully. "Just don't forget—*you're* buying!"

CHAPTER 25

As was usually the case on a Saturday afternoon, Jimmy Francis was ensconced in the tiny garage of the tiny house that he and Kathy rented. His car was parked in the driveway outside; the work area he had devised for himself inside didn't leave quite enough space to share with the vehicle.

On this particular afternoon, he was putting the finishing touches on his latest private artistic endeavor. It was a bust, carved appropriately from oak, of the late General (and President) Dwight D. Eisenhower. The piece had been commissioned by members of a local American Legion Post who were familiar with some of Jimmy's previous works.

The door that led from the garage into the house's kitchen opened and Kathy came out. She usually left him alone with his work. Occasionally, though, she liked to plant herself on a stool and simply watch in silence as he patiently revealed what had been hiding inside an otherwise inert block of wood.

She brought a tall glass of iced tea with her today, setting it down on Jimmy's work table within arm's reach of him before she took up her perch nearby.

"Mmm—mm," he hummed when he finally paused long enough to take a sip of the cold beverage. "That's mighty fine, darlin'. Thanks." A second swallow was put on hold when he glanced at his wife and saw a slightly nervous expression on her face.

"What's up, sweetheart?"

She stared down at her hands, which were fidgeting together in her lap, then back up to him.

"There's something I need to talk to you about, Jimmy."

"Oh-kay." He could tell from her behavior that it was something serious, at least to her. "You wanna go inside?"

"No. This is fine." She looked around. "I like it out here."

"All right. So, what's up?"

She tried to smile but had difficulty doing so. "I might as well just come right out and say it." She exhaled.

"Jimmy...I'm *pregnant*."

"What?" Stunned, unsure he had heard his wife correctly, he stared at her slack-jawed. "How?"

Kathy smiled in a way that suggested sarcasm leavened and softened with whimsy. "Well, you see, Jimmy, when a man and a woman really love each other and they get together in a special sort of way—"

"Dammit, Kathy, I *know* 'how'!" he exclaimed in exasperation that did little to hide his genuine and growing concern. "I mean...*how*?"

The woman of course knew exactly what he meant. Not long after she had returned home following her miscarriage a few years earlier, she and Jimmy had sat down together to have a most serious discussion regarding how they would move forward.

Jimmy didn't tell her that he had already received a loving but stern "mommy talk" from his mother Virginia. She had impressed upon him the need to be sensitive and accommodating to Kathy's feelings, wants and needs. He was fiercely determined to follow those instructions.

He had gone so far as to offer to abstain completely and forever from any future conjugal activities. He was secretly relieved when Kathy met this sincere if ill-advised offer with horror and adamant rejection.

He then offered a far more reasonable and workable solution to the problem of avoiding a possibly fatal pregnancy: he would willingly submit to a vasectomy.

Kathy vetoed that motion as well. It was always possible, she argued, that her own medical condition would improve sufficiently in time to make pregnancy a viable option once more. The reversal of a vasectomy, while possible, was too "iffy" for her liking.

Her counterproposal was that she would get and use a prescription for birth control pills. Seeing her determination and remembering his mother's admonition, Jimmy agreed to this course of action.

At the end of this discussion, which, though painful, also proved to be cathartic for both young people. Jimmy had asked Kathy if he was a bad person because at the moment he did not truly want to even *think* of the prospect of another child.

She assured him he wasn't and even confessed to having similar feelings herself. The sense of loss was yet too fresh, too full upon them both. One doesn't just "replace" a lost child the way you would a broken appliance. Their grieving process was still far closer to the beginning than it was to the end.

Rather tentatively, Kathy did broach the possibility of *adoption*. Not now: maybe not ever.

Jimmy offered to leave any such decision to her, with the heartfelt promise that he would fully support any such choice she might make in the future.

Kathy had never mentioned it again, nor had he.

And now…this.

"Really," Jimmy said. "Talk to me."

"The last year has been really bad for me, Jimmy." The time for jesting was clearly passed.

"It was like I had an actual, physical aching inside me. And at the same time, a numb sort of emptiness.

"I wanted another baby, Jimmy. Not an adopted one, even though that's a good thing. But I wanted a baby that would be my own flesh and blood, and yours."

"I didn't know," Jimmy confessed, feeling shameful guilt.

"I didn't want you to know; tried to keep it from you. I wanted to work through it myself, if I could.

"So, about six months ago…I stopped taking the pill."

"Why didn't you tell me?" Jimmy asked.

"Because you would have been opposed to the idea, wouldn't you?"

Jimmy opened his mouth to say "no," then closed it as his shoulders slumped as in defeat.

"Yes," he said at last, the voicing of that single word so faint Kathy barely heard it. "I'd have been against you doing it. You know what your doctors all told you about your heart." What she knew in the moment was that the anguish she saw in his eyes, heard in his voice matched that in his heart.

"You could both die," he stated flatly.

"We won't, Jimmy. We won't." She reached out to clutch at his hands. "I promise."

"You can't make that kind of promise."

"Maybe not. But you have to try to understand; I want this so much, Jimmy. More than I want a long life for myself. I need it. Some things are worth taking any risk for, and this is one of them. It's something I just have to do. I have to, no matter what." Her grip on him tightened as much as her tiny little hands would allow.

"Does that make any sense to you? Can you understand what I mean?"

"I think so," he replied, but only after the contemplative moment he liked to take before saying anything of import. Prompting this response was the certainty he felt that even if he raised any objections they would fall on deaf ears and do no good.

That and the familiar ache now tingling at the base of his skull that he hoped was telling him this was the right thing to do.

"But this comes with some conditions," he added as adamantly as possible.

"BUT THIS COMES WITH SOME CONDITIONS."

"You're getting under the care of a doctor right this minute, and you're gonna do whatever he tells you to do to make this as safe as possible.

"*Whatever* he tells you. Diet, medication. If he tells you to go to bed and stay there the whole nine months, that's what you'll do. Even if it means I have to tie you down. You got that?" Tears were streaming freely down her cheeks as she threw her arms around his neck. He held onto her for dear life.

"I love you, Jimmy. I love you. And everything will be all right. You'll see."

What she could not see was the worried, even frightened expression he bore on his own face.

It was Kathy's arms that clung tightly to his waist; but it was the hand of *Death* he felt on his shoulder.

CHAPTER 26

As Jimmy Francis made the slow, dreaded walk across the cemetery grounds toward the site of the graveside service, it saddened him that there were so few other people in attendance: no more than eight or nine. Among them he spied his mother and his brother Scooter.

Scooter didn't see his brother till he was nearly upon them. Once he did, he fairly threw himself into Jimmy's arms, desperately clutching at him as he began to sob.

"I was afraid you weren't gonna make it," the younger man gasped.

"You shoulda known better, bubba," Jimmy said soothingly. He smiled as he placed a comforting hand on the back of Scooter's neck.

"It's just that Mr. Santini's ill and I needed to take care of a few things at the shop before I could leave."

With his arm around Scooter's shoulders, he walked with him the few feet to the gravesite. As they drew closer, he finally caught sight of Howdy Watson, standing next to Jimmy's mother.

At just about the same time that Scooter Francis had begun to come to terms with his sexuality a few years earlier, news reports had begun to filter out of California regarding an inexplicable increase in cases of a certain type of cancer. It appeared to be especially prevalent among members of the gay community.

The underlying cause behind this epidemic was eventually isolated, identified and given a name now widely recognized: *AIDS*.

The funeral being held today was for that insidious disease's most recent victim: Scooter's boyfriend, Kevin Jacobs.

While just fresh out of college, Scooter had quickly managed to land a job with a local building contractor. It was a prestigious but small and very staid family owned company. Because of that, Scooter had felt compelled to keep his sexual orientation concealed from them.

Because of that, no one from the firm was here today; they knew nothing about it. Scooter kept even his loss and grief secret from them.

A few friends that he and Kevin shared—some but not all of them also gay—were there now. Tragically, of Kevin's family only his grieving mother was present. The rest of his family, especially his conservative, fundamentalist father, had essentially disavowed and disowned the young man.

To them, Kevin was already dead even before this day.

Earlier, Scooter had told Jimmy that he had even experienced some difficulty finding a clergyman willing to conduct the funeral service: finally settling for one provided by the funeral home.

The service that followed was a brief but respectful one; the man of the cloth delivered a sincere homily about love and hope. Once concluded, most of those in attendance quickly drifted away after offering Scooter final condolences.

Scooter and his mother approached Kevin's mother, who had remained discretely distant from all the others to that point. The suffering woman could do no more than tentatively shake Scooter's hand, but she allowed herself to be hugged by Virginia. The emotional dam within her burst and the two women cried together as Scooter looked on uncomfortably.

"How's the kid doing?" Howdy asked Jimmy, coming over to stand beside him.

"As well as could be expected, I think. It's been a real punch in the stomach, though."

"Yeah." Howdy hesitated but a moment before asking the next question. "And how's he doing...*physically*?"

Jimmy sighed. "He's all right. As soon as Kevin tested positive for HIV, they tested Scooter, too. His results came back negative."

"Thank God. I hope he stays that way."

"Amen to that prayer, brother."

Scooter, leaving the two mothers to their shared sorrow, came over to join Jimmy and Howdy. Both hugged him.

"How's Kathy?" Scooter asked, needing and wanting to talk of something other than his own loss.

"Fat and sassy," Jimmy said with a smile. "She wanted to be here so badly that I practically had to wrestle her back into bed. She sends her love."

Scooter nodded. Now six months into her risky pregnancy, Kathy had been ordered into bed rest until the time for delivery arrived.

"Me and Mom are taking Mrs. Jacobs back to the house," he told Jimmy and Howdy. "Mom fixed a little lunch ahead of time.

"I'd love it if you guys could come, too. But I understand if you have to get back to work."

"Hey," Howdy immediately chirped. "I took the whole day off. And you know I never pass up a free meal!"

"Guess we're all yours, kiddo," Jimmy added.

"Thanks, bubba," Scooter said, his voice quivering just a touch.

An arm around each other's shoulders, the three men walked away from the gravesite.

Behind them, Kevin's mother kissed the top of her lost son's coffin before allowing herself to be led away by Virginia Francis.

CHAPTER 27

"What are you doing out here alone, Jimmy?"

Jimmy Francis looked up from the bench upon which he was sitting in the garden area of Hillcrest Hospital. Even before he did, he knew the question had come from Howdy Watson, who was standing and staring down at him with mild concern.

Jimmy shrugged and smiled up at him. "Mom and Kathy chased me out of the delivery room," he admitted. "They said I was making both of 'em too *nervous!*"

A few hours earlier, though only seven-and-a-half months along in her pregnancy, Jimmy's wife had gone into labor.

Howdy unceremoniously flopped down beside Jimmy and for a minute or two they simply sat together in silence admiring the colorful floral displays all around them.

"I've been sitting here praying, y'know?" Jimmy declared at last, turning to look at his closest friend. "For Kathy and the baby." He tilted his head to gaze skyward.

"Given some of the things I've said about God in the past, I guess that makes me one helluva hypocrite, doesn't it?"

"Naw," Howdy said, placing a hand on Jimmy's arm. "It just means you're scared, that's all."

"I am, Howdy. I really am," Jimmy admitted with an audible catch in his throat. "More scared, I think, than I've ever been in my whole life." He gripped his comrade's hand tightly.

"I could lose both of 'em, Howdy. I could lose everything."

"Not everything, buddy," Howdy assured him fervently. "Never everything."

"I prayed like this the day Dad died, too," Jimmy told him in reply.

"I prayed so hard. I prayed for his life…because I loved him…and because I didn't want to lose him." Tears were flowing unchecked down his cheeks.

"Well, I lost him." The words stuck in his throat, choking him.

"I don't wanna lose again."

"None of us wants that, Jimmy," Howdy said.

When any more words of comfort failed to come to him, he fell back on what he always relied upon in times of stress or despair: humor.

"Hey," he quipped. "You know what they say about prayer, don't you?"

"No," Jimmy replied, trying hard to smile at what he knew was about to follow. "What do they say?"

"They say God answers every prayer. Sometimes His answer is 'yes.' Sometimes His answer is 'no'." He had a slight twinkle in his eye.

"And sometimes His answer is, 'You want *what*'?"

Though he didn't feel it, Jimmy managed to squeeze out a soft chuckle for Howdy's sake and to pat him on the knee.

"Well, if you two don't make a fine pair," a new voice said from behind them.

Jumping to his feet, Jimmy spun to see his mother, Virginia, leaning back against the door leading back into the hospital. Arms folded over her bosom, the weary look on her face was lightened by an indulgent smile.

For the first time ever, something about her look, her bearing, made Jimmy realize how old the woman was growing; she would soon be sixty.

"What is it?" he asked her nervously. "Has something happened?"

"You could say that," she chuckled. "You're a father, Jimmy. That's what's happened.

"You've got a precious little girl."

"Oh, God," he gasped. Then, "Yes!" he exclaimed, coming forward to lightly grasp his mother's arms.

"Is she all right?"

"She's fine, Jimmy. But she's tiny and a little frail." Seeing her son's eyes widen fearfully, she hurried on.

"That's only to be expected, son. She's come more than a month early, remember? They may want to keep her and Kathy here for a few days, just to keep an eye on them."

"Did Kathy come through it all right?"

"She seems to have," Virginia replied, but Jimmy knew his mother well enough to realize the optimism in her voice and in her eyes was somewhat guarded.

"Did something happen to her?" he pressed.

"They told me her blood pressure spiked dangerously high during the delivery," Virginia somewhat reluctantly admitted. "Shot through the roof."

"Oh, my God…"

"Now, hold on," Virginia said firmly. "They've got it under control. It's back in the normal range." Despite her assurance, her face took on a more somber cast.

"But this can't have done that heart condition of hers any good, son. You both knew that was likely. Like your daddy always said, this is going to be one of those times when you'll have to step up to the plate. Be a man."

"How do you mean, Mom?"

"I mean you had a hand in making this baby—now you need to take an equal hand in taking care of her. And taking care of her mother, too. You hear me?"

"I hear ya, Momma."

"For better or for worse, remember?"

"And it don't ever get no better," he said with a crooked smile, finishing his father's old joke.

His mom swatted him on the upper arm for his efforts.

"Get on in there with Kathy, Mr. Smarty-Mouth!"

Jimmy took a quick step, then popped back and kissed Virginia on the cheek. She swatted him again, but with a smile on her face.

As she watched her son hurry off, Howdy came up, slipped an arm around her waist and likewise gave her a loving kiss on the cheek. Turning her face toward him, she reached up and stroked his cheek.

"When are *you* gonna get busy and start making babies, Dickie?" she asked with the bluntness nearly universal in mothers. For as long as she had known this boy, she had refused to call him "Howdy."

"It takes two to tango, Mom." Howdy's real mother had died in a car crash eighteen months earlier. But long before that or the desertion of his father, Howdy had taken to calling Virginia "Mom."

"And I just can't seem to find a dance partner."

"You will," she assured him, patting his chest.

"I hear *you're* unattached," he said with a lecherous wink.

"Hush your mouth!" she exclaimed, slapping him with all the force of a feather. She then locked an arm in his.

"And take me down to the cafeteria for a cup o' coffee. I'm getting too old for these long vigils."

Elsewhere, Jimmy opened the door leading into his wife's hospital room as slowly and quietly as possible, so as not to unduly disturb the new mother.

His breath caught in his chest at his first clear sight of her.

She was in a pose nearly identical to the one in which he had found her on the night that their first baby had died. Her head was turned to one side; she was gazing out the nearest window.

But to his overwhelming relief, as he drew closer he could see that this time she bore a placid, peaceful, even happy expression on her face. She even blessed him with a smile as soon as she spied him.

And resting upon her breast, wrapped in a blanket in her arms, was a bundle so tiny that at first Jimmy didn't even notice it—until he saw it squirm ever so slightly.

"How you doin', babe?" he asked softly, taking a chair beside Kathy's bed and placing a hand tenderly on her arm.

"I'm doin' great, sweetheart," she replied enthusiastically, though even her voice seemed weak. Her eyes looked slightly sunken into darkened sockets.

"I hope you're not disappointed that I gave you a girl this time," she said.

"No...of course not." He smiled and winked. "Like Howdy says, as long as it's got all six fingers and toes, nothing else matters!"

Even the laughter Kathy blessed him with was lacking in strength and robustness.

"Would you like to hold your daughter?" she asked him at last.

"Oh—Oh, God," he stammered nervously. "I don't know. Do you think I should? What if I break her?"

"She's not a China doll, Jimmy. Besides...I've seen those hands of yours carve things that were more delicate than a hummingbird's wing."

"Are you sure? What if she cries?"

"Then you breast feed her."

"Huh?"

"Calm down, little boy. That's *my* job. Here." She lifted and extended the precious bundle toward him.

"Just let her rest in the crook of your arm. That's it. Don't forget to keep her little head supported. It's all right."

Looking down, he found that he couldn't actually see the baby for the enfolding blanket, so he pushed it back with one finger of his free hand.

What was revealed was a gurgling, wriggling, five-pound…something. Nearly sightless eyes bulged behind closed lids. Its pate was almost hairless, its skin splotched like that of an amphibian. Jimmy's verbal reaction to the first sight of the child was spontaneous and bluntly honest.

"Dear…God in Heaven," he murmured, looking up at his wife, who gazed back expectantly.

"Next to you…she's the most *beautiful* creature I've ever seen!"

"Isn't she?" Kathy proudly concurred, bobbing her head while simultaneously crying.

Such is the wonder of new parenthood that, in the moment, she was as blissfully blind to reality as was Jimmy.

Growing more comfortable and confident about holding her by the second, Jimmy brought one finger to her mouth and began to playfully strum at her pouting lips.

"You're a pretty girl," he told her, instinctively resorting to the "baby talk" that is the closest most men come to knowing a second language. "Yes, you is." The pride, joy and love in his heart was reflected in his voice.

"And you'll always be my baby girl."

"'Baby girl' is a fine name, Jimmy," Kathy poked, "if you want our daughter to grow up to be a *stripper*.

"Otherwise, I think we'd better give her a *real* name."

"Well, sure," he huffed. Like all expecting parents, he and Kathy had devoted a fair amount of time discussing the viability of a variety of potential names, both male and female. But they had been unable to reach any mutually agreed upon consensus.

"You brought her into this world," Jimmy now said, "so you should probably do the honors."

"But she's gonna be yours forever, Jimmy," Kathy replied, turning her head away from him and again gazing out the window.

A powerful fist squeezed Jimmy's heart at the unspoken implication that his beloved wife still might not live to see their baby grown.

"I want her daddy to name her."

CHAPTER 28

"Wake up, old man—you've just become a *grandpa!*"

In the place that had become his personal chapel, in the closest he ever came to participating in religious or spiritual ceremony, Jimmy Francis sat in his usual pose near his father Ted's grave.

"You oughtta see her, Dad. She's awful pretty. Full o' piss and vinegar, too, I s'pect." He grew more pensive.

"She's gonna need to be, at least early on. She came too soon, y'know; and that could cause problems. We're gonna have to take really good care of her. *I'm* gonna have to.

"And I will, too. If I don't, you won't have to come back from the dead to whip up on me. Mom'll do that.

"One time, when I was a kid, she told me what a boy should do if he wanted girls to like him. Here lately, she gave me some lessons on what a man should do to be a good father.

"Don't get mad…but we both agreed you didn't do everything on her list.

"But you did most of 'em, as best you could, and Mom's got no complaints about you. Neither do I. None that amount to much, anyway.

"And if you can offer me any more help from wherever you are now, 'y God, I'll take it. I really will.

"'Cause it's not just the baby I'll need to look after. There's Kathy. This has taken everything but the life out of her; I don't know if she'll ever fully recover. She's not complaining; if I know her, she never will. I'll have to keep a mighty close eye on her.

"I know it prob'ly sounds like *I'm* complaining, or feeling sorry for myself; but I'm really not.

"Truth is, I'm feelin' really happy; like I'm one of the luckiest guys on Earth. You know I mean it."

From a shirt pocket, Jimmy extracted an inexpensive cigar and placed it atop his father's headstone.

"I know this might not be totally appropriate, given what tobacco did to you. But it's tradition, and you're beyond being hurt by it now." Jimmy rose to his feet, brushing bits of dried grass off the seat of his trousers.

"I'm sorry you'll never get to hold my baby girl, Dad; never get to know her. But I'll make sure she knows about you."

His gaze shifted momentarily over to the nearby reproduction of *The Pieta*. Over the course of the years he'd been paying these periodic visits to the cemetery, he'd fallen in love with the statue and what it represented. Occasionally, even after concluding his visits with Ted, Jimmy would remain for a time, sitting on one of the benches facing the statue while reading a book.

On this day, at this moment, it almost seemed as if the plaster Virgin's gaze raised from her fallen Son to instead fix Jimmy with that same loving look.

"I think I know the name I'm gonna give the baby, Dad," he told his departed father. "It's as beautiful as her.

"*Mary.*"

CHAPTER 29

Jimmy Francis squirmed in his waiting room chair, shifting from side to side, throwing one leg over the other and then doing the reverse.

He had quickly discovered that being inside law offices made him nearly as uncomfortable as did being inside hospitals.

Given that one of the attorneys in conference just beyond the nearby closed doors was Mr. Santini's son Dominic, Jimmy naturally assumed he had been summoned here on some matter related to the recent death of the elder Santini.

It had happened on a Tuesday morning, now a little over two weeks ago. As usual, Jimmy had arrived early at *Santini's Woodworks*. Mr. Santini had taken to letting him be the one to open the store; the old gentleman was having a harder time getting up and around so early nowadays.

For that reason, Jimmy was surprised when he entered the store to find that the light in the back workshop was on. Adding to the puzzlement was his discovery that the store's alarm system was not turned on.

When he had left the store the night before, he locked the front door but had not activated the alarm because Mr. Santini had chosen to remain behind for a little while, saying he wanted to finish up a little work of his own. But Santini should have turned out the lights and set the alarm when he called it quits.

Snatching up a hammer from a display table, Jimmy quietly made his way to the back of the building. In hindsight, he would rather have stumbled upon a burglary in progress instead of the sight that greeted him.

Mr. Santini was still in the workshop—slumped over his bench.

Unable to find a pulse, Jimmy called 9-1-1. He gently laid the old man down on the floor and, even though his friend and mentor was already cold to the touch, tirelessly attempted CPR until the paramedics arrived.

Jimmy followed the ambulance to the hospital, from where he phoned Dominic Santini with the tragic news of his father's passing. He offered the younger Santini both his condolences and whatever help he might need in making final arrangements.

He'd been glad, even proud, to render what assistance he could, but was frankly puzzled when Dominic called and asked to meet here at the offices of the elder Santini's personal attorney.

Jimmy jumped as if taken by surprise when the door to the inner office opened and Dominic poked his head out.

"Sorry to keep you waiting, Jimmy," he said cordially. "Come on in, won't you?"

He clasped Jimmy's hand, shaking it while almost having to pull him into the office. Dominic motioned toward the other gentleman in the room, a well-dressed man in his fifties who smiled and nodded at Jimmy.

"This is Bill Evans," Dominic said in introduction. "He was Pop's attorney. Please, sit down."

Jimmy almost fell into the offered chair, while Santini took a perch on the corner of Evans' neat desk.

"First off," Dominic said, "I just wanted to thank you again for all your help and for everything you did for Pop. You were a good friend to him."

"It wasn't hard to be his friend," Jimmy replied. "He meant the world to me; I hope he knew that." As was so often the way between men, Jimmy had never actually spoken those words directly to Mr. Santini; nor would such have been expected, acknowledged or openly reciprocated.

"He did." Dominic chuckled. "He always carried on so much about you that I almost feel like you're my kid brother!"

Jimmy also chuckled. "I know what you mean. The first time I ever laid eyes on you, I could have picked you out of a line-up of a thousand men; I'd seen so many photos of you and your family. He was always showing them to me.

"You were his pride and joy."

"Thanks for saying that, Jimmy." Dominic glanced over at the other attorney.

"But now that Pop's gone—what are your plans for the *shop*?"

Jimmy blinked, not fully comprehending. "I assume that's up to *you*, Dom. It belongs to you now."

"Actually...no, it doesn't." Dominic again glanced over at his colleague. "That's what Mr. Evans and I have been discussing. He's the lawyer who actually handled Pop's estate for him.

"The Old Man, God bless him, did leave the bulk of his estate—such as it was—to me and my wife Maeve. He knew well and good, though, that I had no interest in his shop.

"But *you* do, Jimmy."

"I'm not sure I understand what you're saying."

"It's like this, Mr. Francis," the attorney Evans now chimed in. "Antonio didn't actually own the property where his store sits, but we did negotiate a very reasonable, long-term lease agreement with the owner.

"I've already spoken to the landlord and he's willing to continue that same arrangement with you."

"Why me?" Jimmy was looking at Dominic as he spoke, but it was Evans who answered his question.

"In his will, Antonio left you a little money—and all of his tools. And he expressed his wish that you take his place and run the shop."

Jimmy sank back in his chair, genuinely stunned. He had, truly, always been content and happy simply to work for the old man who had almost been like a second father to him.

"It's strictly up to you, of course, Jimmy," Dominic said. "You don't have to take over the shop if you don't want. We can just close it."

"Of course I want to," Jimmy replied. "I love that place almost as much as he did." He gazed intently at Dominic. "You sure that's all right with you?"

"Positive. From this day on—it's *yours*." He sighed softly before continuing. "What *name* do you think you'd like to give it?"

This time, Jimmy felt not the slightest hesitation. "If it's all right with you, Dom, I'd like to keep the name the same as it is right now.

"I may be the one running it from now on...but as far as I'm concerned, it will always be Mr. Santini's."

"I think he'd like that," Dominic Santini replied, and Jimmy could see a mist of tears in his eyes.

As with the father, Jimmy now reached out and shook the hand of the son to seal the deal.

CHAPTER 30

As expected the parking lot of the *Applegate Grill* was nearly full with its lunchtime crowd when Jimmy Francis pulled into it. He'd been exceptionally busy in the six months since Mr. Santini passed away, but when Howdy Watson called him that morning and practically pleaded with him to meet for lunch he felt duty-bound to comply. The last thing of which he would ever want to be guilty was of neglecting the best friend he'd ever had.

An almost frantic movement caught Jimmy's eye the moment he crossed the vestibule of the diner. Howdy, seated in a booth midway down the length of the establishment, was eagerly waving him over.

It was only as he neared the booth wherein Howdy sat, once past a waist-high partition, that Jimmy saw, much to his surprise, that a *woman* was seated in the booth alongside Howdy.

Jimmy paused in mid-stride, looking her over. She was short and slightly overweight; a pair of Coke bottle eyeglasses rested atop a nose just a bit small for the plain face surrounding it. Her mousy brown hair was straight and somewhat oily in texture. When she smiled at him, he saw plainly that her teeth could have used the service of braces in her childhood.

"Jimmy! C'mere, c'mere!" Howdy said just a bit too loudly, standing and wildly windmilling one arm.

"I'd like you to meet Gail Winters," he said with the pride of a man who'd just won an Olympic gold medal.

"Gail," Jimmy acknowledged, leaning forward slightly to extend a welcoming hand. "I'm Jimmy Francis."

"Oh, Dickie's told me all about you!" she gushed. (Was that the trace of a lisp he heard?)

"Really?" Jimmy said, casting a glance to see Howdy squirm slightly before gracing Gail with a smile. "That's funny—'cause *Dickie* hasn't told me *anything* about you!"

"It's hard to believe, Jimmy," Howdy hurriedly interjected. "We literally bumped into each other a few months ago at Comic Con in San Diego. Not that you don't bump into a lotta people there; it's like they've crammed the entire population of a small city into a single building!

"Well, anyway, we both happened to be in costume at the time."

"Let me guess," Jimmy said, enjoying stretching this out. "You were made up like Mr. Spock from *Star Trek*."

"Who else would I be?" Howdy replied. "But the crazy part is...Gail was dressed as Spock's girlfriend Nurse Chapel!"

"Sorta...nerds of a feather, huh?" Jimmy jested.

"Ha-ha. Very funny." Howdy screwed up his nose. "Actually—that *is* kinda funny!"

Gail giggled in response. At least that much of her was kind of cute, Jimmy thought.

"Anyway," Howdy continued on, "we struck up a conversation and that led to us having dinner together."

"Chinese," Gail interjected. "It was wonderful!"

"Turns out," Howdy said, "that Gail lives not far from here, with her parents. Just across the state line. She's a cashier in a grocery store."

"We kept in touch after the convention; I drove up to visit her a few times. And, y'know, one thing led to another."

"Am I old enough to hear about this?" Jimmy said, enjoying himself tremendously at the expense of the couple sitting across from him. He wasn't sure which of them turned the brightest red.

"What I meant was, we fell in love," Howdy stammered defensively.

"I finally got up the courage to pop the question last weekend."

"A question about *Star Trek*?"

Howdy slapped his hand over his face, drawing it downward. "Dammit, Jimmy—you *know* what question!"

"Then don't keep me in suspense," Jimmy said, slyly winking at Gail. "What was her answer?"

"I said *yes!*" the woman practically shrieked, thrusting out one hand toward Jimmy to display the small but tasteful diamond ring circling her finger.

"We're gonna get married this summer," Howdy beamed. "We've timed it so we can honeymoon at Comic Con."

"How romantic," Jimmy drawled.

"That's what I tried to tell my parents," Gail said earnestly. She then motioned for Howdy to slide out so she could exit the booth.

"I have to go to the ladies room," she announced, giving Howdy a quick kiss. "If the waitress comes while I'm gone, just order something for me.

You know what I like." She smiled at Jimmy before heading for the back of the restaurant.

"So, what do you think?" Howdy said anxiously once his fiancée was out of hearing range.

"What I *think*," Jimmy said with mild sternness, "is that the first thing I want to know is why I've never *heard* of this girl before today."

Howdy's mannerisms betrayed his nervousness. "I just didn't want to make a big deal out of it."

"You're kidding, right? You made a big deal out of buying a near mint copy of *Spider-Man* #14. You're gonna *marry* this girl, Howdy. I'd say that qualifies as a pretty big deal. One you've obviously kept secret from me for *months*. How come?"

"It hasn't been a secret, exactly," his friend replied evasively.

"Then why didn't you tell me what was going on, man?"

Howdy stared down at his clenched hands and when he spoke there was a patina of guilt in his voice.

"I was afraid you'd make fun of me," he finally admitted.

Jimmy was nonplussed. "Why would I do that, buddy?"

Howdy now bore an almost pained expression on his face. "Aw, hell, Jimmy. I know Gail's not the prettiest girl in the world. And let's face it— she's kind of a *geek*."

"I would assume that's one of the main things the two of you have in *common*!" Jimmy jested in a gentle tone that made Howdy chuckle. Jimmy then grew more serious.

"Do you love her, Howdy?"

"With all my heart, Jimmy."

"Okay. More important...does she love *you*?"

"She says she does."

"But does she *show* that she does?"

"All the time, Jimmy. In all sorts of ways. I don't think I've ever been happier than when I'm with her."

"Then you were wrong, Howdy."

Howdy frowned. "What do you mean?"

"Sounds to me like she *is* the prettiest girl in the world."

Howdy gave out a short laugh mixed with an exhalation of relief.

"And you'd *better* be planning on having me as your best man," Jimmy insisted.

"I wouldn't even *think* of asking anybody else," Howdy asserted, before hesitating momentarily.

"You wouldn't mind wearing a *Star Trek* uniform while you're standing next to me, would you, buddy?" he asked rather sheepishly.

"Seriously?"

Howdy shrugged.

Jimmy stared at his expectant face only a few moments before throwing his hands up in the air. "Aw, why the hell not? It's not like you wouldn't do the same thing for me." He reached across the table and shook his friend's hand.

"Beam me aboard, Scotty!"

By the time Gail returned from the restroom, Jimmy was already planning in his mind what kind of Trek-themed sculpture he could present to the pair as a wedding present. He had no doubt it would be appreciated far more than would be a toaster oven, by both of them.

The pair eyed him oddly when he let out a sort of snort, suppressing a laugh. The image had just leapt into his brain of what it would take to convince a stripper to paint herself green for Howdy's bachelor party!

He didn't linger long over lunch, however. His wife Kathy had never recovered her full strength following the birth of their daughter. Though she had urged him to keep this lunch date with Howdy, Jimmy knew the demands of chasing after an active three-year-old would be draining on her; so he was eager to return home.

"Congratulations again, guys," he said sincerely as he rose from the booth. He extended a hand toward Howdy's fiancée. "And welcome to the family, Gail."

Instead of taking his hand, the woman flashed him the iconic, split-fingered "Vulcan salute." Clumsily and only partly successfully, he returned the gesture. He shrugged apologetically as Gail and Howdy, heads together, broke into laughter.

As he exited the restaurant, Jimmy smiled and shook his head.

"My God," he faintly muttered aloud. "There really *is* a special someone for each of us!"

CHAPTER 31

Jimmy Francis sat slightly slumped over the workbench in his cramped, makeshift garage woodshop. Friends of his, a couple he had met through Kathy and her work at the hospital, had recently lost a beloved family pet:

a Cocker Spaniel. To show his condolences, Jimmy was sculpting them a wooden replica of their loved one, using a photo for reference.

As was her wont, his five-year-old daughter, Mary, was greatly underfoot, peppering him with the myriad questions both great and small that plague those too young to know all the answers.

Jimmy had long since learned how to compartmentalize his brain so that he could more or less simultaneously focus on his art while tending to the little girl's needs.

Kathy had complained of being tired, so he had given her marching orders to return to bed while he took Mary off her hands.

But even he couldn't maintain concentration when the child now literally popped up between his arms.

"I'm hungry, Daddy," she announced.

"You're always hungry."

"I am *now*."

He set his tools down and leaned forward to kiss her on her button nose.

"Why don't you go ask Mommy if she wants to have lunch, too."

Figuring this would give him at least a couple minutes of peace and quiet, Jimmy returned to his work, attempting to capture just the right soulful expression in his faux Spaniel's eyes.

"Mommy won't wake up."

He straightened and turned to see little Mary standing there, hands behind her back, legs slightly bowed so one foot rested atop the other. She looked slightly apologetic.

"I shook her and I shook her, but she won't wake up."

Jimmy grew instantly alarmed but didn't want to frighten the child. "She's probably just really, really sleepy, baby girl. Tell you what; why don't you go to the kitchen and start getting everything we need out of the refrigerator, while I go get Mommy?"

"Can we have baloney?"

"Huh? Oh, sure we can. Go on."

He managed to restrain himself until she skipped out of sight, then raced to the master bedroom. His heartbeat quickly slowed a bit as he saw that Kathy's breast was at least slightly and slowly rising and falling.

But he, too, was unable to rouse her to any more than a semi-conscious state wherein she was capable of no more than an unintelligible mumble of sound.

He wasted no more time in snatching up the bedside telephone and dialing 9-1-1.

From the kitchen, he could hear the sounds of his daughter humming merrily as she prepared sandwich fixings.

Two hours later, Jimmy Francis was once again consigned to the lonely and heart-wrenching job of sitting expectantly in a hospital waiting room.

His head snapped up as it always did when any movement caught his attention and he saw his younger brother Chuck entering the room.

He leaped to his feet and the two siblings hugged each other tightly.

"Any word since you called?" Scooter asked.

"Nothing. It's driving me crazy."

"Try to be patient, bubba. I'm sure they're doing all they can."

"Yeah." He motioned for Scooter to join him on a sofa.

"Mom wanted to come up here with me," Scooter explained. "But she's still fighting the flu and I insisted that she stay home. I told her I'd call her the minute we knew anything."

"Good. Good. That was a good idea."

Scooter glanced around the small waiting room. "Where's Mary?"

Jimmy smiled wearily. "Howdy and Gail arrived at the house almost as quick as the ambulance did," he said. "They're keeping Mary at their place tonight."

Though their nearly three years of marriage had yet to produce a child of their own, both Gail and Howdy doted on little Mary as if she was their own flesh and blood. Despite their mildly awkward first meeting, Jimmy had soon grown to like the good-hearted Gail. Kathy, naturally, had instantly accepted her as a new "sister."

"At least she'll have plenty of toys to play with," Scooter attempted to joke, referencing Howdy's large collection of action figures and such.

"Yeah." Jimmy managed a wan smile.

The two brothers mostly fell into sympathetic silence then. More than once a nurse entered, not with news but simply as a friend and co-worker of Kathy's, to offer their best wishes and moral support.

Finally, Kathy's doctor came in.

As so often happened to him, Jimmy experienced an unsought impression of a scene from an old movie.

This was one from a John Wayne Western film entitled *McLintock!*. In this particular scene, an old friend of the Wayne character tells him he's turned most of the running of his ranch over to his son, ever since "the doctor gave me the long face."

This doctor had a long face.

"Brian," Jimmy greeted him. As with some of the other doctors in residence here—both those who treated Kathy and those she simply worked alongside—Jimmy had struck up a casual friendship with this physician, allowing for more familiarity.

"How is she?"

"We've always known this day would come, Jimmy," the physician said haltingly. "Kathy's heart is as big as all outdoors…but it's extremely fragile as well.

"It's served her well," his voice choked, "but its service is at an end."

"Oh, God," Jimmy moaned. "How long does she have?"

"Probably only a few hours; quite possibly less." He lay a solicitous hand on Jimmy's shoulder.

"If you're going to say good-bye to her…you'd better do it now."

Jimmy turned to see Scooter with tears streaming down his face, then nodded to the doctor and began the interminable walk to Kathy's room.

He'd had to see her lying in hospital beds more than once in the years they'd been together. As he pushed through the door of her room, it came to him that every time he had come in on her in such situations, she seemed to be always lying with her head turned toward the nearest window.

Today, she lay with her head turned toward a bare wall.

Jimmy stood still in the doorway for several moments. His own heart was torn in two at the sight of her hooked to cold machines, an oxygen tube looped under her nose. The only sound to be heard was the steady beep-beep-beep of her heart monitor.

He had sworn to himself that he would remain strong and maintain a brave front for her. As he approached her bed and saw her looking so tiny, so pale, so lost…all his resolve vanished.

It crumbled around him as he neared her bed and she turned her worn, drawn face toward him. Tears were flowing down her cheeks and her lips trembled.

"I don't wanna go, Jimmy," she murmured helplessly.

He plunged to his knees, clutching at her hand as he too burst into tears.

"Then don't go, baby," he begged. "Stay here with me."

"I want to," she told him. "But I can't."

He began to blubber, squeezing her hand and kissing it. "I don't know if I can live without you."

"Shh," she whispered, stroking his hair with her other hand. "Don't say that."

"It's true."

"I know. I know. But you've *got* to live, Jimmy. You have to take care of Mary."

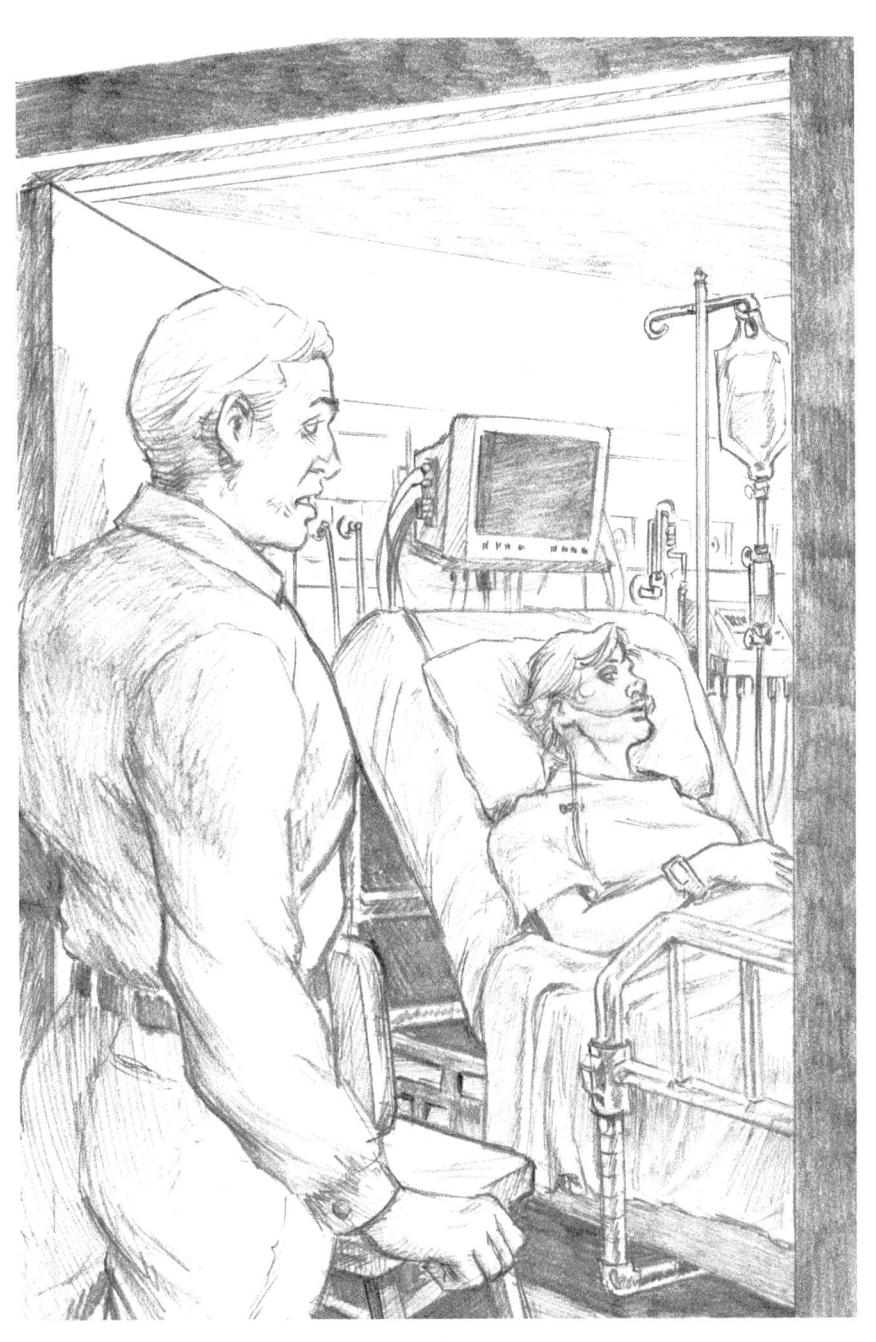

HIS OWN HEART WAS TORN IN TWO AT THE SIGHT OF HER...

"But you always took care of both of us, Kath."

She managed a weak smile as she shook her head. "No. You've always been the strong one, Jimmy."

"No."

"Yes. And now you're gonna have to be a little stronger."

"It's not fair."

"It is…what it is," she said with resignation.

His features darkened and his brow furrowed with a sudden, cold anger. "I can't let you go, Kathy. I *won't!*"

"It's not up to you, sweetheart," she counseled. "It's not up to me."

He said nothing more for a long moment, fighting to suppress a moan. "You do know how much I love you, don't you?"

"Of course I do, darling. I knew it before you did, remember? I know… you love me…just as much as I love you."

He arched upward, lightly kissing her dry and trembling lips. "Walking through life with you has been my greatest joy," he told her.

"And now, here I am breaking your heart," she replied sadly.

"No." He shook his head fiercely. "You're filling it up with even more love."

"Then I'm happy," she said, her words trailing off at the end.

Jimmy buried his face in the bed's mattress, clutching her hand even more tightly as he sobbed unashamedly.

He neither noticed nor heard when the rhythmic beeping noise of Kathy's heart monitor changed to a single, flat drone.

CHAPTER 32

Kathy Francis had been much loved, as was reflected in the large turnout at her funeral.

She had made many friends among the nurses and doctors with whom she worked and in time several of them and their families could be counted among Jimmy's friends as well.

Others knew Jimmy through his woodshop: men who'd worked for and with him as well as regular customers with whom he had struck up friendships. The circle grew even wider when counting acquaintances met through his association with his brother Chuck and with Howdy Watson. Several members of Kathy's family were there as well.

The number of mourners that followed the funeral procession to the cemetery was not noticeably smaller than the crowd that had filled the chapel for Kathy's memorial service.

All would agree that both it and the graveside ritual were beautiful.

As they began to drift back to their parked cars, Jimmy remained standing beside Kathy's bronze casket, holding their daughter Mary in his arms. Inconsolable, she cried uncontrollably and clung tightly to her papa.

"Jimmy?" Virginia Francis said, stepping up and looping an arm through one of his. "Scooter and I are heading back to the house. Some of the wives are already there, preparing food.

"You and Mary need to come along, too. You both need to eat something."

"Thanks, Mama," he said softly, bending enough to kiss the silver hair atop her head. "We'll be along."

As Virginia walked away, Howdy and his wife Gail stepped up to take her place. Both of them, especially Gail, had been devastated by the loss of Kathy and each still looked stunned.

"Anything, buddy," was all Howdy could manage to squeeze from his constricted throat. He gripped Jimmy's arm.

"I know."

"It's not fair," Gail moaned, her heart clearly in tatters.

"No." Jimmy knew of nothing else to say.

"Uh…would you guys mind taking Mary over to Mom's for me? I'd like to stay here a little while longer."

"Sure."

"No, Daddy!" the little girl wailed, tightening her grip on her father as Gail tried to lift her away from him. "I wanna be with you!"

"I know, baby girl," he said soothingly, trying to kiss away her tears. "Go with Aunt Gail and Uncle Howdy."

"Nooo!"

"Go on. You can help Grandma in the kitchen; and I'll be there in just a little bit. I promise."

She was still shrieking and crying as Gail carried her away. Riddled with guilt, Jimmy turned away from the sight, but couldn't block out the sound.

"I won't be long," he said to the groundskeepers standing a respectful distance away, not wishing to keep them from their somber chore ahead.

"You take all the time you need, sir," one of them replied with firm sympathy. On wooden legs, Jimmy approached the coffin.

"You were the best thing that ever happened in my life," he told Kathy.

"And you died giving me the next best thing." Eyes clouded, he turned his gaze skyward.

"I hope I deserve it."

He bent at the waist, rubbing the top of the casket gently before planting a kiss on its cool, smooth surface.

"And I'm glad you always knew I loved you."

He took some small comfort in knowing that, as per her wish, Kathy Francis went to her grave still wearing the wooden ring he had carved for her those all too few years ago.

Jimmy didn't head immediately for his mother's house, though; instead driving only so far as to the section of the same cemetery in which lay his father Ted. This would be the first chance he'd had to talk to him since Kathy's passing.

"Was it my fault, Dad?" he asked, knowing full well he would receive no answer.

"If I'd taken better care of her, made sure she didn't get pregnant again... we might still have her.

"And what do I tell Mary when she asks me why Mommy's never coming home...when I'm asking the same question?"

A sudden but gentle gust of wind ruffled his hair. He desperately hoped this was his father granting him absolution.

Rising from his traditional seat on the ground after planting a kiss on Ted's headstone, Jimmy made the short walk over to the statue reproduction of *The Pieta*.

"I'm still not sure in my own mind if God exists," he confessed to the Virgin, standing close in front of her. "But I *am* convinced that you and your son were real. Flesh and blood and maybe more." He reached up and gently ran his hand across the plaster Mary's cheek.

"And I think I understand your grief. I lost a son and a spouse, too. How did *you* survive it? How did *you* go on?"

The masterful passion in her face was the only reply she could give him.

He stumbled back slightly until his legs hit the edge of one of the benches facing the statue and he sat down heavily. For neither the first nor last time, he covered his face with his hands and wept bitterly.

Jimmy would continue to make his periodic, therapeutic visits to his father's grave...but would find himself unable to do the same with Kathy's.

CHAPTER 33

"*Whooof!*"

Jimmy Francis let loose an involuntary grunt as his ten-year-old daughter practically launched herself into his lap. The newspaper he'd been reading flew from his hands, its pages scattering around the room.

"What's wrong with you?" he demanded irritably.

"Nothin'," she professed, throwing her arms around his neck. But when she then kissed him on the cheek and snuggled closer on his lap, he knew without a doubt something most definitely was wrong.

"Did you break something?" he growled.

"No!"

"You didn't *steal* something?"

"Daaad!"

"Then what's going on here?"

"*Nothing.* I just felt like cuddling."

"Uh-huh." He began to wonder how much this was going to cost him.

"Tell me the truth, young lady, or I'll put you over my knee."

"No you won't," she purred.

"Don't tempt me, baby girl."

"Oh, all right." Straightening up but keeping one arm around her father's shoulders, Mary reached into the breast pocket of her school uniform's blouse and extracted a folded sheet of paper.

It was a typed note sent home by Mary's teacher, Mrs. Richards. Wanting the best he could afford for his daughter, Jimmy had enrolled her in a highly regarded but not overly expensive or exclusive charter school, where she had seemingly thrived. In the note, Mrs. Richards was requesting that Mary's parents contact her and schedule a time for a parent/teacher conference.

"What's this about?" he asked Mary sternly.

"Oh, it's no big deal, Papa," his daughter assured him, flipping her hair. "Mrs. Richards is nice, but she's kinda strict. She's sent lotsa those notes home with kids. You don't even haveta do it if you don't wanna. The parents get to decide."

As he had progressed through his adult years, Jimmy had found that he experienced the tingling aches at the back of his head less and less often. It was throbbing now like the racing heart of a thoroughbred.

Mandatory or not, he thought it wise to speak with this woman.

Despite this resolve, Jimmy was surprised to find himself unexpectedly feeling slightly nervous when he knocked on Mary's classroom door a few evenings later.

In response to his tapping, the door was opened by a handsome woman who appeared to be near his own age. Her lack of vanity was evidenced by the few streaks of gray in otherwise dark hair that was neatly styled. Her eyes were a cool shade of green.

Something about her also seemed vaguely familiar to Jimmy, and this sense was emphasized by an increase in the dull ache at the base of his skull: strong enough to make him reach back and rub it.

Her smile was warm and seemed to come easily as she invited him in and offered him a chair before taking a seat herself on the opposite side of her desk.

"Let me put you at ease right off by saying that Mary's not in any sort of trouble," she began.

Jimmy chuckled slightly and felt some of the tension drain from him.

"That's good to know."

"There are a few issues I wanted to discuss with you, though," the teacher continued, and some of the tension returned.

"I assume you look at the grade reports she brings home every quarter?"

"Of course."

"Then you know that she makes good, solid grades. And there's nothing wrong with that. But I feel certain that Mary is capable of even better, if she just applied herself a little more diligently.

"I don't want to put too sharp an edge on it, but she seems to be a little lacking in focus and discipline. She seems to get bored with class work easily and has a bit of a tendency to goof off and clown around."

"And you think that's my fault?" Jimmy asked, inwardly wincing as he realized his voice sounded more defensive than he intended.

Mrs. Richards, hands folded atop her desk, smiled patiently at him before responding.

"I didn't ask you here to assess any sort of *blame* for anything, Mr. Francis. There's no need to; there's nothing wrong with Mary.

"And the fact that you're here shows that you care; not enough fathers bother to attend these conferences for my liking.

"But Mary *is* an only child, yes?"

"Yes."

Her smile grew wider. "Well, I hate to say this about my own sex, but little girls that age *do* sometimes use their relationship with dear old dad to their own advantage."

This time, Jimmy let her words sink into his skull and rattle around a little bit before responding. Then it was his turn to smile, albeit somewhat sheepishly.

"I see your point," he conceded. "What should I do?"

Relieved that she sensed no animosity from the parent, Mrs. Richards now also relaxed.

"Mostly, just keep doing what you're doing. But maybe be a little more firm with her about things like homework, trying to participate more in classroom activities with the rest of the kids. Feel free to call me for updates on how she's doing. Just be involved. Show her you love her—but remember to be her father and not her friend."

Jimmy nodded. "Those all seem like good points. I'll try to do better in the future."

"I think you will," she replied. "And if you do, she'll do better, too."

Sensing the purpose of the conference had been fulfilled, Jimmy started to rise from his chair. But the nagging feeling that he had met this woman before gave him pause.

"Can I ask you something, Miz Richards?"

"Certainly." She expected a question regarding Mary.

"Can I ask what your first name is?"

Not what she was expecting, but an innocuous enough question.

"It's Barbra."

Jimmy chewed on that for a moment before following up with yet another query. "I hope I'm not sounding creepy here, but by any chance was your maiden name *Newburg*?"

"Why, yes it was. How did you know?"

"Barb!"

When this exclamation was met with a look of blank puzzlement, he continued on. "It's *me*: Jimmy Francis. We went to Rogers High together."

"Oh my God!" she gasped as recognition fully lit her bright eyes. "Jimmy!" She leaned forward, reached across the desk and took his hand in both of hers, squeezing it warmly.

At her touch, he was transported back in time to that night of the junior dance. That night when Barb had stepped onto the dance floor with football star Thad Richards—prompting Jimmy Francis to instead turn his attentions to his future bride Kathy.

"I've never really felt the urge to attend any of our class reunions," he told Barb now. "But I do remember hearing that you and Thad had gotten married. What's *he* up to now?"

"Last I heard," she replied, the smile now fading from her lips, "he was living in Florida with a twenty-year-old stripper he knocked up."

"Oh," Jimmy murmured uncomfortably. "I'm sorry."

"Don't be. I'm not." Her resentful scowl softened.

"It was a mistake from the start," she continued. She seldom spoke of her past to anyone, especially with a man who was virtually a stranger to her. But the look on his face as he leaned slightly forward made her sure that here she would find a needed and sympathetic ear.

"Thad and I got married our sophomore year in college, when we were still just kids."

(Jimmy ignored the renewed tingling in his skull. Though it had intensified, it was incapable of informing him of the fact that in his previous life it had been *he* and Barb who had made this painful mistake.)

"Everything was fine as long as Thad was a football stud," she explained. "Everyone agreed he was guaranteed a bright future as a professional in the NFL.

"He probably would have been a star, too—if he hadn't blown out a knee that fall. He left his dreams on the field that day.

"Football was all he had, all he knew, all he wanted. So he dropped out of school and I had to do the same.

"He was totally adrift; he bounced around from one dead-end job to another. He began to drink to dull whatever pain it was he couldn't handle. The more he hurt, the more he drank.

"When that wasn't enough…he began to exorcise his demons by hitting me."

"Oh, Lord," Jimmy groaned. "I—I'm sorry, Barb. I didn't mean to bring up bad memories."

"It's all right, Jimmy," she replied, actually managing a thin smile. "It might do me good to talk about it. But you might not want to listen."

"Will you give Mary extra credit if I do?"

"Oh!" she gasped after laughing briefly. "Oh, I think that actually did me some good."

"Good. Go on with your story."

"Are you sure? I don't want to keep you from getting back home."

"Don't worry about it. My buddy Howdy and his wife are sitting with Mary."

"Howdy?" Barb's face twisted slightly in concentration. "Not that weird kid you hung around with back in school?"

"The very same."

"And he has a *wife*?"

"Yep. Just as weird as he is. They're the perfect couple."

"Goodness. Who would have thought that I'd make out worse than *him*?" Seeing Jimmy staring at her intently, Barb self-consciously moved a hand up to fuss with her hair.

"So…you left Thad because he abused you?"

"Oh, God, I wish I could say *yes*, Jimmy. But the truth is, I didn't. Not right away. Not like I should have.

"I think…I think he'd done a good job of making me feel worthless. Like I didn't deserve any better. I'd find myself believing that it was my own fault: that I was somehow to blame for his behavior.

"Oh, and he'd cry, Jimmy. Like a baby. Beg for forgiveness and swear he'd never do it again. And he wouldn't—till the next time. And time after time I was foolish enough to believe that would be the last time. That he'd change.

"He didn't.

"Whoo!" Barb looked upward, blinking away tears. "It actually—it actually feels kind of good getting that all out."

"Then keep it comin', girl," Jimmy encouraged.

"The day I walked in on him with another woman in our bed, *he* was the one who behaved like the injured party." Her face took on a more resolute expression.

"That was the last time I let him lay a hand on me."

"Again," Jimmy said, "I'm sorry you had to go through that, Barb."

She waved off his objection. "That one was an 'exotic dancer,' too. Thad was so smitten with her that he didn't contest our divorce at all.

"Of course, he also never gave me a penny of the alimony he had been ordered to pay, either.

"So I supported myself with mostly menial jobs—sometimes more than one at a time—while I went back and finished my education. And ya know, those were some pretty rough times—but they were still better than the last years of my marriage. Isn't that crazy?" She made a waving motion at her desk.

"And I've been teaching here for eight years now."

"But you're still 'Mrs. Richards'," Jimmy observed. "Didn't you ever remarry?"

"No. Not surprisingly, I wanted nothing to do with men for quite a while. Then I was just too busy, too tired. Then too invested in my career.

"What about you?" she asked him. "I don't see a *Mrs.* Francis here with you tonight. Is she out of the picture?"

"I'm afraid so," Jimmy said wistfully. "Mary and I lost her five years ago."

"Oh, I'm sorry. I didn't know, Jimmy."

"No reason you would. It's all right. Actually, you might have known her. Kathy Brown? She went to Rogers, too."

Barb thought on it before replying. "The name's familiar, but I don't think I really knew her. Ours was an awfully big class, you know."

"Yeah." Jimmy didn't add that it was also a stratified one; Kathy and Barb would have circled in entirely different orbits.

But time and events have a way of changing things. Barb had been at the top of their class: admired, envied and desired by nearly everyone. The one sitting across from him now, though, was a battered and bruised version of that girl. But she'd clearly come through it unbroken and unbowed, and thus a better person than when she went in.

At Barb's urging, he then told her the *Readers Digest* abridged version of his life since high school. She promised to visit his woodshop some day to view his handiwork.

"Oh, my God," he said at length, glancing down at his wristwatch. "I've been talking your ear off for more than an hour! I'm sorry for keeping you so late."

"Don't give it another thought," she said graciously. "My only plans are to go home, heat up a can of soup and a cup of tea and watch a little TV."

"It's been nice to see you again, Barb."

"You too, Jimmy."

With a smile and a nod, he rose to leave. The teacher watched him walk to the classroom door, where he stopped and seemed to be rubbing the back of his neck. He turned back toward her, and she looked at him questioningly.

"Was there something else, Jimmy?"

"Yeah. No. Well." Clearly, he was having some difficulty getting the words out.

"It's just that...I mean, I don't know if it would be inappropriate or against some kind of rule...you being Mary's teacher and all."

"What's that?"

Her words drove him partially out the door before he turned back to her. "Well...I was just wondering if maybe you might like to get together for a cup o' coffee some evening. When you're not busy."

Her appraising look made him hugely uncomfortable, even though it was accompanied by a wispy smile. And her reply seemed glacially slow in coming.

"As far as I know," she said at last, "that wouldn't violate any code of conduct." Her words seemed to be as measured as were his own.

"And, yes…I'd like to have coffee with you some time."

"Good," he sighed with relief.

"Good," she repeated. "My number's in the telephone book; just give me a call when you like."

"I will," he said, waving slightly as he backed out of her classroom. Walking down the hallway that led out of the school, he turned his eyes heavenward.

"I hope that's okay with you, Kathy," he whispered.

By the time he pulled the car into his own driveway, he had convinced himself that it would be.

CHAPTER 34

"Is it *true?*"

The harsh, accusatory tone of Mary Francis' voice was unmistakable. Sighing wearily, her father laid down his tools and swiveled around on his stool. Mary stood just a few feet away, legs slightly spread, clenched fists on her hips, looking daggers into him.

"Is it true that you're *dating* Mrs. Richards?"

"Now, where'd you hear a thing like that?"

"From a girlfriend of mine. She saw the two of you together."

"I see. And being such a good 'friend'—she just couldn't wait to come tell you."

"That doesn't matter. Is it true?"

Jimmy frantically sought a way to parse his words before replying. "No. Not exactly, no. We've met for coffee a couple of times, that's all."

"That's called a *date*, Papa. How could you do that?" She threw her hands up in the air in exasperation.

"Do you know how gross that is?"

"No…I—I can't say that I do, Mary."

"Not to mention embarrassing to me. You should hear what the other kids are saying!"

"And *you* should stop listening to them, hon. Trust me, they'll lose interest just as soon as something juicier—something *grosser*—comes along. After all, the school year is nearly over; Barb won't be your teacher then."

"*Barb*?" Jimmy was startled to see how much venom could drip from lips so young.

"Besides," he said tightly, "you always told me you liked Mrs. Richards."

"Not *that* much." Clearly, the girl would not be mollified.

"What is it that's *really* got you so hot and bothered, Mary?" he pressed softly.

"Don't you *know*?"

"Well, clearly I don't. No. So tell me. Please."

"I never thought you'd *cheat* on Mama," she finally hissed through clenched teeth. Her eyes had become small, cold agates.

"Don't you *ever* say anything like that to me again, you hear?" he snapped angrily.

"It's *true*," she shot back.

Rather than escalate what was already an overheated situation, Jimmy simply glared at the pouting girl, inwardly urging himself to calm down. He didn't need a tingling pain in his skull to tell him this was a critical moment.

"Sit down, baby girl," he finally said softly, patting the seat of a second nearby stool. "Let's talk about this, okay?"

Mary looked as if she was suspicious of his motives, but she took a seat. Her arms were folded across her body and she was clearly still angry.

"Your mother's been gone a long time now," Jimmy said gently, wiping his hands on a chamois cloth. "Five years."

"That doesn't mean you have to replace her."

"I couldn't 'replace' her, Mary, even if I wanted to. There'll never be anybody like her. I still really, really miss her."

"I know you do, too. And that you still love her. But that doesn't stop you from having fun with your friends. It shouldn't."

"You got plenty o' friends," Mary retorted. "Like Uncle Howdy and Uncle Scooter."

He chuckled lightly. "Yeah. Thank God. But as much as I love them—as much as I love *you*—I still get lonely sometimes.

"You don't think your mama would want me to be lonely, do you?"

"No." The admission came grudgingly, as would the acceptance, but he knew it would be better now.

"Just do me one favor, Papa."

"Sure, sweetheart. What is it?"

"Don't get Mrs. Richards in trouble."

CHAPTER 35

"Teenagers. God help me."

Jimmy Francis paced the floor of his living room, while Barb Richards, his brother Chuck and Howdy and Gail Watson looked on anxiously.

In the three years since Jimmy and Barb had become reacquainted, they had continued to date: tentatively at first, then eagerly, having soon discovered that they were very comfortable with each other.

Neither was entirely sure when "comfort" had turned to "love," but neither had any doubt that it had. That realization brought each another kind of comfort of which both were sorely in need.

Today was the day they were to solemnify that love, in a wedding ceremony to be held outdoors in a nearby park. The weather had chosen to cooperate: it was a cool and sunny day. At least three dozen invited guests were probably already there, joyfully awaiting the arrival of the wedding party.

And now young Mary Francis had decided to balk, refusing to leave her bedroom.

"Maybe I could talk to her," Gail finally volunteered.

"No," Barb said. "Let me."

Gail bristled slightly, though she said nothing. When Jimmy had first introduced Barb to her and Howdy, Gail's initial reaction to her was somewhat similar to that of Mary.

She saw Barb as a rival for Mary's affection, a usurper who might take Gail's place in the girl's heart.

Nor had Barb been so instantly and totally accepting of Gail and her… eccentricities…as had been Kathy Francis. They did not share many (All right—*any*!) common interests.

But that wasn't entirely true, as they came to discover. They did share two paramount points of agreement.

Each loved Mary. And neither wanted to become a source of friction between Jimmy and Howdy.

Their unspoken truce had gradually grown into at least the semblance of a friendship, though Gail still felt a certain proprietary claim to Mary's attentions.

After tapping lightly on the door and receiving no response, Barb entered to find Mary lying propped up on a pillow in bed, sulking.

"I can't get married without my maid of honor," Barb said, acting as if everything was normal. "What's wrong, sweetie? Don't you feel good?"

"I'm not goin'."

"Why not?"

A chill went up Barb's spine as Mary's head slowly turned toward her. The deliberate movement and the hateful look on her face reminded Barb of the horrifying scene in *The Exorcist* wherein the possessed girl's head swirled around 360 degrees.

"I don't want you to marry my dad," Mary stated bluntly. "You know that. He knows that."

Barb sighed deeply and long. "Well, all right then. I guess we'll call off the wedding."

"Huh?" Mary looked stunned; this was the last response she had been prepared to hear. "You'd do that?"

"Of course," Barb replied with no rancor in her voice. "Why would I want to marry Jimmy when I know you hate me?"

"I don't hate you," Mary blurted. She exhaled loudly in exasperation as her not yet fully developed brain sought the right words.

"I just can't stand the thought of you taking Mama's place, especially here in her house."

"Ah." Barb nodded. "Sweetheart, that would never happen. I have no intention of trying to take your mother's place, or to make you or your Papa forget about her. But I guess that doesn't matter now.

"It's been really nice knowing you, Mary. Good-bye." Barb turned her back on the girl and headed for the door.

"Wait! What do you mean, good-bye?"

Barb turned back and smiled sadly at Mary while slowly shaking her head. "You don't think your father will want me around anymore after I call off the wedding, do you? He'll never want to see me again.

"So...good-bye."

"I didn't mean I wanted you to break up," Mary stammered. Clearly, this was not playing out the way she had imagined.

"It's all right," Barb said in an almost casual tone of voice. "Your father's still a relatively young man. Good lookin'. Runs his own business. He'll find somebody else.

"I just hope it's somebody you'll like better." She turned again to make her exit.

"Hold on," Mary pleaded, swinging her legs over the side of the bed and sitting more upright.

The thirteen-year-old's face scrunched up in concentration as her mind frantically worked on deciding what options remained for her. Barb stood patiently at the door, letting the girl reach her own conclusion.

"All right," Mary at last said petulantly. "I'll come to your darn ol' wedding."

"That will make your Papa and me very happy, Mary."

"But I'm never gonna call you *Mama*," Mary insisted. Barb was wise enough to know that the girl needed at least this much of a victory.

"You can call me anything you like, Mary—so long as it's not something nasty.

"Now, get a move on; freshen up if you need to. We don't want to be late."

Jimmy Francis, nervously pacing the floor, looked up expectantly as Barb entered the living room.

"Well?" he asked.

"Well…I have good news and I have bad news. The good news is that Mary's coming to the wedding."

Jimmy looked relieved, then wary. "Wait. What's the bad news?"

Barb shrugged.

"I think we're gonna have to buy a new house."

CHAPTER 36

Jimmy Francis jerked awake just as he was starting to nod off.

He was seated in a reclining chair in the living room of the house he and Barb had purchased shortly after they were wed.

There was nothing extravagant about it, but it had all the amenities one could realistically desire. It sat in the middle of a nice, quiet, middle-class neighborhood called Hawthorne Hills and both Francis's had quickly fallen in love with the house and its pleasant environs.

(Such was not the case with the "previous" Jimmy Francis, for this was the exact same house he looked upon with loathing as the symbol of his financial and personal failings. With changing tides, one man's dungeon can be another man's castle.)

Rubbing the sleep from his eyes, he glanced at the wall clock and frowned. It was well past the time he had set for Mary's curfew.

His eighteen-year-old daughter had graduated from high school a few weeks earlier. Barely so, despite his pleas and threats and Barb's efforts to help tutor her. None was capable of making her interested in academics.

The girl had grown increasingly surly and distant in the past six months. She avoided her parents as much as possible. Jimmy knew only a few of the people she called friends, and most of them were a sort of which he did not approve.

Just as he rose to his feet, Jimmy heard a key turning in the lock of the front door. When Mary shuffled into sight, some of his worst fears were confirmed.

It was obvious from her demeanor and the unfocused look of her bloodshot eyes that the girl was stoned.

"You're late," was all he said.

"Leave me alone," she mumbled, starting to shamble past him.

"Hold on," he said, grabbing her arm. As he did, the cloth of her blouse was pulled slightly to one side and near her exposed collarbone he saw the image of a tattooed butterfly.

"How long have you had that?" he demanded.

"A while," she snapped, pulling away from him.

"Where were you tonight?" he then asked.

"None o' yer bus'ness," she slurred, trying to turn away from him. He moved around to block her path.

"It *is* my business, young lady."

"No it isn't. You can't tell me what to do, where I have to be."

"That's where you're wrong, Mary. This ain't no hotel. (He couldn't believe he'd just used one of his dad's old sayings, but he was now committed to this line of reasoning.)

"This is *my* house, and as long as you live under my roof—you'll follow *my* rules."

"Then mebbe I'll jus' move out."

"That's up to you."

Slightly weaving on unsteady legs, the teen fixed her father with a look that spoke of utter contempt.

"You'd like that, wouldn't you?" she accused drunkenly. "Then you and your bitchy little *slut* would have the place all to yourselves."

The words were nearly driven back down her throat as Jimmy slapped her with his open right hand.

She staggered back, slapping the palm of her own hand over the burning flesh of her cheek. She had a look of horrified amazement on her face; replaced quickly by a look of unbridled hatred even as tears welled up in her eyes. Sobbing, she pushed past her stunned father, rushing into her bedroom and slamming the door behind her.

He was as horrified as she was; this was the first time he had ever laid a hand on his "baby girl." He stood turning in slow circles in the hallway, clenching and unclenching hands that hung lifeless at his side.

At last he retreated toward the back of the house, past the closed bedroom door behind which Barb slept oblivious to what had transpired and out the back door. Near the far end of the backyard sat his pride and joy: a small work shed he had constructed with his own hands. This was where he worked on his personal art pieces, surrounded by the sweet smells of various cuts of wood.

On this night, he simply sat and stared at his latest creation until weariness led him back to the house and sleep.

CHAPTER 37

"Mary's gone," Barb said, shaking Jimmy just firmly enough to awaken him the following morning.

"Huh?" Jimmy muttered, only half awake. "Where'd she go?"

"I don't know," Barb said, a slight quiver detectable in her voice. "I think she's run away."

"Oh, don't be silly," he gruffed. "She wouldn't do that."

"Don't be so sure, Jimmy. I went to see if she wanted some breakfast, but her bed didn't look slept in. She's nowhere else in the house, either.

"And there's more. I checked back in her room and discovered her backpack's gone, along with some of her clothes and toiletries."

Now equally worried, Jimmy threw off his covers and bounded from the bed. He didn't bother with dressing before he was on the telephone. Fighting to remain calm, he began to place calls to the parents of any of Mary's friends that he knew. (Why hadn't he bothered to get to know them all and how to reach them?) None could offer him a substantial clue as to his daughter's possible whereabouts.

As the day progressed with no news, Howdy and Gail and Scooter

Francis all came by to offer all they could: moral support.

"Maybe we should call the police, Jimmy," Barb urged at last.

"And tell them what, honey? We have no idea where she is or where she's going. And in their eyes, she's an adult; free to go anywhere she wants."

"This is all my fault, isn't it?" Barb moaned, fresh tears welling up to replace the old.

"Mary's never accepted me. If I hadn't butted into your lives—"

"That's silly, Barb," Jimmy said, dismissing the very notion while taking her into his arms. "You've been nothing but kind to her; gone out of your way to do so.

"If anyone's to blame, it's me," he confessed, while not giving the full details of the confrontation from the night before.

"She and I have been banging heads for the last five years now. She was bound and determined that everything had to go her way or no way at all.

"I guess she just got tired of me trying to tell her different."

All of them jumped nervously as the telephone suddenly rang. Jimmy released his hold on Barb and raced for the receiver.

"Mr. Francis?" an adult male voice said in response to his greeting. "This is Carl Renfrow. My son said you called earlier looking for me."

"Yes. Actually, I was looking for my daughter Mary. I thought maybe your girl might be able to help."

"Well, she's right here. Let me put her on."

"Hello?" The new voice that came on line was so soft Jimmy could barely hear it.

"Linda?"

"Uh-huh."

"Linda, this is Mary Francis' dad. I was hoping you might be able to tell me where she is."

"I haven't seen her in a couple of days."

"Oh." His hopes sank. "Listen, Linda. I, uh, I think she may have run away from home. Do you have *any* idea where she might go in that case?"

There was a painfully long pause on the other end of the line. "I don't wanna get her in trouble."

"You won't, I promise. I just need to know that she's all right."

Another pause that left him fighting the urge to start pounding the tabletop with the telephone receiver.

"There *is* a guy."

His heart shriveled. "What guy?"

"I don't really know him. I think his name's Alex. He's a couple years

"LINDA, THIS IS MARY FRANCIS' DAD."

older than us; Mary met him at a concert and they've been hangin' out ever since."

(This was the first Jimmy had heard of any "guy" in Mary's life.)

"I think he was kind of a drifter. Mary said he'd been trying to talk her into taking off with him and heading for California."

"Do you know this guy's last name? Where he's from? What he does?"

"I'm sorry. Mary wouldn't talk about him much."

Now the silence came from Jimmy's end of the line.

"Mr. Francis?"

"Huh?"

"Are you okay?"

"Yeah. I'm fine."

"I wish I knew more."

"It's all right, Linda. Thanks for your help."

Jimmy stood staring down at the receiver after he replaced it in its cradle before turning to report what little he had learned to the others.

"What if this guy hurts her?" Barb exclaimed. "I still think we should call the police."

"I'm afraid Jimmy's right," Scooter interjected as diplomatically as possible. "She's no longer a minor and there's no evidence that might indicate she was coerced or forced to leave against her will. *If* that's what she's done; we still don't know for sure."

"California's a mighty big place," Jimmy added. "And her girlfriend didn't seem to have any idea *where* in California they might be headed for."

A dark look such as Barb had never seen before seemed to be closing in over Jimmy's face, and she grew even more worried.

"They may not even make it to California," Jimmy glumly continued. "I know Mary doesn't have any money, and I suspect her boyfriend doesn't, either. They could run out of cash in any number of towns between here and the coast and end up slinging hash in some hick diner."

"Then, what do we *do*, Jimmy?" Barb asked tremulously.

"Nothing," Jimmy replied, with a coldness in his tone that chilled everyone in his presence.

"What do you mean?" Barb pressed.

"I mean she's made her bed...and now she's gonna have to sleep in it."

"Jimmy, no. We can't just turn our backs on her," Barb pleaded. "She's just a *baby*!"

"She's a grown woman," Jimmy retorted. "Which she constantly liked to throw in my face. It's her who's turned her back on us.

"She knows our phone number. If she comes to her senses, she can call us." He then turned toward the others, who were simply staring at him in uncomfortable silence.

"Guys, thanks for coming over. There's nothing more you can do."

Without another word, Jimmy turned his back on all of them, walking to the rear of the house, out the door and across the yard to his workshop.

"I'm sorry," Barb told the others. "He's upset, but he doesn't want to show it."

"It's more than that," Scooter stated. "He's hurt."

"Yeah," Howdy concurred. "I haven't seen that look on his face since—" He caught himself before he could say, 'since Kathy died.' "Well, in a long time."

"We should go, fellas," Gail said. She then walked over and enveloped Barb in a sisterly hug.

"If there's anything we can do, you call me, Barb. Day or night."

"I will. Thanks."

Out in the woodshed, Jimmy tentatively approached what had been his latest wood sculpture, sitting covered with a square of cloth.

His hand shook slightly (From anger, from sorrow, from fear? Yes.) as he lifted the cloth to reveal the nearly but not quite finished bust of Mary he had been working on for weeks.

Littering the table around it was an array of photos he had taken of his daughter from multiple angles, for reference. He'd spent several days going over blocks of wood to find just the right one to use; the one he felt sure was wrapped around the perfect likeness of his baby girl and was just waiting for someone like him to uncover it.

He had hoped to finish it in time to present it to her as one of her graduation presents, but his drive to make it exactly right and the demands other things made on his time had made that impossible.

Jimmy lifted the bust carefully in his hands. His face looked intense yet calm as he examined it with a critical eye and ran his fingers lightly over its curves. Any unbiased observer would have declared it, even in its unfinished state, to be a masterful work of art. It captured not merely her physical looks, but her very essence.

Sliding off his stool, he carried the bust over to the small buzz saw installed against one wall of the shed.

Inside the house, Barb could hear the whirring sound of the saw and wondered if her husband and her life would ever be the same.

CHAPTER 38

B arb Francis had made up her mind that things could not go on this way
any longer.

It had been a month since Mary had run away, and there had been no
word from her. Inside the Francis household in that time, there had at best
been long stretches of tense silence passing between Barb and Jimmy. At
worst, there had been several brief but heated arguments about Mary.

Jimmy had taken more and more to retreating to his workshop,
isolating himself from Barb.

She seldom entered the shed, knowing his art required his full
concentration and attention and that his psyche required a space that was
solely his. Exceptional times called for exceptional actions, though, and
this, she felt, was surely one of those times.

Jimmy had his back to the door and was so immersed in the current
project on which he labored that he was not aware of Barb's presence in
the shop until she placed a hand on his shoulder.

Jumping with surprise, he threw his arms up in an effort to block Barb's
view of his work, but the gesture came too late.

"Oh…my God," she whispered breathlessly.

She stared as if in a trance at the wooden bust of Mary. Despite his
initial, impulsive decision to destroy it on the night the girl ran away,
Jimmy had found himself incapable of letting the ruthless teeth of the
buzz saw touch even a mere representation of his only child.

Save for a bit of delicate, fine sanding, the bust was nearly finished,
ready for the final step of preserving the wood with a light coating of a
lacquer of Jimmy's own devising.

"Don't stop," Barb told him. "I'll just sit over here and watch you, if
that's all right."

"Sure." He said nothing of the fact that as a little girl Mary used to sit
and watch him in just that fashion.

He held the bust in one hand while with the other he used a small
square of the finest grain of sandpaper to smooth out some of the carving
around the figure's nose.

Then he put down both bust and sandpaper and sat in silence with his
head hanging down between his shoulders. When he raised it and turned
toward Barb, she was appalled to see tears in his eyes and an anguished

expression contorting his facial features.

"I hit her, Barb," he moaned. "I hit my baby girl."

"What?"

He could do nothing but shake his head fiercely.

"Talk to me, Jimmy," she urged firmly.

He sucked in his breath and his tears and finally told her the details of the night before Mary ran away: of the horrible fight they had.

"Then," he finally confessed, "when she said that vile and contemptible thing about *you*...I just lost control. I slapped her, Barb. I slapped her really hard." His body slumped like that of a defeated boxer who had been dragged back to his corner stool.

"It was all my fault," he murmured. "I'm the reason she ran away."

"You don't know that, Jimmy."

"What else could it have been?"

"Lots of things. She was a troubled little girl. I think it may even have been *my* fault."

"What? No. Why would you think that?"

Barb, her hands on her knees, arched her back and took in a gulp of air to momentarily staunch any flow of tears.

"Because I've always felt I was the cause of *all* the problems between you and Mary. After all, you two seemed to have had a wonderful relationship with each other until I entered the picture."

"Dammit, don't you *ever* think that," Jimmy demanded almost harshly.

"Before I found you again, our house and our lives were pretty empty, even if we didn't realize it at the time. You filled both up with light and goodness that had left us.

"If Mary never recognized that truth—it was *her* fault, not yours." His eyes narrowed in thought.

"She just wouldn't listen to reason," he said. "Wouldn't think things through, that's all. Obstinate, that's what she is."

"Or maybe just a little too much like you?" Barb gently teased.

"Yeah. Or maybe just not enough like her *mother*."

Barb studied him intently. "You still miss Kathy, don't you?"

"Would you think I was awful if I said yes?"

"No. I don't think so."

"But her face has never once come between mine and yours," he hurried to assert. "I want you to know that."

"It better not," Barb jested, flipping her hair. "I'm much prettier than she was!"

They shared a short burst of laughter and then Jimmy returned his attention to the bust of his daughter. Barb slid off her stool and came to stand beside him.

"But why didn't you tell me everything about that fight that you and Mary had?" she asked him.

"Because I was ashamed of what I did," he told her, then averted his eyes.

"And I was afraid that if you knew what I'd done to her…that you'd leave me, too."

"Why would you think that?" She was genuinely puzzled by his words.

"Because of what happened to you before, with Thad," he said. "I was afraid you'd think *I* was the same kind of man he was."

"No such thought would ever enter my head, Jimmy. We've been together for eight years now. I've had plenty of time and opportunity to see your bad side, same as you've had to see mine.

"But never once has your behavior toward me risen anywhere close to the level of being violent. And believe me, after all the years I spent living in terror, I know all the signs." Barb punctuated her declaration with a soft smile.

"You just raised a slightly spoiled and greatly stubborn child—and that night you pushed each other too far." She reached out to stroke the hair on the back of his head.

"So, no, Jimmy," she whispered, laying her forehead against his. "I'm not afraid of you. And I'm not going to leave you. Ever."

Jimmy took his wife in his arms and held her tightly. He was glad the deep sobs that now racked her drowned out the sounds of his own sniffling.

When they finally drew apart, Barb reverently placed a loving hand atop the bust of Mary.

"When it's finished, we'll put it in her room," she said.

"So it'll be there when she comes home."

CHAPTER 39

Jimmy Francis still hated hospitals.

They were the sites of his greatest losses—his father, his unborn son, his beloved wife Kathy—and thus the repositories of his deepest grief.

He tried rationalizing internally that a *nursing home* was not the same as a hospital.

He wasn't able to fool himself.

Over the course of the past eighteen months, Jimmy's mother Virginia had suffered three strokes: the last one major. Left partially paralyzed and confined to a wheelchair, she was no longer able to live alone and care for herself.

Jimmy's brother Chuck was no longer around to help with her care. He had recently accepted a job offer from a major construction company on the West Coast and was still in the process of getting firmly established in his new surroundings.

Jimmy and Barb had implored Virginia to come live with them; Barb had even explored her options for retiring early from her teaching position. While loving them for their sincere offer, Virginia had stubbornly refused to accept it.

"If you think I'm gonna let my *children* feed me and change my diaper, you're crazy!" she had declared adamantly.

"I'd rather let strangers do it. At least they get *paid* for performing unpleasant chores."

As was often the case when he paid one of his frequent visits to the home they had all agreed upon, an attendee directed Jimmy not to his mother's room but to the facility's nicely kept courtyard garden.

There, he found his mom contentedly sitting alone, eyes closed with her face tilted up toward the sun.

Jimmy started toward her, then stopped for a beat as a sudden jolt of the old tingle in the back of his neck caused him to wince.

In this instance, the tingle was simply an unconscious translation regarding the vastly different direction in which Jimmy's current life had diverged from his previous one. While mostly small when viewed alone, those many and diverse changes had spread outward and grown to form an entirely new life.

Before, with her own very being so tightly bound to that of her husband, and without the need to care for a small child, Virginia had died within a year or two of Ted Francis' passing.

Because this time around she had been with Jimmy so much longer, she had exerted much more influence on him than before. Her soft and gentle nature had been added to her son's character, whereas before he had mostly reflected the tough, irascible nature of his father.

"This" Jimmy Francis was more well-rounded: still capable of stubborn sternness, but also more understanding and compassionate. (*If you want to be loved—be lovable.*)

The previous Jimmy had also been denied the diverse and life-altering affects of a relationship with his first wife Kathy. And Howdy. And Scooter. And Mr. Santini. And so many others.

As in the way that ripples often meet and change the course of other ripples even as they become one with them, so too did the new Jimmy Francis in essence create a new world in which to live.

The simple effort of reaching out more to his father than he had dared do before had forged a different, better and stronger bond between them; which in turn made his father a better, more layered individual whose life was the richer for it.

Without that, Scooter might never have been born; his mother might long since have gone to her grave.

Sensing the positive effects of his father letting down his stony, defensive guard just a little had in turn led Jimmy to open himself up more to others; to the benefit of them as well as of himself.

Without Jimmy Francis and the choices he made, Howdy Watson would have spent a lifetime alone, devoid of much purpose other than his own continued survival. Without his second "son," Mr. Santini's shop and thus his legacy would have ended with his life.

Kathy Brown would have gone home alone that night from the junior prom.

Having come through the dark tunnel of her first marriage, Barb Newburg was able to find the deep and fulfilling relationship with an older Jimmy that would have been impossible had the two of them married as immature teens.

Jimmy Francis was unquestionably the same *man* he had been when he'd met the odd little fellow at Irish Mike's Pub.

But he was now a vastly different *person*.

"Working on your tan, Mom?" he asked Virginia as he stepped up beside her.

She greeted his arrival with a warm, glad smile. Or part of one, at least; a sad legacy of her last stroke was that the left side of her mouth, of her face, now perpetually sagged downward.

Jimmy wheeled her a short distance, to one of the several patio chairs sprinkled along the garden's pathways.

"So, how are things?" she asked as he took a seat.

"I'm having trouble sleeping," she told him.

"Oh? What's wrong?"

"With me, nothing. But there's an old fart in here who seems to think he's still a teenager. The horny old goat's pestered the poor woman in the next room until he's convinced her she's a spring chicken, too. After lights out, he slips into her room.

"The two of 'em make more noise than a concrete mixer!"

Jimmy laughed. "I guess it's good to know you're never too old."

"Well, a person *oughta* be!" Virginia declared, then cast a somewhat conspiratorial glance about.

"And I think one of the nurses is stealing *meds!*"

"What makes you think that?" Jimmy asked, mildly concerned now.

"'Cause she's *way* too happy in the morning. No one's that chipper about changing bed pans unless they're hopped up on something!"

"Maybe she just loves her job," Jimmy said with a smile.

"*This* job? Ehh!"

"Are they at least feeding you proper?"

The old woman shrugged her right shoulder. "Define 'proper.' There's enough of it, I guess—and way too much pudding. But if I was up to snuff, I could teach their cook a thing or two." She sniffed.

"It's like they never even *heard* of *salt!*"

"They're just trying to do right by you, Mom."

"Hmmph. I get more sympathy from Barb when I complain to her. Where's she at?"

"Oh, she's buried in final exam papers that she has to grade. But she sends her best and told me to tell you she'll be out here to see you this weekend."

Virginia turned her head and gazed silently at the various types of flowers blooming in the garden.

"Why doesn't *Mary* ever come visit me?"

With this, Jimmy was forcefully reminded that the strokes had left his mother impaired not just physically but mentally as well. He reached out and patted her arm.

"Mary left home," he said, gently reminding her of what she had momentarily forgotten, "and she hasn't come back yet." A look of confusion briefly clouded Virginia's face, then cleared away.

"Oh. Oh, that's right. How long has she been gone?"

"Four years now."

She slowly turned to look directly at him and her eyes—including the one permanently half-closed—were completely clear and lucid.

"That's just not right, Jimmy," she said softly but emphatically.

He shook his head slowly. "No, Mama. It's not. But I don't know where she is. I don't know how to find her.

"There's nothing I can do."

"I'll pray for her, Jimmy," his mother said, trying to smile reassuringly. "And for you, too."

He rose out of his chair. "You do that, Mom. And, y'know, God wouldn't mind if you asked Him for a little help for yourself, too."

She waved his words off with a swipe of her right hand. "There's nothing more He can do for me, son. I'm gonna die here."

"Don't say things like that, Mom," Jimmy said firmly. It always disturbed him whenever it seemed to him that she was giving up.

"It's all right, Jimmy," she assured him. "I've had a long life…and a good one." Again she smiled as best she could.

"And I'll get to be with your father again."

"Well, when you get there, tell Dad I said 'hi'," Jimmy replied as cheerfully as he could manage. He bent to stroke her hair and kiss her cheek and give her a sly wink.

"And don't let him get you in trouble either, y'hear?"

CHAPTER 40

"I guess you won't really need me to come talk to you anymore, Dad," Jimmy Francis said somberly. He was sitting in his usual spot near his father Ted's headstone at Calvary Cemetery.

Just a few feet away, the earth filling Jimmy's mother's grave was still fresh. Her headstone would be laid in place the following week. Between the graves of his parents, Jimmy had also arranged for a permanent bronze vase to be installed as well, for flowers.

"You've got Momma to keep you company now, old man—though she's prob'ly busy ding-donging St. Peter about how he should visit his mother more often.

"Still—if you don't mind—I'd like to keep paying you these visits from time to time.

"I don't know if they do *you* any good. Hell—pardon my French—I'm still not really sure if you're even still here at all or if I'm just talking to myself.

"Guess it doesn't matter, though. It does *me* good, so I hope you won't mind if I keep droppin' in and bending your ear."

After his ritual of kissing his fingertips and pressing them against his father's headstone, Jimmy repeated the process, pressing his fingers lightly into the loose soil covering his mother's resting-place.

He groaned slightly from the effort of rising to his feet. (He wasn't getting any younger, either.) As he walked away in the direction of his parked car, he stopped—as was also almost ritual—at the plaster statue of *The Pieta.*

"Keep an eye out for my momma, would you?" he asked of the Virgin. "And don't let her talk ya into playin' bridge with her." He shook his head slightly.

"She doesn't look it—but the old lady's a *shark.*"

CHAPTER 41

At first glance, Jimmy Francis didn't recognize the young woman he saw standing on his front porch when he answered a timid knock at the door.

Her hair was long and stringy, badly in need of the services of both shampoo and a comb. She stood shifting from foot to foot nervously. Eyes that darted back and forth and failed to make contact with his own were slightly sunken.

Jimmy's stomach twisted and his heart sank rather than soared when he recognized with sickening suddenness who this sad specimen that stood forlornly before him was.

"Mary?" he almost moaned.

"Can we come in?"

No "Papa" from her cracked lips, even after being away for ten years. And "we?" Only now did Jimmy notice that his prodigal daughter was not alone.

Standing behind Mary, down at the foot of the porch steps, was a young man, probably in his early thirties. He was dressed in frayed and faded blue jeans. He wore no shirt, merely a black leather vest that exposed arms covered from shoulders to wrists with ornate tattoos. His hair was buzz cut close to his scalp.

A small ring in one nostril glistened above a mouth that seemed to be permanently locked in a condescending sneer.

Somewhat numbly, Jimmy stepped aside and with a waving motion invited them to enter.

"Mary!"

Entering from the kitchen, Barb Francis instantly recognized her wayward stepchild. Rushing across the room, she threw her arms around Mary, hugging her warmly and kissing her cheeks.

Jimmy noted that Mary's arms remained stiffly at her sides.

"C'mon! Sit down!" Barb practically babbled, dragging a reluctant Mary over to a chair. The boyfriend remained standing, arms folded over his chest, leaning against the doorway.

"Geez, the guy looks like he's *casing* the joint!" Jimmy thought but was discrete enough to refrain from saying aloud as he too took a seat.

"Can I get you two something?" Barb offered. "Something to drink?" She glanced sadly at Mary's overly thin figure. "Something to eat, maybe?"

Her partner began to open his mouth, then closed it when Mary responded with a curt "No."

Uncomfortable silence then descended over the group. Seeing that Jimmy seemed incapable of anything more than staring sternly at his daughter, Barb tried to break the ice.

"So, is this Alex?" she asked, motioning toward the sneering man.

"Who?" Mary seemed almost baffled by the question. "Oh. No. We made it as far as Montana before that prick took off on me."

Barb saw Jimmy flinch almost imperceptibly. "So is that where you've been all this time?" she asked Mary. "In Montana?"

"Oh, God no. My nearest neighbor there was a mountain goat." The short laugh that issued from her rattled rather than rolled from her throat.

"I've mostly been knocking around the Pacific Northwest," she continued, nervously and unconsciously flicking at the nail of her middle finger with the nail of her thumb.

"What did you do there? What kind of work, I mean."

"Oh, this and that. I met Jock (This was the closest she came to actually introducing the lump leaning against the door.) at a...at a *club* I was working at in Portland."

"Sounds like you've done real good for yourself, sister," Jimmy said coldly. The look Barb shot him told him she would have preferred he maintain his stony silence.

The gent now known as Jock pushed himself away from the door and proceeded to arrogantly rearrange the crotch of his trousers.

"I'll be waitin' for ya outside, babe," he said, then made his exit without any further farewell.

"Looks like you got yourself a real *keeper* there, Mary," Jimmy drawled sarcastically.

"Got him tried and convicted in only five minutes, do you?" his daughter snapped back hotly.

"Oh, hush, you two!" Barb scolded. She reached out and patted the arm of an unresponsive Mary.

"We're just glad to see you, Mary. What brought you back after all these years?" Barb noticed that Mary seemed to brighten ever so slightly at the question.

"Me and Jock…we're gonna get *married!*"

"Oh." Barb hoped her utterance didn't too greatly reveal her disappointment. "So—does that mean you'll be living here from now on?"

"Naw. We'll prob'ly head back to the Coast pretty quick."

Jimmy, grown suddenly suspicious, determined to re-enter the conversation. "You mean you came all this way just to deliver that little gem of news?"

His bad feeling began to intensify as he saw Mary begin to wring her hands together nervously.

"Jock—me and Jock—thought you might like to hear it in person."

"Uh-huh. *And*—?"

"And *what*?" Mary's eyes narrowed warily.

"What else do you want, Mary?" he replied, struggling mightily to keep his voice calm and measured.

"Well…you know. You need a lot of things when you get married. We just thought…" Her voice trailed off to nothingness.

"So you just came back looking for *money*," Jimmy said. Barb heard the sadness and the pain in his voice; Mary did not.

"Not a *lot*," she said defensively. "Just—you know—just maybe a little somethin' to help us get on our feet."

"And would you use it to buy a refrigerator?" Jimmy asked. "Or just more of whatever it is the two of you are on right now?"

"Yeah, I took a little somethin' before I came over here," Mary admitted with acid dripping from her tongue. "I thought it would help me cope with the crap I knew you'd throw in my face." Her gaze was now more glaring than glazed.

"Obviously, I didn't take *enough!*"

"Mary," Barb said with a pleading tone.

"You stay out of this!" her stepdaughter barked at her.

"Hey!" Jimmy shot back. "Save your venom for me, not her."

"You always did side with her against me," Mary accused.

"Only in your twisted little brain," Jimmy countered. "But let's get back to the point of your visit.

"What have you and Jock been doing for money up till *now*?"

"I've been working as a waitress," Mary replied. "The tips aren't bad."

"Uh-huh. And while you're on your feet eight hours or more a day—what does *he* do?"

"He's been working really hard, trying to find investors. He wants to open his own tattoo parlor."

"In other words," Jimmy said, shaking his head, "he sponges off *you*."

"It's not like that."

"It sounds *exactly* like that to me," Jimmy said, wishing he were wrong. "Look, it's obvious the guy's a low-life, Mary. You'd be better off without him."

"It's *you* I'm better off without!" Mary shrieked, jumping up from her chair. "I don't know why I ever came back here. You haven't changed a bit!"

"Not one *damn* bit, sister!" her father snarled.

Jimmy later convinced himself that it was an optical illusion that caused him to think he saw tears welling up in Mary's eyes. She didn't give him the chance to confirm it as she spun and bolted from the house, savagely slamming the front door behind her.

Casting a pained look at her husband, Barb raced to follow Mary out the door.

Jimmy sat stewing in his chair for several long minutes. Only then did he hear the harsh, coughing sound of a motorcycle engine turning over, followed by the blatting sound of the machine roaring off down the street.

Moments later, a dejected Barb slunk back into the house, looking as if she had taken an emotional beating.

"Well," she said with a sigh, "that certainly could have gone better." She walked over to Jimmy and slid down onto his lap. His arms circled her waist as hers snaked around his neck.

"You *know* you could have handled that better, Jimmy."

"I'm sorry," he growled, squeezing her tighter. "But the idea that Mary would show up on our doorstep after all these years, just so she could put the touch on me…That just went through me like a knife, babe."

"I know," Barb commiserated. "But maybe that wasn't *all* she wanted."

"What do you mean?"

"I mean our phone number hasn't changed since she left here. If all she wanted was money—she could have just called."

"Maybe she thought I'd be more likely to cough up some cash if I saw how pitiful she looks with my own eyes."

"*Or,*" Barb persisted, "maybe this was the only way she could think of to reach out to you after all this time; to at least start to re-establish some sort of relationship with you, Jimmy."

"You're reading an awful lot into someone showing up on our doorstep unannounced, half-high and with her hand out," Jimmy demurred.

"You intimidate the poor girl, Jimmy. I know you don't mean to, but you do." Barb smiled wanly.

"Plus, she's always been too stubborn for her own good. You know that."

"Then she needs to get over it," he said gruffly.

"You could have made more of an effort tonight, sweetheart," Barb told him.

"So could she."

"Maybe so. But if you ever get another chance with your daughter, you need to remember something a pretty smart fella once told me."

"What's that?" Jimmy asked warily.

"If you want to be loved—be lovable."

Jimmy turned his eyes away from her.

"I expect she still knows our phone number."

"And I hope she uses it," Barb said, brightening up a bit and kissing him on the cheek.

"Do we have any of that meat loaf we had for supper left over?" he asked, desperate to change the subject. "I could go for a cold meat loaf sandwich right about now."

"Comin' right up!" Barb chirped, hopping off his lap. She then pointed a finger at him and affected a stern expression.

"So long as afterwards you go with me to walk some of it off."

"Yes, mother," he said with resignation.

"But as long as I'm gonna hafta work for this sandwich—throw a slice o' cheese on it, too."

CHAPTER 42

"I think Mary's in trouble."

Jimmy Francis looked up in puzzlement as his wife Barb entered the den of their home. He was sitting there with Howdy Watson, who had come over to proudly show him the battered but intact copy of the *Amazing Spider-Man* #1 comic book he had recently purchased online.

"What do you mean?" Jimmy asked Barb. "What makes you think that?"

"I just got off the phone with her."

It had been two years now since his daughter Mary had popped back into and then stormed out of their lives.

Jimmy knew that she and her boyfriend had not subsequently left town; he'd seen the two of them tooling around astride Jock's cacophonous clunker of a motorcycle just a few months back.

But he'd had no personal contact with Mary, had not spoken to her since the night of their caustic confrontation. Until this moment, he had assumed the same would be true of Barb.

"She called you?" he asked his wife.

Like a contrite child, Barb found it difficult to look at Jimmy and to frame her words in just the right way.

"I should have told you," she finally said. She inhaled and exhaled several times before continuing. "I've been in contact with Mary all along."

"Oh?" Only a single-word response, yet it managed to pose a question, make an accusation and question the woman's loyalty.

"You remember I followed her out into the yard the night she huffed out of the house? She and I only talked for a few minutes, but I did manage to calm her down a little bit.

"I—I'm sorry, Jimmy—I told her that she could call *me* if she didn't want to talk to you."

"And why would you do that?" he asked.

"Because she's still our *daughter*, Jimmy." Barb's voice now flared slightly with anger. "Because I didn't want to just throw her away—along with any chance we might have to have a real relationship with her!"

Though his expression did not change, inwardly he took note of the pronouns "our" and "we" rather than "your" and "you." It showed him Barb was as emotionally invested in Mary's well-being as was he: maybe moreso, he admitted with discomfort.

"Anyway," Barb resumed her confessional narrative, "a couple weeks later, she *did* call me—at a time when she knew you'd probably still be at the shop.

"She told me she and Jock had gone down to the courthouse and gotten married."

"Without asking you to be the flower girl?" Jimmy quipped sarcastically.

Barb wisely took a breath rather that shooting back at him. "Instead of immediately heading back to who-knows-where, they decided to stay here in town, at least for a while.

"So I asked her to let me take her to lunch: my treat. Somewhat to my surprise, she accepted. It was a little uncomfortable for both of us, but we managed to make our way through it without biting each other's head off.

"Since then, we've stayed in touch by phone; gotten together from time to time."

"Have you given her money?" Jimmy asked in an icy voice.

"A little, yes," Barb admitted. "But only a little. And it's always been my idea; she's never once asked."

"And you've kept all this secret from me for two years?" The ice in Jimmy's voice had given way to a slightly pained tone.

"That's the way she wanted it, Jimmy, and I didn't want to risk losing her for good, so I went along with it.

"I thought—I hoped, I prayed—that in time she'd come around enough to reach out to you on her own."

"Uh-huh. Any *other* secrets you've been keeping from me?" Both Jimmy and Barb instantly regretted that he had spoken such, and each drew in an outraged breath.

"Hold *on*, people," Howdy suddenly and unexpectedly interrupted. He was sure both of them had forgotten he was even there and a party to the exchange.

"Have you guys forgotten how this conversation *started*?" He fixed Barb with an intent gaze.

"You said you thought Mary was in trouble. What *kind* of trouble?"

Barb sat down beside Jimmy and gripped his hand tightly before explaining her comment.

"I think that worthless slimeball...I think he's been *hurting* her, Jimmy. Physically, I mean."

Jimmy's own grip tightened painfully around her small hand. He had not experienced one of his tingling headaches for years, but he had not forgotten the squeezing sensation that now pressed on the back of his neck.

"What makes you think that, Barb? Did she tell you so?"

"No. Not in so many words. And every time I've tried to broach the subject with her she strongly denies it. But I know the signs, remember?"

"So you think she's covering up?"

"I *do*. Even her denials are all familiar to me. And when I talked to her a few minutes ago, I could tell she was very upset. I think she'd been crying.

"She wouldn't tell me what had happened...but I think it was bad."

Barb's voice broke slightly.

Jimmy sat in silence for a minute or more, chewing on what he'd just been told before asking his wife, "Do you know where she lives?"

Even now, in this dire moment, Barb hesitated to break a confidence: hesitated to reply.

"Do you know where she lives?" Jimmy repeated, slowly speaking words that had to escape through clenched teeth. Impossibly as it seemed, his grip on Barb's hand tightened further.

"Yes," she said meekly. At that, he rose to his feet.

"What are you gonna *do*, Jimmy?"

"What do you *think*?" he replied, snatching his car keys up out of a nearby bowl.

"I'm gonna bring our baby home!"

There were tears spilling over the lids of Barb's eyes and rolling down her face as she looked up at him, but there was a hopeful smile on her lips.

"*I'll* drive," Howdy said, rising from the sofa and tossing aside his now forgotten pulp prize.

"There's no need for *you* to get involved in this mess, buddy," Jimmy said.

"The *hell* there *isn't*," Howdy snapped back with uncharacteristic assertiveness. "She's *my* little girl too, remember?" Brooking no further argument, he grabbed the car keys from Jimmy's hand.

"Now, let's get goin'!"

CHAPTER 43

Mary Francis only opened the front door of her apartment a few inches —and then only after repeated, persistent pounding on it by her father.

Her head was bowed, her long hair covering and concealing most of her face.

"What do you want?" she asked, though not in an overtly hostile tone. It was more like one of tired resignation.

"For starters, I'd like to come in, Mary," he said.

His voice was calm and flat. Howdy had lectured him on the entire ride over on the importance of Jimmy remaining cool and keeping his emotions in check. That became harder for Jimmy to do the minute he realized what part of town his daughter was living in. Low scale, high

"SHE'S MY LITTLE GIRL TOO, REMEMBER?"

crime; the dull throbbing at the base of his neck had become a rolling thunder pounding against the back of his skull.

Mary merely grunted before turning and shuffling into the apartment's cramped living room. The look of the place made Jimmy's skin literally crawl, and when Mary flopped down on a ratty sofa he remained standing.

"How'd you know where to find me?" she asked, raising her head only enough for one glassy eye to gaze up at her father.

"Barb told me."

"She shoulda kept her mouth shut."

"Don't bad-mouth her, Mary," Jimmy replied, striving mightily not to lose control. "Right now, that woman might be the best friend you've got." He shook his head.

"Maybe the *only* one."

"What's *that* s'posed ta mean?"

"It means she cares about you, girl. And she's worried."

"About *what*?"

He decided not to dance around the subject any longer. "She thinks your husband's been hurting you."

"Well, she's wrong. I *told* her that. I'm telling *you* that!"

"Yeah? Why don't you raise your head and look me in the eyes while you say that again, little girl?"

"I'm *not* a little girl!"

"Well you sure as hell don't act like a grown-up."

"How would *you* know how I act?" she snarled. "You've barely seen me for half my life!"

"And whose fault is that?"

"Why don't you just go away?"

She heard a low, rumbling sound in her father's chest and throat. "All right," he said at last. "I *will.*"

Seeing her posture relax at the words, as he had hoped, Jimmy quickly stooped, put one hand under her chin and forced her head up. As it rose, the hair fell away from the side of her face it had been masking.

Jimmy let out an involuntary gasp, horrified by the purplish bruise covering much of her left cheek; the eye on that side was swollen nearly shut.

"What happened?" he practically growled.

"Nuthin'. I fell down the steps getting the mail yesterday."

"That's bullshit, Mary, and we both know it. Now, why'd the greasy sunovabitch hit you?"

"It was *my* fault, okay?" she said, her voice taking on a whining pitch. "I said something that upset him."

"What could you possibly have said that would cause him to do something like that?"

She was bent slightly at the waist and rocking slowly back and forth. "I just gave him some bad news, that's all."

Jimmy felt his heart sink like a rock in a shallow pond. "What bad news?"

Mary shrugged and said nothing.

"What did you tell him, dammit!" Jimmy roared.

Mary's head snapped up at the command, her eyes blazing with an angry fire.

"I told him I'm *pregnant*, all right?" she screamed. Her head and shoulders then slumped as if all her strength had been swept away by the exclamation.

"I told him that I'm pregnant."

Jimmy shook his head, not in sympathy but in disgust. "I tried to tell you he was no good. But you wouldn't listen to me."

"Is that why you're here?" she demanded, flicking one hand as if she was trying to shoo away an annoying insect. "Did you come all the way over here just to say I told you so?"

"I came because your mother's worried about you."

"My mother's *dead*!"

The snarled words were like a punch to the stomach. Jimmy breathed in and out several times deeply, determined not to lash out physically at his daughter as he had done on that awful night so many years and tears ago.

"Do you think Kathy would be any *more* worried about you if she were still alive, still here? Or any *less*?"

"Tell Barb I said thanks for her concern," Mary replied in a rather petulant tone.

"And tell her I won't be calling her any more."

"Don't punish her because of me, sister," Jimmy said. "Or yourself. Barb will always be there if you need her."

"That's nice to know," Mary said, looking at him with disdain.

"And where will *you* be?"

Jimmy's fists clenched and unclenched several times before he responded.

"That's it," he said at last. "Get a bag, pack whatever you think you'll need. We're getting you outta here."

He was puzzled when his daughter's expression changed to one of anger rather than of gratitude.

"Just like that?" she said.

"Just like that."

Mary made a short, scoffing sound. "You really *haven't* changed," she said in an accusatory tone of voice.

"All my life, it was the same with you. It never mattered to you what *I* thought; what *I* wanted.

"You never asked, you just told." Her lips twisted into a sneer.

"Like all those times you went off to visit your dead daddy. But never—not one, single time—did you ever take me to *my* mom's grave. Never asked if I wanted to place a flower on it." She threw her head back and issued a short and sardonic laugh.

"Hell, old man...you're no better than *Jock* is!"

Mary quickly dropped her head between her shoulders, steeling herself for the angry verbal if not physical retort she expected from her father.

But none came. In fact, no sound issued from Jimmy at all.

Tentatively, anxiously, she raised her head to see he was simply staring down at her. He was rubbing the back of his head and had a stricken look on his face that Mary instantly feared for a moment meant that her contentiousness had triggered a stroke or heart attack in him. He was, after all, sixty years old now.

Her fear intensified as the man ever so slowly lowered himself to his knees in front of her. Yet he was showing no other signs of physical distress as he hesitantly reached out and took both her hands gently in his.

"Is that *really* what you think of me, Mary?" he asked hoarsely. "Is that really what I've been: what I am? Because, if it is...I am so, so sorry." He fiercely blinked away tears.

"No wonder you hate me."

Mary inhaled almost as sharply as she had when Jimmy slapped her on that hated night long ago, then shook her head.

"Oh, no," she moaned. "I don't hate you. Not really."

"I love you, baby," Jimmy professed. "Always have, since the day you were so tiny I could practically hold you in the palm of my hand. Always will. I truly did believe I was only doing what was best for you. I hope you can believe that."

"I know you were."

Her father smiled tightly. "But you're right. You're a grown woman now, with all the scars to prove it. So now, *you* tell *me*.

"Tell me what you want, Mary, what you think you need…and I'll do everything I can to help you make it happen."

Tears welled up in the battered young woman's eyes and began to roll down both cheeks at her father's obviously sincere and heartfelt concern and intent. Her lips moved soundlessly up and down several times before actual words came spilling out.

"I wanna go *home*, Papa!"

With a choking cry, Jimmy pulled her off the chair and into his protective arms. The two of them clung to each other as if to the life preserver from a sinking ship.

"We need to get you outta here right now," Jimmy said at last, softly wiping the tears from his child's face.

"Throw whatever you need the most into a suitcase or a trash bag or whatever you've got. We can come back later for the rest or just replace it. Okay?"

"Okay."

It didn't take long; the poor girl didn't have much. Hustling her to the front door of the apartment, Jimmy flung it open—to find a startled Jock standing on the other side.

"What the hell are you doin' here, old man?" Jock demanded of Jimmy, and the words spewed out on breath that reeked of alcohol.

Fighting the urge to say the words that immediately sprang to mind, Jimmy turned to his daughter and simply said, "Mary?"

"I'm leaving here, Jock," she said defiantly. "And I'm never coming back."

"Yeah?" her husband replied, that seemingly permanent sneer twisting his lips. "And what if I say yer stayin'?"

"Get out of our way, you slimy little chickenshit," Jimmy said harshly. The sneer and the cold, dead eyes that accompanied it now turned toward him.

Jock let loose a short, guttural laughing sound. "And what are you gonna do if I don't, grandpa?"

"Papa," Mary said, a plea in her voice as she tugged at her father's arm, silently urging him to be careful and back away.

"Let me tell you something, boy," Jimmy said, ignoring his daughter's entreaty and fixing Jock with a glare even colder and harsher than the one the younger man had mustered.

"I may be sixty years old, but on the *worst* day of my life I could still pound a gutless pissant like you into the ground without breaking a sweat."

Inwardly, Jimmy was cursing his mouth for having just written a check he was pretty sure his ass couldn't cash. But he let no such self-doubt show in his demeanor.

"As it is," he pressed onward, "the divorce lawyers I intend to hire are gonna chew you up and spit you out like the worthless worm feed you are. Don't make things even worse by having criminal charges filed against you.

"Now get the hell out of our way!"

His brain being not the sharpest tool in the shed even when not addled by liquor, Jock just stood speechless, his eyes blinking rapidly in dull incomprehension.

"Get outta the way, asshole," Jimmy repeated with exasperation, pushing Jock aside with one arm while gently guiding Mary with the other arm around her shoulders.

He stopped after they had moved out of the confines of the apartment and a few feet down the sidewalk, turning back toward Jock.

"Don't you ever come within a mile of me or my family, Jock," he warned ominously.

"And if you ever lay hands on my little girl again, you'd better hope the police are on hand to throw your sorry ass in jail.

"Because if I get to you first—won't man nor God be able to stop me from gutting you like a fish!"

Without another word, Jimmy turned and again directed Mary down the sidewalk.

When they were well out of earshot of Jock, Jimmy whispered to Mary. "Is he coming after us?"

Mary hazarded a quick glance back over her shoulder.

"No. Looks like he's gone inside."

"Thank God!" Jimmy exhaled. "I figure it would have only taken him about ten seconds to whip my old ass up one side and down the other!"

Mary chuckled despite the seriousness of the situation and pressed herself even more tightly up against her father's side.

As they neared Jimmy's parked car, they saw Howdy Watson standing up on the curb. He was wielding a tire iron and vainly trying his very best to look menacing.

"What the hell are you supposed to be doin'?" Jimmy asked.

"I saw that fella coming up to the door and thought you might need some help. He looked like a pretty tough bruiser!"

Jimmy started laughing, as much from relieved tension as anything, and threw his free arm around the narrow shoulders of his lifelong and best friend.

"Put your bullet back in your pocket, Barney," he said lightly, "and get back behind the wheel. He looked lovingly at his daughter and smiled.

"Our baby girl's come back to us!"

CHAPTER 44

Jimmy Francis had set his alarm clock when he went to bed the night before, but found he didn't need its monotonous beeping to awaken him bright and early on the morning of his sixty-fifth birthday.

He felt fully alert, rested and refreshed, but chose to remain snuggled in the comfort of his covers a little longer.

After all their years together, Jimmy could tell simply by the feel of the bed that his wife was no longer in it with him. Barb had doubtless already risen and was probably busy preparing breakfast in the kitchen.

She had retired from her teaching post (save for occasionally making herself available as a substitute) five years earlier, having worked long enough to receive a nice pension.

Jimmy had held off retiring a couple years longer, then arranged an amicable deal whereby his longtime and faithful employees bought out his woodcraft business. He still spent an hour or two each week visiting with them and some of his loyal customers.

(One non-negotiable part of the transfer of ownership, which was met with no resistance, was Jimmy's insistence that the shop continue to be called *Santini's*.)

Jimmy and Barb's combined incomes plus savings they had wisely invested and managed allowed them to live modestly but comfortably. They were well off enough to finance the occasional car trips they both enjoyed. Two years earlier, they had even enjoyed a weeklong cruise in the Caribbean.

Jimmy heard the sound of his front door opening and closing, and whispered words being exchanged. Smiling, he rolled onto his side so as to face away from his bedroom door.

He distinctly heard the slap-slap of small, sneaker-clad feet, followed by a momentary silence—and then a wriggling bundle landed right on top of him.

"Help me, Mother!" Jimmy screeched in feigned terror.

"I'm being attacked by a *monster*!"

As was always the case at the climax of this scenario, his pleas were met by the beautiful sound of a child giggling.

"It's not a monster, Grandpa," a small and slightly breathless voice said. "It's *me*!"

"Me, who?"

"Me, who—that's who!"

Jimmy used his arms to push himself up to a sitting position in the bed, leaning back against the headboard.

Still sprawled across his legs, pinning them down, was his precocious four-year-old grandson *Teddy*.

(Naming him after his great-grandfather had not been Jimmy's idea, but that of the boy's mother, who had doggedly insisted on it.)

"Get off your grandpa," Mary Francis lightly admonished as she now breezed into the bedroom.

"You'll squash him."

"Nuh-uh. No I won't, Ma. Will I, Grandpa?"

"I don't know, Slugger," Jimmy demurred. "You're gettin' mighty big. How much do you weigh now—two hundred, three hundred pounds?"

"No! Elephants (the word came from Teddy's mouth as "eph-elants") don't weigh that much!"

"Well, maybe you're a *super* elephant," Jimmy replied, lightly tugging on his grandson's lobes. "Your ears *are* awful big!"

Teddy giggled again.

"Get up and let Grandpa get dressed," Mary said. "Grandma's about ready to serve breakfast." Before steering Teddy out of the bedroom, she leaned over and kissed her father atop his snowy head.

"Happy Birthday, Papa!"

As he swung his legs over the edge of the bed, Jimmy glanced at his nightstand. Sitting atop it near the head of his bed, as it had been every night for the past sixty years, was the tiny *hourglass* he had discovered on the morning of his fifth birthday.

He held it in his hand for a moment before turning it over and setting it back down on the nightstand. He had never figured out where the little trinket came from, but he wouldn't part with it for the world.

By the time he dressed and walked down the hall and into the combined kitchen/dining room area, he saw that little Teddy was already ravenously devouring a helping of bacon and scrambled eggs.

"You sit down and eat something too, sister," Barb told Mary, handing her a plate.

"Thanks, Mama," Mary said, giving Barb a peck on the cheek as she took the plate from her stepmother.

Jimmy smiled as he stood in the doorway, absorbing and enjoying the Rockwellian tableau spread out before him. Everything about it illustrated how well all their lives had gone since the night he first brought Mary back home.

Mary's subsequent divorce had gone smoothly, thanks in part to her making no request for either alimony or child support. To sweeten the deal (and with Barb's unflinching approval), Jimmy had tapped into part of his savings account to entice Jock into signing an ironclad agreement whereby he permanently forfeited any and all parental rights.

(Jimmy had declined to tell Mary how much it had cost him to buy off Jock and get him out of their lives forever. Not because the sum was so large—but rather because the worthless slug had been more than happy to accept an amount barely enough to buy the new motorcycle that doubtless took him out of town. Jimmy didn't want his daughter to ever know just how little value her ex-husband placed on her and their child.)

None of them had seen or heard from Jock since, nor was his name ever brought up in conversation. Mary had insisted on taking back her maiden name of "Francis."

Surrounded by as much love as he was, little Teddy had not yet shown any curiosity about the identity of his father. Jimmy frowned slightly at the thought of the inevitable day when the boy would want to know. On that day, it would be mightily tempting to simply tell Teddy that his father was dead (as, if there was any justice in this world, he actually would be).

Jimmy hoped they would all resist that temptation. Honest answers, he felt, were usually the best answers, even if they brought pain in their wake.

Following Teddy's birth, Jimmy and Barb had provided support for Mary to attend some secretarial classes. This in turn had helped her get a good job in the offices of the small law firm that had handled her divorce.

She now had her own apartment and was dating a young attorney from the firm: one who seemed to be a good and decent man. He treated both Mary and Teddy kindly; that's what was most important in Jimmy's assessment of him.

Having started in on his breakfast before any of the adults, little Teddy naturally finished first. He was impatiently hopping up and down in his chair like a Mexican jumping bean on steroids by the time the last dish was being cleared away.

"Give Grandpa his present!" he insistently harangued his mother.

Smiling indulgently, Mary went into the living room and quickly returned with a package wrapped in festive foil.

"Ohh," Jimmy exhaled when he opened the package, touched by what he saw revealed.

Mary, through the marvels of e-bay, had found and purchased for him a pristine, vintage Davy Crockett collectors plate identical to the one her father had described to her from his childhood.

"Thank you, Mary," he said. "And thank you, Teddy," he remembered to add. "This is the best gift *ever*." The little boy's face fairly glowed at the words.

"This reminds me," Jimmy then said, carefully handing the plate to Barb. "I have something for *you*, Slugger."

Teddy's brow furrowed in puzzlement.

"Yer not s'posed ta give *me* a present on *your* birthday, Grandpa!"

"I know. But this is something I've been wanting to share with you. I'll be right back."

As Jimmy headed toward the central hallway of the house to lower the stepladder that led up into a small attic, Mary cast a questioning glance at Barb. Equally baffled, all she could do was shrug in response.

They could hear Jimmy rummaging around above them for a few minutes before he descended back into the main house, carrying a large plastic bag with him. Motioning for Teddy to follow him, he carried it into the middle of the living room. Setting it down on the floor, he extracted a large box from inside the bag.

"What is it, Grandpa?" Teddy asked.

"It's my original *Fort Apache Playset*, Slugger."

"Wow," Teddy marveled, looking down at a box that was remarkably well kept. Then he cast Jimmy a questioning look. "What's a Fort Apache?"

Jimmy explained all about it to the rapt little boy, and of how his parents had given it to him when he was the same age Teddy would soon be and how it was one of his "favoritest" presents in his whole life (Next to the Davy Crockett plate Teddy had just given him, naturally).

He then opened the box and rather unceremoniously dumped its contents out on the living room floor. With equal abandon, he and Teddy began to assemble its various components.

"Should you be letting him play with that, Papa?" Mary asked with some trepidation. "That's got to be a collector's item."

"Oh, it's a lot more than that, baby girl," her father said, looking up at her with a broad smile. "It's a *toy*!"

She smiled in return, seeing that he was growing genuinely excited as he turned his eyes back to the grandson upon whom he doted.

"And toys are meant to be played with. Right, Teddy?"

"Right!"

The two children became so engrossed in their play that it finally behooved Barb to literally chase them out of the house so that she and Mary could clean up and make things ready for the small birthday party they planned to host that evening in Jimmy's honor.

"What say us *men* go for a walk, Teddy?"

"Okay."

"Just don't feed him while you're out, Papa," Mary admonished. "Especially junk food."

"Yes, sister," Jimmy replied meekly, but he cast Teddy an exaggerated wink.

He and the boy first paid a brief call at Jimmy's backyard workshop before starting their meander. There, Jimmy proudly showed off his latest project: twin busts of him and Barb; both attached to a single base of polished cedar. Jimmy intended to present it to his wife as a gift on the occasion of their impending wedding anniversary.

"Who are they?" Teddy innocently asked, carefully running his tiny hands over the curvature of the sculpted wood.

"That's me and your grandma."

Teddy cast him a somewhat apologetic glance. "But…they don't *look* like you."

Jimmy chuckled. The boy was absolutely right, of course. The sculpted figures did not look the way he and Barb did—*today*. He had instead decided to present them as they were the way they had looked on the day of their marriage.

"Let's go for that walk now," he said to Teddy.

"Where we goin'?"

Jimmy glanced toward the house as though fearing the women inside would be able to hear his reply, then leaned close to give his grandson a conspiratorial look.

"Can you keep a secret?"

"Uh-huh."

"Okay. I thought we'd walk down to the woodshop—and then maybe go to the ice cream parlor."

"O-*kay!*" No surprise there, that the little boy would be fully in favor of this notion.

As the two of them walked hand-in-hand down the sidewalk lining the street, Teddy spotted his grandpa's neighbor: old Mr. Crowley. The little boy waved to him when their eyes made contact, but the curmudgeonly Crowley's only acknowledgment of the gesture was a cold glare.

"He don't like me," Teddy said sadly.

"Oh, he don't like *anybody*, Teddy," Jimmy assured him. "It's not your fault. He's just lonely and unhappy—and shows it by being mean to people."

"Sounds like *he* needs some ice cream," Teddy philosophized.

"I think you're right, Slugger," Jimmy concurred. "That might be just the thing for him."

Dale Leon immediately and warmly greeted them when they entered *Santini's Woodworks*. Dale had been Jimmy's assistant manager in the shop for years; he was now the principal owner, with three other former employees holding the rest of the shares. They were all in the shop this day, too, and all called out greetings to Jimmy and Teddy before going about their work.

"What brings you two out?" Dale asked.

"We've mostly come for the ice cream next door," Jimmy replied, patting his grandson on the shoulder. "Teddy here's helping me celebrate my birthday."

"Your birthday?" Dale repeated. "I didn't remember it being your birthday, Jimmy. You should have said something."

"Oh, it's not a big deal," Jimmy insisted. He could tell by the way that young Teddy was gazing longingly toward the door that the boy felt they had spent enough time on the amenities; he was ready for ice cream.

More than once over the years, others had encouraged Jimmy—as they had Mr. Santini before him—to try to push out the tenants of the ice cream parlor and to use the space to expand the woodshop. Both men had been loath to do so and had adamantly resisted any such idea.

A married couple—the Hogans—had long since left the running of the parlor in the hands of their children, and Jimmy had made friends of all of them.

Two of the Hogan siblings were in the parlor on this day; and upon being informed by Teddy that it was his grandpa's birthday they had insisted that the ice cream was on the house. Jimmy had a single scoop of vanilla. Teddy had chocolate—two scoops.

With the weight of such confectionery ambrosia weighing down his little belly, Teddy's short legs began to give out on him when he and Jimmy were still about a block away from returning home. Teddy rode the rest of the way on his grandfather's back, still relishing the sweet aftertaste of the ice cream.

In the little boy's mind, all was right with the world.

When Jimmy deposited him on the front porch of his house, Teddy looked up earnestly at him. "Don't tell Ma I had ice cream, okay, Grandpa?"

"I won't say a word, Slugger," Jimmy pledged. "I promise."

Jimmy had to work his facial muscles greatly to suppress a grin. The little boy was oblivious of the chocolate "moustache" coating his upper lip that would surely tell his mother at a glance what the two of them had been into.

"I said no junk food, young man," Mary scolded as they walked into the kitchen. Teddy spun and stared incredulously at his grandpa.

Jimmy shook his head and shrugged. Better all around if he simply left Teddy with the impression that mothers possessed a psychic ability that alerted them when you broke the rules, no matter how hard you might try to hide that fact from them.

"I've got a little errand I need to run," he then said, scooping up his car keys. "I'll be back in about an hour."

"Hunh. What could he possibly need to do today?" Mary wondered aloud.

Barb smiled and patted Mary on the arm. "Oh, that's just what he says when he means he's gonna go visit his father."

Jimmy didn't sit on the ground anymore when visiting his father's grave. As he jovially but truthfully said, he could get *down* about as easy as ever—it was the getting back *up* that had gotten a little difficult. Such was his pride that he did not want to risk even the slightest chance of a stranger seeing him struggle to get back on his feet.

"If you were still around, Dad," he said, "you'd be nearly a hundred." He chuckled. "Tough as you were, I'm kinda surprised you didn't make it that long.

"Myself? Well, I'm thinkin' I still have at least ten more years in me: maybe more. No reason to think they won't be mostly good ones.

"My baby girl's doin' real well. She's come a long way since the night me and Howdy brought her back home."

He glanced off to the south. Though he couldn't discern it from this distance, he knew that the grave of his first wife lay in that part of the cemetery.

A few months after Mary had come back into his life—when her physical wounds had healed and her emotional ones had at least begun to scab over—he had visited Kathy's grave with her. Both had spoken to her of their abiding love.

Jimmy had not returned for another visit since, but he knew Mary paid regular visits and he was glad of it.

"And you should see little Teddy," he told his father's spirit. "He's a good boy. I believe he'll become a good man.

"You'd like him and his mama both. I sure do."

As one of the parts of his cemetery ritual he had not abandoned, Jimmy managed to go down on one knee, kiss his fingertips and press them first against the headstone of his father and then that of his mother.

He rose back up with relative ease and only mild discomfort from the arthritis that had taken up residence in his lower back some years earlier.

As was the usual postscript to his funereal ritual, Jimmy then walked over to view the reproduction of *The Pieta*. Two years ago, much to his horrified dismay, unidentified vandals had invaded the cemetery grounds. Among other unspeakable acts of desecration, they had spray-painted graffiti on the statue and taken a hammer to the Virgin's plaster head.

Jimmy had personally spearheaded a fundraising drive—including the raffling of an original woodcarving rendered by him—to raise enough money to pay for the restoration of the statue. It now looked as good as new.

"It's always good to see you, dear Lady," Jimmy said to the reproduction of the Holy Mother. "I hope all is well with you."

He leaned forward and respectfully kissed the Virgin on the forehead before turning to head for home.

CHAPTER 45

"I can't believe this," Barb Francis said, looking out the front window for at least the fifth time.

She turned back to look at the small group currently assembled in her living room. Besides herself and Jimmy, the only people there were Howdy and Gail Watson (Mary having finally departed to put young Teddy to bed).

Jimmy had insisted on keeping his birthday celebration small and low key, so only a few friends had been invited to attend. But one by one almost all of them had phoned to excuse themselves from being able to attend. Those who had not called had simply not shown up.

Jimmy had done a game job of masking his disappointment, but couldn't hide his eager reaction when the phone rang again and Barb told him the call was for him.

"Haaaappy Birthday, bubba!" his brother Chuck fairly shouted through the receiver.

Jimmy had known Scooter would not be at the party. A few years before, he had moved to the East Coast, where he was now designing some of those skyscrapers he had longingly envisioned in his youth.

"Lee sends his best too, Jimmy," Scooter added. It had meant more than he could ever verbalize when Jimmy had flown out the previous summer to stand beside his baby brother at Chuck and Lee's wedding.

"Did you get the gift we sent you?" Scooter asked.

"Yeah. I'm lovin' it."

They spoke for several minutes and even when Jimmy hung up he kept his hand on the receiver, wistfully patting it.

"I'm sorry things got screwed up, sweetheart," Barb said, laying her hand on his shoulder and rubbing it.

"Why don't you and Howdy go down to Irish Mike's?" she suggested. "You can at least celebrate with a drink or two."

He smiled and nodded. "What do you say, Howdy? Wanna bend an elbow or two with me?"

"You had me at 'drink'!" Howdy replied enthusiastically.

Jimmy walked down the hall to his bedroom to retrieve a jacket and Barb followed after him. She withdrew a small package from her dresser and handed it to him.

"In case you boys don't make it back before midnight," she said. "I want to make sure I give you my present to you while it's still your birthday."

He opened the package and the small case within to see a new watch he had admired in one of the local malls a few months prior to this day. On the back of the watch was an engraved inscription.

To Jimmy: Who is loved because he is lovable. Barb.

"Our time together has been mostly good, hasn't it, sweetheart?" he said as he slipped the watch onto his left wrist.

"It's been mostly *great*," Barb replied, taking him into her arms and kissing him deeply.

"And don't you drink too much tonight," she warned him, using the tip of her thumb to wipe away the lipstick she had left behind on his mouth.

"'Cause when you get back home—I want you in shape to enjoy the *rest* of the 'celebration' I have in mind."

"I'll be as sober as a judge," he professed—then pinched her on the bottom. "And horny as a goat!"

Howdy was waiting for him at the front door. "Are you gonna drive," Jimmy asked him, "or should I?"

"I thought we might just walk," Howdy replied. "That way, neither of us has to be a designated driver!"

"Sounds good to me, pardner."

Barb stood at the front window, watching as the two men set off into the evening. Once they were nearly out of sight, she then turned to Gail.

"All right," she said. "Let's pack up the food and give the girls a call!"

Jimmy and Howdy took their time as they walked toward the pub, enjoying the coolness of the night air.

"Y'know," Jimmy said, "it's probably just as well that it ended up being just the two of us, Howdy. We've been a team for a mighty long time now."

"Yeah. Most of our lives."

"And just think; it all started because you were afraid you were gonna get blown up."

"Sometimes I'm still afraid of that."

"I hear that."

"But we've helped see each other through both the good times and the bad," Howdy ruminated. "And I reckon we'd help each other through a nuclear war, too."

"Aww, they ain't built the bomb powerful enough to blow us up."

"Yeah. I guess we're kinda like an old married couple: till death do us part."

Both chuckled at that.

When they reached Irish Mike's, Howdy rushed ahead enough to hold the door open for the birthday boy, affecting an exaggerated bow at the waist and ushering Jimmy into the pub.

Entering the place, Jimmy's jaw dropped and his eyes widened as a loud and collective cry greeted him.

"*Surprise!*"

CHAPTER 46

Irish Mike's Pub was packed on this night—in honor of Jimmy Francis.

Almost dazed, he staggered into the bar to the accompaniment of cheers, whistles, applause and much backslapping.

He quickly realized that all of the friends and spouses he had had invited to his home that evening (and a fair number he hadn't) and who had "canceled" out on appearing at his birthday party had merely done so in order to set him up for this far bigger and more elaborate surprise party.

"Sorry, buddy," Howdy practically shouted in his ear to be heard above the din, "but we weren't about to let you enter your *twilight years* without a big bang!"

Barb Francis and Gail Watson—having driven rather than walked— entered the pub just moments later. Jimmy pretended to give his wife a disapproving frown before bursting into laughter and sweeping her into his arms.

The guys and gals from *Santini's* and the ice cream parlor, all of whom had done such a masterful job of pretending ignorance that this was Jimmy's birthday, were also on hand for the festivities.

Almost as impatient as had been young Teddy earlier, the crew from the woodshop couldn't wait a minute before wheeling out the present they had collectively bought for their former boss.

There was much "oohing" and "ahhing" as they unveiled a brand new workbench, upon which rested a set of expensive new carving implements.

"People! People!" a loud voice called from behind the bar. The voice belonged to the owner of the establishment, Timothy Clancy (who, in his previous life, Jimmy had known with at most passing interest simply as the pub's bartender. Jimmy had never known then, as he did now, that Clancy had inherited from his father Michael.).

"The man's *bound* to be dyin' o' *thirst*!" Clancy boisterously declared. "Make way and let him find his way to the bar!" The crowd obligingly parted.

"The first one's on the house!" Clancy magnanimously told the guest of honor.

"I'll take it, Timmy," Jimmy said, "but only if you then let me buy *you* one—and you join us in the party."

"Done and done!" Clancy replied cheerfully.

As Jimmy reached for his drink, he felt a hand come to rest on his shoulder as an oddly accented voice whispered in his ear.

"Happy Birthday, *Champ!*"

Jimmy spun on his stool, nearly spilling his drink, irrationally but understandably expecting to see his father—the only one who had ever called him "Champ"—standing behind him. Such wasn't the case, of course. Still, the solicitation—whether real or imagined—brought a warm glow to Jimmy's belly.

But there were plenty of other well-wishers all around him, and they now began to chant with one voice.

"Toast! Toast! Toast! Toast!"

A beaming Jimmy turned his head from side to side, casting his eyes on the many friends who were gathered together this evening on his behalf. He considered himself to be well and truly blessed.

And he hoped he was worthy of it.

Before he could respond to their chanted exhortations, a flickering light near the back of the pub caught his attention.

Rising slightly on his stool to get a better look, he saw two men (not participants in the birthday party) huddled together in one of the establishment's smaller booths. One of the men he recognized immediately and surprisingly as being his curmudgeonly old neighbor Mr. Crowley. The old crank was staring intently down at a small object sitting on the table in front of him.

It was a tiny *hourglass.*

As seen from across the room, it appeared to be virtually identical to the one Jimmy himself owned and treasured—with one notable exception.

This one was emitting a warm, pulsing, orange glow.

Jimmy couldn't identify the fellow sitting beside Crowley. He was a little man of indeterminate age, whose reddish hair and elfin face gave him the look of a leprechaun.

The little man swung his head away from Crowley and toward Jimmy. As he made eye contact from the other side of the pub, he smiled broadly, lightly tapped the side of his nose—and gave Jimmy a wink.

"Toast! Toast! Toast!"

As the chanting grew louder and more insistent, Jimmy turned his eyes away and returned them to the beaming faces of his many friends. As his wife Barb leaned in to kiss his cheek, and with a smile that almost gave off a glow of its own, James Francis raised his glass skyward.

"*To Life!*"

THE END

ABOUT OUR CREATORS

AUTHOR

R.A Jones — His credits include newspaper and magazine columns, articles and short stories. He has been a movie reviewer and commentator in newspapers and on radio. He assisted actor Gary Lockwood (*Star Trek; 2001: A Space Odyssey*) in the writing of Lockwood's autobiography, 2001 Memories: An Actor's Odyssey. With Michael Vance, R. A. co-wrote the syndicated comic book and comic strip review column Suspended Animation for five years.

The readers of *Comic Buyer's Guide* magazine voted him "Favorite Writer About Comics" in 1985, and in 2006 he was inducted into the Oklahoma Cartoonists Collection Hall of Fame. He has scripted more than 100 different issues of various comic book titles in his career. Among the more noteworthy are Wolverine and Captain America for Marvel Comics; *Harlan Ellison's Dream Corridor* for Dark Horse Comics; and Star Trek: Deep Space Nine for Malibu Comics. He also co-wrote, for Image Comics, *Bulletproof Monk*, which served as the basis for the 2003 movie of the same title. His comic book stories, "Cold Hard Facts" and "Three On A Match" which originally appeared in the magazine *Metal Hurlant*, were short films in France.

His novels include *Deathwalker, Global Star* (written with Michael Vance and Mel Fox), *The Equation* (co-written with Michael Vance), *The Steel Ring*, a superhero book based on characters from one of the earliest publishers of comic books, Centaur. He also wrote the Western thriller, *Gun Glory*.

INTERIOR & COVER ILLUSTRATOR

ROB DAVIS - began his professional art career doing illustrations for role-playing games in the late 1980's. Not long after, he began lettering and inking, then penciling comics for a number of small black and white comics publishers- most notably for Eternity Comics, which eventually became Malibu Comics in the 1990's, on their book SCIMIDAR with writer R.A. Jones. Branching out to other black and white publishers and eventually working at both DC and Marvel, Rob worked on likeness intensive comics like TV adaptations of QUANTUM LEAP and STAR TREK's many incarnations mostly on the DEEP SPACE NINE comics for Malibu. At Marvel he worked on the Saturday morning cartoon adaptation PIRATES OF DARK WATER. After the comics industry implosion in the late 1990s, Rob picked up work on video games, advertising illustrations and T-shirt design as well as some small press comics like ROBYN OF SHERWOOD for Caliber. Rob continues to do the odd self-published comic book as well as publisher and designer for his small-press production REDBUD STUDIO COMICS. Rob is Art Director, Designer and Illustrator for the New Pulp production outfit AIRSHIP 27, partnered with writer/editor Ron Fortier. Rob is the recipient of the PULP FACTORY AWARD for "Best Interior Illustrations" in 2010 for his work on SHERLOCK HOLMES: CONSULTING DETECTIVE and has been nominated for the same award every year since. He works and lives in central Missouri with his wife and two children.

HIS NAME WAS MANKILLER

Young Jason Mankiller never believed his surname was an omen of his future until the Civil War broke out and he joined the Union Army. Fate took him to the fields of Gettysburg. By the time the battle ended, he was sitting atop a small rise surrounded by the bodies of dozens of Confederate troopers. Days later, while drunk, his fellow soldiers had tears of blood tattooed onto his face. From that day forward, the Man Who Cried Blood's reputation spread far and wide.

Ten years later, Jason Mankiller is in Ft. Rogers, Texas, hoping to find a job and bury his past. But the blood tattoo won't let him escape the gunfighter's trail. Writer R.A. Jones delivers an old fashioned western adventure in the grand tradition of Max Brand and Louis L'Amour. Here are pioneering men and women facing the birth of a new American destiny that will demand their blood, sweat, tears and sacrifice. For Jason Mankiller, that promise of a better life will be claimed at the end of a smoking gun.

LAWMAN BASS REEVES

In all the annals of frontier history, there was no lawman as skilled or tireless in meting out justice then former runaway slave, Bass Reeves. Having lived with the Five Civilized Tribes during the Civil War years, Reeves was taught tracking and hunting by the natives of that rugged land. After marrying and starting a horse ranch, he soon realized raising a large family (he would have ten children) was expensive. Thus when offered to pin on the U.S. Deputy Marshal's badge, Reeves accepted for two practical reasons; his own respect for the law and the fact that Marshals got to keep whatever bounty was posted on the outlaws they hunted.

In this volume, writers R.A. Jones, Terry Alexander and Mel Odom put the legendary Marshal to the test in three brand new adventures. From facing an old deadly foe, hunting a killer in Indian country and going after a preacher who believes himself to be God's own avenging angel. This is the Wild West at its wildest, challenging the one man who could not be beaten, Marshal Bass Reeves.

PULP FICTION FOR A NEW GENERATION!
FOR AVAILABILITY: AIRSHIP27HANGAR.COM

AIRSHIP27HANGAR.COM

NEW PULP